D1825586

Please return/renew this item
by the last date shown.
Books may also be renewed by
telephone and internet.

Telford & Wrekin Libraries
www.telford.gov.uk/libraries

989900633241

DEDICATION

I'd like to dedicate this book to Gabrielle Phoebe, who has been asking me for years to write something she might enjoy. Here it is, Gabbii - I hope you like it.

I would also like to dedicate it posthumously to my mum, who always encouraged me to keep writing stories and hoped that one day she could read a published version of one. Sorry it's a bit late, Mum, but I'm sure even angels get to read novels and have the odd giggle, so enjoy!

ACKNOWLEDGMENTS

I would like to thank everyone who has helped and encouraged me in the writing of this novel. I couldn't have done it without you! You know who you are.

COPYRIGHT

Spellings are in British English

Editing by Writer Marketing Services

Cover Art by Wicked Women Designs

Formatting by Helen Bright

1

SINGLE? *SINGLE?* HE COULDN'T EVEN PUT 'IT'S complicated'? I suppose Facebook doesn't do a status for 'ended a perfectly good relationship to run off with a floozy East End barmaid with boobs like barrage balloons' does it? What's worse is that now *I* have to put 'single' on *my* page. Otherwise it looks like I'm either pining for him to come back like some hopeless wimp, or that *I'm* the one that split us up and flipping well cheated. I suppose I should be grateful he hasn't put himself down as being in a relationship with *her* – which is obviously the truth – but then I suppose everyone would know right away what a slimy scumbag he's being. And my *mum's* on Facebook!

'Miss? Are you serving?' An old woman's voice invades my thoughts, making me look up from my phone. I'd completely forgotten I was in the hotel restaurant.

She's a rather rotund, grey-haired old dear with pale blue eyes and a mouth which looks like it needs to smile more.

'Yes, of course.'

'I'd like the full English, please – but no tomato. I can't eat tomatoes. They give me the worst indigestion, you know. And make sure they poach the egg properly. I don't want it all congealed like yesterday.'

I drop my phone into the large pocket of my apron and pull out a notebook and pencil. In my head I also throw Connor Worthington into a large pocket – or a well, or a black hole, or the depths of hell maybe, which, I notice, must be where this old dear got the hideous gold necklace that looks like it's attacking her scrawny neck.

'Coming up.' I take the menu from her and plonk it on the dumbwaiter (which sounds a bit insulting of a perfectly nice piece of furniture, in my opinion – the hotel hasn't invested in the modern type with the mini-lift, yet). Then I make my way to the kitchen. I may be seething on the inside but my outer smiley professional strives to force her way to the fore.

'The grumpy cow in room 109 wants her usual,' I yell over to Justin, the breakfast cook. 'And she said don't congeal the eggs like yesterday.' Okay, maybe smiley didn't strive *that* hard.

'Flippin' cheek!' He sounds just like Gino D'Acampo – which is odd, considering he's from Croydon. I assume it's a 'chef' thing.

I throw him a sympathetic smile. 'Her words, not mine.'

'I never congeal *anything*. She should eat it faster, while it's still nice and soft. Congealed indeed!'

Justin's clearly ticked off and I just nod in agreement as I hoist myself onto the counter and idly swing my legs from side to side as pans clatter and bang all around me.

'Libby. A word.'

My heart sinks even further than it did when I checked Facebook earlier. My inner smiley retreats even further into the abyss. Mr Partington's frowning at me – again. I know he doesn't like me, but flipping Nora, couldn't he find someone else to pick on just this once? Doesn't he know what day it is? Boyfriendless Day 1 is what it is. You'd think he'd cut me some slack. Maybe even give me the day off to recover. Perhaps that's what he's about to say? *Libby, I read on Facebook that Connor's changed his status to single, which must mean you two have split up. I'm so sorry. It must be awful for you. How about taking the day off – or even a week? Go and take a holiday while you get over it. I'll pay you, of course – double, in fact. You deserve that much, at least.*

'Liberty?'

Oh no. He's using my full name. That doesn't sound very sympathetic. Actually, he doesn't *look* very sympathetic either. In fact he looks quite angry—he's red-faced and scowling at me impatiently. Behind his back we all call him 'Party', because of his name and partly because he's *anything but* the life and soul of the party. It's our ironic sense of humour. Which is something Party's totally lacking – a sense of humour, I mean.

I hop down from the side and walk over to him, my heart pumping like a steam engine. *I need this job*, I remind myself. *I really can't lose this job.*

'Come to my office.'

This can't be good.

'But the order—'

'Cheryl can take it.'

I give Cheryl, the kitchen porter, a nod of thanks and she gives me back a grimace of sympathy, eyeing the boss. *Yeah, thanks. I know.*

I wouldn't mind so much, but I'm not even a waitress. I'm only filling in while Fiona's got the flu. I'm actually junior management, though you'd never know it. General dogsbody, more like. Part of my job is to draw up the staff rotas but every time someone's absent I have to fill in for them. It becomes a juggling act with the rest of my admin duties as well as working in marketing and promotion. I'm in the middle of trying to organise the hotel's first wedding fair – if I can ever get around to it. This certainly isn't the job I thought I'd applied for.

I step into the manager's large, plush office and take a deep breath. It smells of lavender and polish. Or maybe lavender-scented polish. It's hard to tell. All I know is it's a damn site bigger and posher than the corner of the cupboard I'm assigned to, behind the reception desk. It's actually a large, walk-in stationery store where they've squeezed a desk at one end for me to use. It wouldn't be so bad but the admin staff aren't even that friendly. Even Frances, the white-haired receptionist wears a fixed smile and always seems gracious even when you know she doesn't really mean it. I secretly wonder if she's a robot. Anyway, I spend as little time back there as I can, to be honest, preferring to loiter in the restaurant and kitchen when I get the chance – there's a much nicer bunch of people working there.

My shoes, which clicked in an extremely professional, businesslike manner across the tiled floor of the kitchen, now sink silently into the thick, cream carpet. *Cream.* In a food establishment? Well, food and beds, really. And booze – red wine, even. It's a hotel. A really nice hotel, I grant you, but still, there's a lot of stuff that can spill onto a cream carpet – as well as mud and... well, you know. *Other stuff.* Talking of which, I wonder about the dark spots dotted about the floor in here. They'll take some cleaning off.

Mr Partington's sitting on that luscious swivel chair of his with the high back and thick, squidgy leather. I'd love to sit there. I once tried to sneak in when he wasn't around, just to sit in that chair. The door was locked, though. It's always locked. Even the housekeeping ladies have to borrow a key from Reception when they need to vacuum in here – it's the only room that won't open with a master key. I know, I've tried.

He leans forwards in his seat, looking wearily at me

over his black-rimmed Ted Baker glasses. I've seen some much nicer Gucci ones that would suit him better and I know he could afford them on his wages. Crikey, a general manager of a hotel this size, in London, he must be on at least—

'What did you think you were doing out there?' His voice is sharp and snappy – unlike his suit.

'Serving breakfast.' *What does he think I was doing – having a bath?*

'You do *know* that the door to the kitchen was still wide open when you shouted over to the chef about the order you were placing, don't you? I could hear what you called your customer from the other end of the restaurant.'

I frown. I didn't realise he was even *at* the other end of the restaurant. Has he been spying on me?

'And you know you shouldn't be on your mobile phone when you're working. I've told you about this before.' He's almost growling at me now. Yep, he was definitely spying on me.

'I wasn't actually *on* the phone,' I try to explain, 'I was checking something on—'

'It doesn't matter what you were doing.' His lips have gone all tight and his eyes have shrunk. 'You know the rules. You've been working here nearly two years now, Libby, and I'm sorry to tell you we're going to have to start looking at cutting back on staff. If I were you I'd have a long, hard think about whether or not your future lies in the service industry at all. In the meantime, you *don't* insult customers, sit on the food surfaces in the kitchen, or use mobile phones in the restaurant. Is that clear?'

'Yes.'

'Yes, what?'

'Yes, it is.'

'Yes, it is what?'

'Yes, it is *clear*.' *What does he want – blood?*

'*Sir*!' he barks. 'Sir, or Mr Partington.'

I resist rolling my eyes – but only just. 'Sir.'

He huffs.

I stare at the floor. Those dark marks look almost like holes in the carpet. They leave a trail from the door, over to the filing cabinet, and from there across to the safe in the corner of the room. Hmm, I wonder if perhaps the boss has been carrying his coffee while he's been working, and has dripped it around the floor. That'll take some shifting, dried in coffee.

'Just what were you thinking?' Mr Partington runs his hand through his grey hair with a sigh.

'White vinegar, sir. And soap.'

'What?' He'd look so much nicer if he'd stop frowning. Well, maybe not *that* much nicer. Polish and turds spring to mind – *lavender-scented* polish at that.

'Just mix it with some water and blot.'

'*What*?' He's frowning so hard I can't help wondering why he doesn't invest in some Botox.

'Coffee stains,' I explain – or at least, I *think* I'm explaining; he seems more confused than ever. It's a good tip, though. Beryl from Housekeeping told me it when I had a little 'accident' in my room upstairs. That's one of the perks of living-in – you've got experts on hand for everything. Though you *do* have to keep the place tidy. And keep quiet. And you can't have visitors. Actually, I'm thinking I might move out soon.

Just then Mr Partington's desk phone rings. He picks up, and I hear Frances telling him the painters and decorators are on the line. He waves me out of his office while he takes the call.

With a sigh, I leave the room, carefully closing the door behind me. He is certainly upset over something. And no-one ever calls him 'sir'.

———

IT'S MID-MORNING WHEN THE BAR STAFF ARRIVE FOR the lunchtime shift, and I'm straightening up chairs in the restaurant, feeling more than ready for them. It's definitely a Spanx day – I could give Bridget Jones a run for her money any day of the week with the size of these knickers, and I'm even wearing Spanx tights to make my legs look thinner, too. My hair and make-up are immaculate, even if I do say so myself. They should be – I've spent enough time in the ladies' loo, preening myself. Cassie, my room-mate and best friend in the whole world, gave me some of her expensive miracle-cream last night, once I'd finished bawling my eyes out, along with some designer make-up and I'm really pleased with my new look.

I've got my hair in a smart, professional-looking chignon, with tendrils curling around my face, just to soften my look a little. We even re-dyed it last night, so it's blonder than ever, though not in an obviously fake way, like Bianca's, just enough to lighten it a bit. I've done this smoky-eyes thing I saw in *Cosmo*, which has really made the blue stand out, and I've used one of those long-lasting lipsticks that doesn't come off when you have a cup of tea, or – God forbid – on your teeth. Connor's going to take one look at me and wonder what he ever saw in that skinny, long-legged Bianca Morrison-Wright. Apart from her money, of course – although, I did hear somewhere that her family's not as loaded as everyone assumes. Something to do with bad investments or something, I think. Oh, and her false boobs. You can't forget them. You can't *miss* them, either. But then, they're just that – false. Just like her eyelashes and her—

'Libby, have you finished laying up?' Mr Partington's really got it in for me today, and I wonder if he meant all that stuff about me not staying in the service industry. Surely he can't actually mean I could lose my job? No, he probably thinks I should be doing more managerial tasks – like I'm supposed to do anyway - instead of filling in with the serving jobs every time someone's off sick. That's it! He's going to promote me to a more senior management position. That's what he meant, I'm sure of it.

I study his face hard, looking for signs of him telling me I'm about to be made Assistant Manager, but he's not giving anything away. In fact, it's quite disconcerting that he's spent so much time in the restaurant and kitchen this morning, watching *me*. Usually he's holed away in that big, lavender-scented office, or having meetings with Mr Ainsworth, the Finance Manager, who's also the Deputy Manager, and is on holiday at the moment.

I gasp as a thought occurs to me; maybe Mr Ainsworth *isn't* on holiday – maybe he's left. Perhaps that's why Party thinks I shouldn't be in the service industry; I should be in Accounts. I'm taking over as Finance Manager. There's just one problem – I'm hopeless with numbers. *Damn it!* But Gabby, one of the admins, is great at all that stuff and she's Mr Ainsworth's assistant. So now she'll be *my* assistant. That would work – I can delegate all the difficult sums to her, and I'll do the important stuff like taking the money to the bank. Yes, I like the thought of that. There are several boutiques on the High Street I can visit while I'm there.

And there's another thought – I'll have a much bigger office. Mr Partington will have to show me around it and say things like 'Feel free to put in any nick-nacks you like, Libby. Make it feel like your second home.' I hope he's having it redecorated, too. A couple of the second floor bedrooms are having a makeover – maybe he'll decide to have the whole hotel done. Something bright and cheerful instead of the corporate cream he seems to favour. I might even ask about hanging up some pictures.

I've just remembered he asked me a question, and take a good look at the dining tables all set up for lunch.

'Yes, I think so.' Everything seems to be in place. In fact, I think it looks pretty brilliant considering it was all done by a non-waitress. 'Are you expecting someone special today?'

His face has turned red again—he's clearly fuming. Damn it. I forgot to say 'sir'. But I did *think* 'Mr Partington' so that should count, right? Okay, maybe not, judging by his scowl.

'Sir, is everything all right?' I'm trying to sound polite and concerned at the same time, but not sure if I'm actually pulling it off. It's hard to tell with him.

Just then there's the click-clicking sound of someone walking behind the bar, and Mr Partington looks over. You can't actually see into the bar from here, but further into the restaurant you can, as there's a hatch on the corner where the waiting-on staff place their drinks orders.

I recognise the sound of the ladies' heels on the tiled floor. Stiletto heels, I surmise. Size nine stiletto heels, at a guess. Nine, for goodness' sake. What's that all about? I mean, I know Bianca's tall, but *size nine shoes*? I'm dying to go and see what she's up to but the boss cuts me off before I can move.

'There will be a staff meeting this afternoon at three o'clock in the Remington Suite,' he informs me, pouting. 'Pass the word around, will you?'

My jaw slackens as I gape at him. 'Today?'

He looks back at me, his eyebrows raised in surprise. 'Yes. Today.'

'Oh, *yesterday*. Damn, that means I've missed it,' I say, thinking aloud. 'So why tell everyone now?'

'Not yesterday. *Today*.' He's frowning again. He often does that when he's talking to me.

I wish he'd make his mind up. 'But I have plans for—'

'Cancel them,' he says, his voice tight. He struts across to the bar, presumably to spread the good news. Ha. My only consolation is that Bianca won't be happy. It's Tuesday and she always has her nails done on Tuesdays.

I hear her moaning and I snigger, heading for the kitchen. The staff there are as thrilled as I was to hear that we've got to stay back after our shift. I wonder if it would cheer them up if I told them I'm about to be promoted. But then, maybe the boss wants to tell everyone. Yeah – that'll be what the meeting's about. He's going to announce it to the whole staff today. Although... Party's not really one for surprises. Even when the hotel was awarded an extra star last year he didn't make a big fuss. He just stuck a notice on the wall of the staff loos.

'We're only paid until three,' Margaret complains. 'Surely they can't make us stay any longer than that? It must be against the rules.'

I stare at her. She's only been at the hotel for two weeks, and obviously has no idea how things work around here. I smile at her sympathetically. She'll learn. She's in her sixties with a shock of white hair – which isn't the only shock she's going to have today, if that comment's anything to go by.

There's a loud rustling sound and Cassie rushes through the kitchen's back door, laden with carrier bags. Her face is flushed with a mixture of exhaustion and excitement. Looks like she's been to Selfridges, Harvey Nichols…ooh, and I wonder what's in the little Dior bag. I can't wait to take a look later.

'I'll just put these away and I'll—' She stops short, clearly sensing the uneasy atmosphere. 'What? What's happened?'

Cassie's such a lovely friend and I really don't want to ruin her day, especially as she's only just got back. It's obvious she's had a great morning in town and will feel bad enough having to come to work as it is. She's on the late shift this week, working splits, and I know she had a busy time last night. Poor thing, she's the best waitress we've got and works like a slave for even less money than me. The first thing I'll do when I get my promotion is to give her a pay rise. Actually, she doesn't really need the money. That's not why she's here. But that's a secret only I know about. Maybe I'll keep the pay rise for myself and just promote her.

'We've got to attend a meeting at three.' Stan, the chef, only arrived a few minutes ago, too, and he tells her through gritted teeth about the impromptu meeting. 'I wish I'd asked Justin to do lunch now. Then he could've stayed instead.'

Justin's not as experienced as Stan, and usually only

cooks breakfast and then sometimes comes back as a commis-chef in the evening when it's really busy.

Cassie looks crestfallen. 'Oh no. I was hoping to try this lot on and take back anything that doesn't fit this afternoon. The fitting rooms were rammed and I didn't have time to hang around.'

I feel sorry for her. The window of opportunity on a split isn't usually that big, and I know she won't have time to get to town and back before tonight's shift if she's kept in a boring meeting for an hour after the lunches have finished.

'Party's in a foul mood today,' I explain. 'He's been on my back all morning.' *But I think he's going to promote me*, I want to add. But I daren't. Maybe that's what's making him so cross? Perhaps he doesn't *want* to promote me. Could it be that I've been talent-spotted by someone from head office? A mystery shopper-type thing? I'm sure they have mystery hotel guests. They spotted me working and have given the order that I simply *must* be given a much higher rank than just junior management. Ah, now it makes sense.

Cassie grimaces. 'Something must have happened. I'll quickly take these up and—'

'You're late.'

Shit. I didn't notice the boss walking in behind me. He's glowering at my bestie who's turning a perfect shade of beetroot.

'I stopped her to explain about the meeting.' My hopes of placating him go straight out the window when the vein in his neck starts pulsating rapidly. It only does that when he's really mad.

'You need to see us all at three o' clock, I hear?' Cassie's got that obstinate look in her eye. *Oh double shit!* That look and his vein are a bad combination.

'That's right. Everyone must attend. It's very important,' Mr Partington says authoritatively.

'Even those of us who only get paid until three?' Crikey, Margaret really has no idea what she's doing, riling him like this. I cringe. The old dear's certainly got a death-wish!

His face is red with fury as his chest heaves and he stares at the older woman as though she's an alien. '*Everyone.*' He growls the word out from the back of his throat, and Margaret just gawps at him.

'I only asked,' she mutters as soon as he's left the room.

Everyone just smiles at her sympathetically, except Cassie, who disappears up the back stairs to our room with her shopping. It's the best part of living-in, getting to share a room with her. She's fab.

I retreat back into the restaurant as the cooks start grumbling about how unfair it all is, though I know none of them would have the nerve to tell Party that to his face.

I fold a few napkins into swans while waiting for the first guests to arrive. My stomach is roiling with disappointment. Not only because of Connor – oh no, I haven't forgotten about him – but also because I wanted to go into town later with Cassie. I've seen some Jimmy

Choos online that would be perfect for a summer wedding. They're pale blue and have little flowers and hummingbirds on them. I've always promised myself a pair of Jimmy Choos. I can't actually afford them at the moment, but I'm saving up. I thought it would be good to check if they've got them in Selfridges and ask if I can try them on, just to see how they look.

Then I could start a whole collection of Jimmy Choos. And maybe some Manolo Blahniks and Diors – and, of course, my absolute favourites, some Louboutins. Though not those fake ones Bianca gets off the market – I'd have proper ones with red that stays on the sole, even in the rain.

Wouldn't they look great all lined up in my built-in wardrobe that I'm going to have when I can afford my own place, which might be sooner than I thought if this promotion comes with a decent pay rise. I've already got a pair of Stella McCartney red court shoes – or 'pumps' as they call them in America, which seems really odd to me as I always think of pumps as those gym shoes we used to wear at school with the sort of rubber tyre over the end. I bought them in a sale. I only wear them on really special occasions, of course, or, at least, I *will* wear them when I go to a special occasion. Nothing that special has cropped up yet since I bought them, but at least I'll be ready for it when it happens.

I've also got a pair of Kurt Geigers that I bought second hand from eBay. They're a bit old but I wear them quite a lot as I still think they're really impressive.

I'm getting some new ones just as soon as I can afford it.

'Shit!' Bianca's shriek hauls me from my shoe plans.

I was trying to forget she was there, although to be honest, she was one reason I was thinking about Jimmy Choos in the first place. I was so upset about her stealing Connor last night that I'd immersed myself in some online window-shopping to cheer myself up. That's when I decided to treat myself to a new designer wardrobe. Or, at least, start saving up for one.

2

I HEAD OVER TO THE SERVING HATCH TO SEE WHAT THE drama queen's yelling about. She's dressed in her usual uniform, burgundy skirt and white blouse – which, I notice is more *un*buttoned than buttoned to show off her massive cleavage – and she's staring at the dirty floor, moaning about how sticky it is. I stare down, too.

She's got those fake Christian Louboutins on, with the pointed toes and five-inch stiletto heels, but she's standing on one leg, scowling at the sole of one of them. I wonder if she's noticed that some of the red colour is peeling off again – I often see flakes of it all over the tiled floor behind the bar – but she's more interested in the heel right now.

'It's disgusting,' she says with a sneer. 'Honestly, if it's not chewing gum, it's sticky drinks! It's about time they got a proper cleaner in here.'

Connor's leaning over the bar from the customers' side, peering in at her. He's been the bar manager for the past eight months and in that time has become well-used to dealing with drama. God, he's gorgeous. But I'm not going to think about that right now. His hair is slightly damp, and I wonder if it's raining outside, or if he just got up late. He's got the palest blue eyes I've ever seen, like aquamarines. His dirty-blond waves are slightly tousled around his neck and he's wearing a tight white shirt that shows off his muscles. My stomach flips at the sight.

Tears prick the edges of my eyes and the lump that was in my throat all night has just returned for an encore. *Damn.* I was determined not to get upset today. I'm all cried out and have convinced myself it's definitely for the best. After all, it's not like we'd been together for ages — only six months. *Six months I won't get back.*

I sniff and watch him make doe-eyes at Bianca.

'What's wrong, babe?'

Babe? *I* was 'babe' up until yesterday. I narrow my eyes and suddenly notice how badly his hair needs re-highlighting and a good trim, and his shirt needs to be a size bigger as it's bulging over his flab. God, he's ugly, I try to kid myself.

I shove my nose in the air, glad that I look so good today.

'Just look at this!' Bianca's voice is getting so shrill that only dogs and bats will be able to hear her in a minute.

She's twisted her leg around to show him the stodgy mess on the tip of her heel and he cranes his neck over the bar to look. He frowns. I frown too, as he admires her mile-long legs. *Typical man!*

'There.' As she hoists her massive foot around a little further, like a demented flamingo, her other foot slips on the tile and her eyes almost pop out of her head as she hurtles along the floor, screaming as she crashes into the bottle bin.

I can't stop the loud snort which escapes as I try not to laugh, and she stares up at me with a mixture of horror and hate. Her yelling has brought everyone rushing out of the kitchen and Stan and Cassie are standing behind me, guffawing uncontrollably, while Margaret stares into the hatch, stunned.

Connor is the first – actually, the *only* – one to rush around and offer Bianca a hand, and she makes a big scene of pulling herself to her feet in a rather ungainly manner. She teeters for minute, a bit like that scene in Bambi when he's learning to walk, and I wonder if it's just an excuse to hold onto Connor for a little longer. *Bitch.*

Then something catches my eye and I can't help giggling. The brownish, sticky mess on the floor has attached itself to her pristine white blouse, and she glares at me before noticing it for herself. It looks like a mixture of beer, whiskey and dirt.

'*Now* look at me!' she shrieks. 'I can't possibly serve like this.'

Connor scowls at me and I notice how unattractive it makes him look. While we were dating I thought he was the most handsome guy on God's earth – well, barring

Chris Hemsworth, of course. And Jamie Dornan. Oh, and that guy in the Diet Coke ads, and…come to think of it, he wasn't *that* good-looking, after all. Anyway, he looks even less attractive now. Not *awful* exactly, more…*plain*. Okay, *plain awful*. I can't think what I ever saw in him in the first place.

I raise my eyebrows as innocently as I can manage under the circumstances and look away, suddenly very interested in a rather wonky swan-shaped napkin on a nearby table. The thought of the swan immediately reminds me of the 'flamingo' behind the bar and I can't stop giggling again.

'Serves her right,' Cassie mutters as everyone else goes back to their positions. 'She's only trying to get out of cleaning the floor.'

Cassie's not only pretty, with a thick, wavy pony-tail, colour-matched with her big, brown eyes, but she's also right.

'She doesn't think it's her job,' I reply, polishing a spoon with the corner of my apron. 'Although *I* always do all the cleaning when I work behind there.'

Being the junior manager means I get all the best jobs. I'm supposed to help the management team with the day-to-day running of the facilities and ensure that each department is fully-staffed. In fact, I end up filling in for anyone who's absent and the only thing I've had a hand in running so far is a wedding fair which is coming up soon. Even then, I'm only involved as it was my suggestion and Party's too busy to give it his full attention.

'Me, too.' Cassie nods. 'I wouldn't dream of expecting Beryl to do it.'

Beryl's one of the housekeeping staff, who usually works downstairs, while all the rest work in the bedrooms on the upper floor. Apart from servicing the few disabled bedrooms down here, Beryl's job includes vacuuming and cleaning the offices and reception area and polishing all the glass in the foyer, but we'd never expect her to clean in the restaurant or the bar area – unlike Bianca. According to the drama queen it's what Beryl's paid for, and she spends half her time filing complaints about the older lady's 'negligence' and 'incompetence'. I know this because I spend half *my* time throwing them in the bin.

Connor used to roll his eyes and explain to Bianca that the poor woman had enough to do without adding the bar to her list of duties, and that each member of staff was responsible for cleaning their own area. He's not saying any of that now.

He helps her hobble over to sit at one of the little round tables in the bar, making soothing noises while she rants about whose fault it was and how she couldn't possibly work her shift in this mess. I hear something about 'where there's blame there's a claim' and decide to get closer so I can listen. This could get interesting.

I pick up a couple of Paris goblets from the dumb-waiter and wiggle my hips as I walk through into the bar, placing the glasses on the counter.

I glance up at the massive mirror on the wall behind the bar to see that I'm still looking totally stunning. I smile, hoping that Connor will have noticed too, which is probably why he hasn't spoken to me yet. He's obviously just realising what he's thrown away. Ha!

Suddenly I see something – or rather some*one* – that makes my whole body heat up practically to boiling point, and my face turn scarlet. There's a man flicking through a newspaper – a drop-dead-stunning man – and he's now looking straight at me in the mirror. He must have seen me smirking about Connor, and now he's frowning — probably wondering if I'm insane. Without looking directly at the handsome hunk, I turn to the couple at the little table.

'Don't worry, Connor. I can always help you with the bar today if Bianca's not up to the job,' I offer with a sickly sweet smile. *I'll show him how professional I am and how being dumped hasn't affected me in the slightest.*

Bianca's face reddens and her jaw drops as she gapes at me.

Connor looks questioningly at her, as though considering his options. *He's a brave man, I'll give him that.*

'I can manage,' Bianca snaps. 'I just need a clean blouse, that's all.'

'Perhaps I could lend you one of mine.' I'm trying my best to appear innocent and helpful, but the way Connor's narrowing his eyes suggests that it's not working.

'No, that won't be necessary, thanks,' she says dryly. 'Besides, I don't think anything of *yours* would fit me.' She pushes out her large bosom to make her point.

'Oh no, I'm only a size ten,' I say sympathetically, secretly hoping that Mr Handsome Hunk is listening in. 'You're obviously much bigger than me, aren't you?' Actually I'm more like a size fourteen, or a sixteen if I'm in one of those trendy shops that skimp on the size, but I'm not going to admit that in front of Connor – or Mr Handsome.

She snorts in disbelief and then frowns and I can tell she's trying to figure out if I'm pitying her or insulting her.

I turn and stroll back towards the restaurant. I take a quick glance back just before reaching the first dining table, and speak in a soft, kind voice. 'Just remember, Bianca, you're welcome to my cast-offs any time.' I stare pointedly at Connor who glares at me, his face turning red and his jaw tense.

My work here is done.

I spin around with a flourish – or at least I mean it to be a flourish, but in fact I whizz around so fast that my head feels a little woozy and I have to grab a nearby chair to stop myself falling over.

'Are you okay, hon?' Cassie brushes my arm as she studies me. She smiles at me sympathetically.

'Yeah,' I say as brightly as I can. 'I'm beginning to wonder what I ever saw in him.' I look back towards the bar where Connor is still soothing Bianca. A pang inside me suggests that this non-caring malarkey's not quite as easy as I'm trying to make out, but I'll be damned if I'm going to let him know that.

'I got some great stuff today,' Cassie tells me. 'We can try it all on later.'

I'll look forward to that. I love borrowing Cassie's clothes. They're all much more expensive and designery than mine.

'Your dad paid up, then?' I grin at her.

'Yup. Four grand, as promised. I said I'd stay until the end of the month, though, just to give Mr Partington some notice.'

I shake my head. 'Incredible. I mean, it's not like you'll need a reference from here, is it?'

Cassie pouts thoughtfully. 'No, but it's only manners. I mean, he doesn't know I'm only here to fulfil a bet with my parents, does he? He probably thinks I need the money like—'

'Like the rest of us,' I finish for her.

'Sorry, hon. I didn't mean it that way.' She blushes. I'm well aware she didn't intend to offend me – she'd never do that in a million years.

'I know.' I give her a warm hug. 'But it *is* true.'

'Maybe Dad can get you a job somewhere really swanky,' Cassie suggests, her eyes wide and shining. 'I can ask him if you want?'

'No thanks.' I shake my head again. It's kind of her to offer, but I need to stand on my own two feet. Even though my parents couldn't afford to bet me four thousand pounds that I wouldn't stick a job for twelve months, they did make it perfectly clear that they didn't think I would *ever* get a job in London – let alone a managerial position (well, on paper anyway). They weren't being nasty; they just didn't think I should up sticks and move here. But I couldn't stay in Broadstairs. Not after what happened with Jonathan Parker. I cringe at the memory. He dumped me very publicly and humiliatingly. The thought of facing anyone after that made me feel physically sick.

'Well, if you change your mind...'

I suddenly become aware that Cassie's still speaking to me.

'Thank you. I really don't want *you* to leave, though,' I tell her. It's true. The place just won't be the same without her. I don't know what I'll do without my roomie and best friend to chat to.

'Maybe you should leave, too? There must be other jobs—'

'Who's leaving?'

We both turn around to see Margaret standing behind us.

'What?' I frown.

'Who's leaving? Cassie said you should leave too. Who's going?'

I'm stunned that this woman knows we're aware she's been listening in on our *totally private* conversation, and instead of having the grace to pretend she hasn't heard a thing – which is what I would do, incidentally - she actually asks us about what we were discussing. *Privately*.

'Oh look, our first customers.' Cassie quickly picks up a couple of menus as two handsome young guys saunter across to us.

'Table for two, gentlemen?' I say brightly, and lead them over to a window table. They sit down while Cassie follows on and politely informs them that the soup of the day is potato and leek, and that the lamb's off.

The lamb's always off. It's since the price went up and hotel management decided not to buy it anymore. The trouble is, if they took it off the menu it would leave a gap and that would look even more obvious that something wasn't there – and Tania in the admin office refused to amend the listing in case it suddenly needed to be written back on. She said it was all to do with time and motion, or something like that. We think it's more to do with laziness and her lack of knowledge of how to format a nice menu.

One of the men smiles at me. He's got fair hair and big green eyes. Quite good-looking, actually. How did I not notice that when he walked in? Oh yeah, I was concentrating on not telling Margaret that Cassie's leaving. Or that her family's rich. Or anything, really. It's none of her damn business.

Cassie takes their lunch order and disappears into the kitchen. Margaret is still waiting by the dumbwaiter. She'll start probing again if I join her, and if I don't go over there she'll think I'm avoiding her – which I am. I decide to stay put and make conversation with the customers until Cassie gets back.

'So, are you here on a business lunch?' I ask nonchalantly.

'Sort of,' the fair one says, raising his perfectly-shaped eyebrows. 'We've got something to discuss, haven't we, Rob?'

The other guy – Rob – looks up at me with a smile. 'Yeah, just some boring details about a story we're running.' He's really handsome, too, with dark hair and a neat moustache.

I know I should take the hint and leave them to talk, but I can't help being curious. 'Are you reporters, then?' Something ignites inside me. I always wanted to be a journalist. Mum and Dad said I'd never make it, not in London anyway, but this junior management lark's so not what it's cracked up to be and I'd love to do something really exciting like working for a newspaper.

'That's right. Hey, you should be a detective. What d'you think, Ben?' He grins at his friend.

'Sorry...I didn't mean to be...' I can feel my face getting hot.

'No, it's fine. He's only joking,' Ben assures me, placing a warm, well-manicured hand on my arm. 'We work for the *Daily Chronicle*. We've got to put our heads together to come up with a good local story, that's all.'

'That sounds intriguing. What's it going to be about?'

Just then Cassie arrives with two bowls of soup and a basket of bread rolls which she places in front of the men.

'Enjoy,' she says, smiling at them before giving me a quizzical look.

'Yes, have a nice… er… meal,' I say in my professional voice.

'Is everything all right?' Cassie frowns at me as we go back to join Margaret at the dumbwaiter.

'Yes, of course.'

'Was something wrong?' Margaret asks with a scowl. I wonder if she's guessed that I was keeping out of her way until I had back-up.

'No, everything's fine. They're just a bit chatty, that's all. You know what it's like – some customers think we've got all day to stand around talking. At least they can concentrate on their food now.' I'm rolling my eyes and waving my arms about, trying to seem as perplexed as I can, but by the looks on the women's faces I'm not sure it's working.

'Anyway,' Margaret says when I stop to draw breath.

Damn, I hate having to do that – it always gives my opponent the chance to butt in.

'Yes, anyway,' I say quickly. 'How about this meeting? What do you think it's going to be about?'

They both stare at me in surprise, but at least Cassie has the good grace to put on a really thoughtful frown.

'I don't know,' she says. 'Mr Partington didn't look too happy, did he? I mean, it doesn't look like he's about to offer us all a pay rise, does it?'

I try not to giggle. Cassie's a brilliant actress – she should be on the stage. Of all the people to think about a pay rise, Cassie Beaumont is the last person I would expect to mention it. Not with all her money. Not that anyone else knows about it, of course. Cassie told me in confidence. The last thing she needs is people asking her why she's working in a place like this when she doesn't need the cash. Besides, she's afraid people might resent her taking a job which someone more needy could have. That's probably the other reason she's leaving at the end of the month – to free up the job for someone else. She's thoughtful like that.

'Isn't that exactly what it ought to be about?' Margaret chips in. 'I've never worked for minimum wage before in my life. What *are* they thinking?'

'Er – that we all need a job?' I offer.

'Yes, and that's precisely what they're banking on,' Margaret goes on, pointing at me. 'If we all told them that we didn't need to work here, they might get worried and offer us more money to stay. We could stage a strike. I think it'll work, you know, but we *all* have to do it. That's the name of the game – solidarity. Do you think everyone else will agree with us? The kitchen staff, housekeeping, admin? The girls on Reception seem quite nice — I'm sure we could count on them. We could start by signing a petition or something. Maybe the Prime Minister will get involved. We might all be famous. The TV, the papers—'

Talking of which... 'I think those men have finished their starters,' I interject.

'I'll clear, you fetch the mains,' Cassie offers, nodding at me vehemently.

Glad of the chance to get out of there, I head straight for the kitchen.

'I'll help Cassie,' Margaret says, following her over to the table.

I sigh with relief. That woman's dangerous!

So why the hell did I just leave her in there with two story-hungry reporters from a regional newspaper?

3

WHEN I TAKE THE MAINS OUT, MARGARET IS TALKING to the men animatedly. And if I'm not mistaken, she seems to be flirting with them, too. *Oh no!*

'Here we are, gentlemen. Your vegetables will be here shortly.' I place the plates in front of them with a smile. I always tell customers that the rest of their meal is on its way in case they start eating without it. Or complain that we haven't filled the order correctly. Or post pictures of their plates on Facebook with a caption saying 'don't eat here; this is all they give you!' That's the trouble with silver service. Not everyone under-stands it.

'Margaret, perhaps you could help?' I suggest, subtly trying to prise her away from the reporters.

She frowns. 'Can't you manage?'

I stare at her, my jaw dropping at her audacity. 'Yes, but I thought you might like something to do.' I smile as best I can while my heartbeat thumps nineteen to the dozen.

'I'm okay, thanks.'

'Right. Fine.' My voice is more like a squeal as I try to hide my anger, but I somehow manage to keep the smile pasted onto my face as I return to the kitchen.

Cassie catches my eye from where she's seating some guests at table four, and gives me a look which says 'I know, what a cow!' I give her a look back that says 'Ha – I bet she doesn't realise one of them's gay.'

The kitchen's quiet today and they've got the radio playing in the background. I take some deep breaths and count to ten...well, seventeen actually – that's just how angry I am.

A minute or so later I'm heading for the table by the window with a double-dish of carrots and peas. I'm surprised to see Margaret polishing cutlery at the dumb-waiter, and Cassie smiles at me conspiratorially on her way to the kitchen with her order. I'm not entirely sure what she's trying to tell me – our telepathy is usually bang on, or at least, I *think* it is – but I'm sure I'll find out soon enough.

'Peas, sir?' I start loading peas onto Ben's plate. As the younger-looking guy—the one I suspect is gay—he gets to have the lion's share. That way he might remember me. Gay men are considerate like that. He might even put an article in his paper about me. *Everyone should come and dine at The Chalfont and ask for Libby. She gives really big portions.* Actually, that sounds a bit rude. Maybe: *she's very generous with her vegetables*. No, that doesn't sound right, either.

'Okay...okay, I said that's enough!'

I suddenly become aware of Ben groaning into my ear and realise I've only left one little pea for Rob. Damn!

'Er...I'm terribly sorry. Perhaps I could...um.' I try lifting a couple of peas off Ben's plate but somehow they get caught up in the prongs of my fork and flick into the air.

'What *are* you doing, Liberty?'

Suddenly Mr Partington's right beside me, frowning. *Shit*. Where the hell did he come from? Ah, now I understand what Cassie was telling me.

'Um...I...er...' My face heats up, and around me customers are sniggering.

'Just serve those vegetables before everything goes cold,' Mr Partington snaps. He turns to Margaret. 'Margaret, go and fetch the potatoes for table fourteen, please.'

She scurries off to the kitchen while I serve the carrots.

Cassie suddenly appears with more peas which she heaps onto Rob's plate. I notice him wink at her and she beams.

'Enjoy your meal,' I mutter as I hurry away with the empty dish and a red face.

Service gets quite busy after that, and I try to avoid the reporters' table as much as I can. We don't worry about designated work stations at lunchtime; we just serve whoever needs it at the time. It's never as busy as dinner, and we all prefer it a little more relaxed.

'I think they're interested in the story,' Margaret informs me when we meet up at the dumbwaiter a while later.

'What?' I'm busy watching a yummy copper-haired guy who's just walked through from the bar and is looking around. It's *him*. It's Mr Handsome Hunk himself.

Oh my God.

My heart pounds like a bass drum.

Cassie's nearest and goes up to him, seating him on table twelve, just next to the deuce by the window. That's a table of two, by the way, not just a tennis term.

I quickly pick up a menu and head over, trying not to catch the attention of the two reporters on the next table. Cassie's eyes flash at me as our paths cross, and I suspect she's thinking the same as me – *what a stud!*

'Good afternoon, sir.' I smile as I hand him the menu. 'The soup today is potato and leek, and I'm afraid we've run out of lamb.'

He doesn't even smile as he takes the menu from me. There's a thud in my stomach.

'Pity, I quite fancy lamb today.'

I daren't tell him what – or rather who - *I* fancy.

'Sorry, sir.'

He frowns; I hope it's not because of the lamb.

'Just be careful of the vegetables,' Ben calls over from the next table.

'You're okay if you just want a pea, though,' Rob chimes in with a chuckle.

Very funny. I shoot them a dirty look, stick my nose in the air and walk away. Or at least, I *would* have walked away if my heel hadn't got caught in the table-cloth as I spun around. I yelp as my ankle twists and there's a clatter of silverware as the contents of table twelve hurtle through the air, firing all around me like bullets as I fall with a hefty slam, ending up sprawled across the floor in between the two tables.

'Libby, are you okay?' Cassie's there in an instant. I peer up gingerly, having covered my head with my arms in case the wineglasses came crashing over me.

'I think so,' I say, sitting up carefully.

The reporters on table fourteen are laughing hysterically, while the man on twelve is shaking his head and holding two glasses in his hands.

'I'm really sorry.' I slowly stand while Cassie gathers the cutlery.

'I saved these.' The man hands me the two wine-glasses. 'Perhaps I could sit at table thirteen instead?'

'I'm afraid we don't have one,' I murmur. 'It's considered, um...*unlucky*.'

The two guys next to us hoot even louder, while I feel myself colouring up again. Damn. The man gawps at me incredulously – and I can't really blame him.

'Table fifteen is free,' I offer, gesturing with one of the glasses to another table. 'Would that suit?'

'I suppose it'll have to,' the man grumbles, leaving the table and going over to the other one.

'I really am sorry.' I can't say it enough, but the guy doesn't seem to be listening. I limp along behind him, stifling a wince. My ankle really hurts, especially when I put my weight on it. I bet it's broken. Not that grumpy-guts here would care. He didn't even ask if I was okay. *I'm really going off him now.*

'Is everything all right here?'

Oh great, that's all I need.

Mr Partington shoots me a glare before apologising to the customer on my behalf.

Cassie's quickly re-laying table twelve with clean cutlery, and I was hoping the manager hadn't heard anything. From the corner of my eye I see movement at the hatch to the bar and turn to see Bianca smirking at me. Now I know how the boss got to hear of the commotion. *Bitch!*

'It's fine,' the customer says wearily. He addresses me. 'I'll have the pâté followed by bœuf bourguignon. No peas.'

The guys on table fourteen erupt into laughter again and I quickly scribble on my pad while making my enfeebled retreat.

'How's it going out there?' Stan asks, frowning at my limp as I place the order and pop some melba toast into a basket.

'Oh, you know. Same old, same old,' I reply, airily. 'But I think I might have broken my ankle. I caught it on...*something* and wrenched it.'

'Probably a sprain,' Cassie says following me into the kitchen. 'You might need to get it in some ice.'

'Fat chance. We've still got meals to serve, remember?'

'Could you fasten an ice-pack to it?' Adrian, the sous-chef, suggests. 'Hang on, I've got some in the freezer.'

He comes over with a big blue bag and a roll of surgical tape. 'Sit there.' He points to a rickety old chair next to the still machine at the coffee station.

'I'm not sure,' I say, plonking myself down anyway. It's a relief to get the weight off my feet. Especially the left one.

'It's swelling already,' he says, pouting at my foot. 'Have you got any flat shoes? Those heels must be crippling you.'

I stare at him in horror. He might be great at first-aid but he clearly knows nothing about fashion!

I always wear heels for work. And they're my Karen Millens. They make my legs look longer and thinner...usually. Currently, my injured one looks like a balloon. Even my Spanx tights can't contain it.

'I'll go fetch some,' Cassie offers and whizzes up the back stairs before I can object.

The ice feels heavenly against my sore ankle, and I wish I could just sit here all day and savour the relief, especially when Adrian takes my shoes off.

'It should be elevated,' he says. 'In a perfect world you should be sitting comfortably with your foot on a soft stool.'

I close my eyes for a second, imagining I'm in that

perfect world. It would be in my new penthouse, of course. Decorated all stylishly and modern. Soft music would play in the background – maybe a harp or something, and I'd have a luscious man to look after me. The man from table twelve...er...table fifteen comes into my mind. My eyes suddenly snap open as the dream is shattered. He won't be handing me a glass of wine and a box of chocolates – he'll be shouting 'where's my pâté?'

'Here you go.' Cassie arrives with my ballet pumps.

'I can't wear them for work!'

'You'll be lucky if you can get them on, to be fair,' Stan calls over. He's scowling at my foot from his position at the grill.

'But I've got to get this starter out. The guy's mad enough already.'

'Who's serving table fifteen?'

Oh great. Mr Partington's found me.

'Liberty, what on earth are you doing?'

'Er...just coming.' I wince as I force my left foot into one shoe, then easily slide on the other. Adrian helps me stand up.

I put my weight on my left foot. 'Ow!'

'She shouldn't be walking. Looks like a bad sprain,' Stan tells the boss, waving a spatula in my direction.

Mr Partington rolls his eyes. 'How on earth did you —no...never mind. I really don't want to know. Can't you just manage until the end of your shift?' He's fuming and I wonder just what Bianca told him.

'I'll do my best,' I mumble, hobbling past him with

the pâté and toast. Apart from the pain, it's not easy to walk with a big, heavy ice pack strapped to your ankle, but I don't see that I have much choice. I just can't wait to finish my shift and go and rest my leg.

Then it hits me. The staff meeting. *Oh God!*

I place the food on the table in front of my customer, who gawps at me in bewilderment. 'Are you all right?'

I'm about to leave him in peace – well, okay, make good my escape – when it registers that he's speaking to me. I turn back in surprise. 'I think I might have sprained my ankle.' *And you didn't give a shit*, I add in my head.

He nods knowingly. 'You need to elevate it. And keep your weight off it.'

I stare at him, dying to say 'well I would if I didn't have to serve your stupid meal' but I stop myself just in time.

'I will when I've finished here,' I say, smiling as sweetly as I can under the circumstances. My stomach flips. Maybe he does care, after all – even if he is a bit pompous about it.

Joining Margaret over at the dumbwaiter, I watch her folding napkins into some really weird shapes. 'Those look...interesting,' I say, trying to be tactful and not just ask *'what are they?'* 'What are they?' (Okay, I failed).

'Can't you tell? They're birds of paradise, of course.' Margaret gawps at me as if I'm stupid.

I stare at the napkins blankly. I try turning my head

first one way and then the other. Nope. They still don't look anything like birds of any kind to me.

'Anyway, I started to tell you.' Margaret's eyes light up as though a thought has struck her, and she suddenly appears quite animated.

I'm glad of the change of subject. Until I hear what the subject is. 'Those men over there are reporters and they are really interested in our story,' she says, pointing to the table by the window.

I frown. 'What story?'

'About the strike. I told them how we are all planning to take industrial action over our wages and they said they'd be really interested in covering it for their paper.'

My blood runs cold. 'But it's not decided yet, is it? I mean, we haven't actually discussed it or anything. We need to have meetings and all sorts before we can do something like that.'

'Why? We're determined, aren't we? We all agreed we're on rotten wages and we want more money. All we have to do is pick a day and then all go on strike until they give us a raise. Those men, Rob and Ben, said to just let them know when it's happening and they'll come down if they can – with a photographer and everything.'

'Oh...er...right.' I'm not actually sure what else to say to that.

Luckily the man on table fifteen's finished his pâté so I clear away his plate and the bread basket. For some reason I feel really nervous around him, and my hands tremble as I collect his dishes. I can't help noticing his aromatic after-shave, too. I hobble off into the kitchen for his main course.

'Is Mr Happy ready for his beef, then?' Stan shouts up as soon as he sees me.

'What? Oh...er...yes.'

Mr Partington frowns and comes towards us. Oh shit! He picks up the order and stares at it.

What did I write? *Think, think, think.* Oh god. I *did* write Mr Happy. It's my ironic sense of humour – not that Party *has* a sense of humour, of course, and I'm pretty sure the gorgeous-but-grumpy customer hasn't, either. I hadn't asked his name and I was trying to get out of there quickly and I—

'Here you go.' Stan hands me a plate of bœuf bourguignon. 'You okay?'

'Yes, thanks.' I'm not really. I'm in a lot of pain, but I'm also in a rush to get out of there and escape Mr Partington's beady eyes which seem to be boring into the back of my head as I reach the door.

'I'll bring your veg,' Cassie offers.

'Thanks,' I mutter, and limp into the restaurant to give 'Mr Happy' his lunch.

Most of the diners have left now, but I'm a little rattled to notice that the reporters are still hanging around.

'Have they had dessert?' I ask Margaret on my way back to the kitchen to fetch the potatoes.

'They said they wanted to wait a while,' she says with a shrug.

Hmm. I can guess why. They obviously enjoyed the floor show earlier – and thought it hilarious when I emerged with my ankle strapped up – and are hoping for another instalment. I suppose I should just be glad they don't have a photographer with them. Although I wouldn't put it past them not to have taken a snap on their mobile phones. I really wasn't taking any notice while I was diving into the carpet at a hundred miles an hour.

'Potatoes for the Happy meal,' Stan shouts over to Adrian, and everyone in the kitchen bursts into laughter.

'Does he want fries with that?' Adrian replies.

Mr Partington narrows his eyes as he stares at me and I suspect he's dying to know if my customer really *is* called Mr Happy. I'm going to be in so much trouble when he finds out what his real name is...although, it *could* be Mr Happy, couldn't it? I mean, *someone* must have that surname – why not him? Perhaps I should ask him...or maybe not.

I manage to serve the potatoes without asking him anything except whether he'd like a glass of red wine to accompany his meal.

'No, thank you.' He seems a bit nicer than he did earlier and I suppose he must have just been wound up about something. I noticed his very determined jaw and I think that might be what makes him look so stern, too. The bloke's probably a really good laugh when you get to know him. I smile at him, hoping he'll reciprocate. He doesn't.

'I think table fourteen are ready for their desserts now.'

I look up in horror. Mr Partington's right behind me. He must have followed me out. Was he hoping I'd ask Mr Happy what his name is? Is he going to sack me for making fun of a customer? Hmm. I'm glad I kept my mouth shut now. I'm really banking on that promotion.

I plaster on my fake smile again as I give the reporters the dessert menus.

'Can we just have ice cream?' Ben asks, looking a little warily at my ankle. He obviously feels guilty for laughing at my accident. Good.

'Of course,' I say brightly, just to make him feel worse. 'One scoop or two?' I burst into laughter at my own news-related joke, but they don't seem impressed. I take the menus from them and hobble back to the kitchen, still chuckling at my own journalist-humour.

I tell Cassie my joke and she chuckles as she helps me prepare the ice-cream sundaes.

'They must be really miserable not to have found that hilarious,' she says with a tut. Cassie always gets my jokes.

'Some people just don't have a funny bone in their body,' I say, shaking my head. Then I realise what I've said. 'Ha-ha – funny bone, get it?'

We crease ourselves laughing again, and I actually feel my eyes watering.

'Liberty.' Mr Partington's voice cuts into our fun like a knife through mashed potato – or *creamed* potatoes as we say in the food trade.

'I'll take these out,' Cassie offers, picking up the sundaes.

'No, actually, the men on table fourteen have specifically asked to speak to Liberty,' Mr Partington says with a frown. 'Something to do with *industrial action*, they said.'

4

IT'S A RELIEF TO FINISH THE SHIFT, BUT A REAL PAIN—literally!—to have to go into the Remington Suite for the staff meeting afterwards.

I managed to fob the reporters off by telling them Margaret was a bit senile and had got the wrong end of the stick. 'Besides', I'd told them, 'we're all thrilled with our jobs and wouldn't dream of taking any action against the management'. I didn't mention that *I* am also management. I don't know if they actually believed me but they left without leaving a tip.

Cassie stayed behind to clear away Mr Happy's coffee while Margaret and I came through to grab the best seats.

We're sitting right at the back, and I've turned around one of the chairs from the row in front to rest my foot on. God, it hurts—I wish the painkillers would hurry up and kick in.

The admin girls, Tania and Gabby, file in and take

the front row – more fool them. That'll be the first place Party looks when he wants to haul someone out of the audience. Actually, on second thought, I doubt he's going to be performing any magic tricks or anything so they might be safe, after all.

The housekeeping ladies have dispersed around the room, as they don't get on with each other that well.

The kitchen staff look a bit disgruntled that we've got the middle back row seats which they always want, but sit either side of us anyway.

Frances, the receptionist, looks a bit uncomfortable being on her own, and sits at the end of a row. The maintenance men are standing up at the sides of the room, apparently too manly to sit down.

The bar staff take the only remaining seats, and I can see Bianca gloating, even through the back of her head, as she sits near the front, beside Connor.

Everyone's talking at once, and I look up as Cassie joins us just before the start. She grins at our choice of seats as she wiggles past the cooks on her way to sit next to me, where I've saved her seat with my ballet pump, which I just *had* to remove as soon as I could.

'Can I have quiet, please?' Mr Partington's puffed his chest out as he stands at the front, frowning at us all. His hair looks greyer than ever under the stark fluorescent lights, which really bring out his wrinkles. I might have to tell him about that later...or maybe not.

The chatting turns to murmuring before he evidently gives up his hope of silence and begins anyway. 'Now, I need to talk to all of you about a very serious matter. A matter which I can't divulge too much about at this stage.' Sounds mysterious.

It's my promotion, I just know it. I hope he doesn't expect me to stand up for a round of applause, though. Trust this to happen to me today of all days.

Stan tuts loudly, causing the boss to look up irritably. 'Why call a bloomin' meeting then?' he murmurs under his breath, but we can all hear him.

Mr Partington looks like he's about to have a coronary, his face turning bright red and that pulse on his neck working overtime.

'What I *can* say, however, is that I need every member of staff to be on your guard.' He stares daggers at Stan. 'Something is going on and you need to be extra vigilant. Money has gone missing – I can't say where from at this stage, but you need to be extremely careful. Keep your belongings locked away. Don't bring valuable items into the workplace.'

No - that's not what this is supposed to be about!

'You think one of us is a thief?' Stan doesn't mince his words – unfortunately.

Mr Partington's lips are thin and tight and it's clear he's holding back his anger. He's about to explode at any minute. (I know the feeling!)

'I didn't say that,' he spits out. 'What I *am* saying is that someone – I'm not accusing any of you – has stolen some money from this hotel and you should all be aware of the situation for your own good. If you see anything suspicious you must report it to me immediately.'

'Suspicious in what way?' Oh God, Margaret's at it

now, too. Why can't everyone just nod and murmur so we can finish the sodding meeting?

The throb in my ankle has escalated up my leg and I'm desperate to get up to my room so I can get into my sweatpants and put my foot up on a heap of pillows. Not to mention go to sleep for a while so I don't have to feel it hurting, especially now that it looks like I won't be celebrating all night.

'Well, anyone that might seem to have more money than normal, I suppose,' Mr Partington says, fidgeting uncomfortably.

'So anyone splashing the cash is the thief, you mean?' Stan shakes his head incredulously.

'They could be.' Mr Partington looks our way and my blood runs cold. I was hoping it was just Stan he was frowning at, but now I can see it's a little closer to home. He's staring at Cassie! And now Margaret is, too, and soon everyone in the room turns around and gawps at her.

Oh shit! Just because she did some lousy shopping they think *she's* stolen the money – Cassie, of all people. The one person in the room who doesn't need any more money. They've got to be kidding.

There's murmuring all around us which grows louder. Cassie shrinks back into her chair, her face pale. She's shaking.

'Well, as I said. Be vigilant and report anything – no matter how trivial it might seem. Oh, and if the person or persons who took the money returns it within the next twenty-four hours I *might* reconsider pressing charges. I can assure you that such action will certainly make me treat that person or persons much more leniently, anyway.' He glances around the room in a non-accusing manner. 'Thank you.'

Mr Partington is the first one out the door.

Cassie shoots to her feet. 'I know what you're all thinking and it isn't me!' She pushes her way to the door and I try to heave my leg off the chair so I can follow her but it's not as easy as it sounds. Not only because it hurts like the devil, but because everyone else is now crowding around the doorway.

'No wonder she wasn't bothered about my strike idea,' Margaret mutters next to me, standing up.

I stare at her in disbelief and horror. Surely she can't think...? 'Cassie is *not* a thief, for your information,' I snap. 'I don't know who took the stupid money, but I can promise you it definitely wasn't her. How can you even think like that?'

'Well, you saw all that shopping she had earlier,' Margaret says sullenly. 'That must have cost a small fortune. And Mr Partington did say to look out for someone who suddenly seems to have lots of cash.'

'That doesn't mean she stole it!' I scrabble to my feet, trying my hardest to steady myself on the chair in front to avoid putting my left foot on the floor.

My blood boils and everyone is staring at us, since the hubbub has died down and no-one seems in a hurry to leave anymore. *Damn!*

'But you have to admit it looks odd. Money goes

missing and suddenly she's out shopping like that.' Margaret's not giving up.

'Cassie often shops like that,' I tell her, shaking my head. 'What are you saying? She robs a bank every week?'

'Well she certainly seems to make her wages go a lot further than the rest of us if today's anything to go by.'

'Well, it isn't. She just happens to have a richer family than most of us,' I blurt out. 'Not that it's anyone's business. And besides, we don't even know how much money went missing or when. I'm sure other people have been shopping recently and no-one's accused *them* of stealing the money. Just because it's announced today and she went shopping this morning doesn't prove anything.'

'No, but it *does* look a bit suspicious,' Margaret insists.

'You haven't been here five minutes. You don't know anything,' I bite back at her. 'Don't you dare accuse my friend of anything. You don't even know her!'

Margaret storms out and the rest of the staff slowly disperses. I finally manage to hobble to the doorway, using the chairs for support. It's a shame Margaret and I have just fallen out as I was kind of hoping she might help me to my room, but she's flounced off now, anyhow.

'Here you go.' Stan's suddenly standing next to me with his arm out. 'I'm sure no-one's going to mind you using the lift in the circumstances.' He puts an arm around me and helps me down the corridor. Lifts are only for customers and senior management but I'm really not bothered about the rules right now.

'Thanks ever so much.' A lump in the back of my throat muffles my voice. I'm so angry and upset I don't know whether to cry or scream – mind you, with the pain in my ankle I could easily do both right at this minute.

'We all know it wasn't Cassie,' Stan assures me with a lopsided grin. Actually, everything about his face is a bit lopsided. His nose kinks dangerously to the left and his eyes look like they've fallen out with each other as they're not only keeping their distance, but they always look in opposite directions. I'm never sure which one to focus on when I look at him, so I normally stare at his hat – which he's not wearing right now so I'm completely flummoxed. His hair's all flattened at the front, I notice, concentrating on that instead. The bit in the middle of his head is all raised to a peak. I've often wondered how much of his chef's hat was just hollow and how much actually had hair in – looks like it's mostly hair.

'I can't believe Margaret would even *think* that,' I tell him, tightening my lips.

'Don't worry about her,' Stan says airily. 'She'll eat her words when they find out who really took the money. If anyone actually *did*, that is.'

I stare at him, despite hearing the ping of the lift arriving on our floor. 'You don't believe it?'

'Well it seems a bit odd that the boss is saying

money went missing but can't tell us where from, when or even how much.' Stan shrugs. 'Hardly worth holding a meeting for, was it?' He helps me into the lift. 'Can you manage from here?'

I nod. 'Yes, thanks.'

The door closes and I lean back against the wall, deep in thought.

CASSIE'S LYING ON HER BED SOBBING INTO HER PILLOW when I almost fall into the room. I knew I shouldn't have put all my weight on the door, but it was such a relief to have something to hold onto after having to cross the damn corridor.

She looks up in surprise as I bump into her bed on my way to my own. The room's quite small and there really isn't room for two of us, but we like sharing. I spent my first year here on my own before Cassie joined the staff, and it wasn't half as much fun.

Banging my leg on her bed isn't much fun either, and I howl as the pain ricochets through to my ankle.

'You need more painkillers,' Cassie says, getting up to help me over to my bed. She sniffs loudly as she fluffs up the pillows behind my head and then grabs the cushions from the chair and piles them up under my foot.

'Thanks, love.' I don't like seeing her with her eyes all red and puffy. 'You know no-one believes it was you, don't you? In fact, Stan doesn't think that *anything's* gone missing at all.'

She hands me a couple of paracetamol and a glass of water from my bedside table.

'I don't care. I'm leaving anyway.' Her voice is quiet and croaky.

'Yeah, but not like this.' I stare at her.

She shrugs. 'I've done what I came here to do. I've proven to Mum and Dad that I can keep a job for a whole year – despite what they thought.'

I grin. 'Well, you can't really blame them, can you? You told me yourself you never lasted more than a few weeks at any of those shops you worked at.'

'True.' She sniffs again. 'I just got bored, that's all. That's the trouble with clothes shops, they don't change their stock often enough for me. Once I'd bought everything from that season's range with my staff discount I just wanted to try another shop. It's the same when you're out shopping though, isn't it? You can't spend months shopping in just one shop. You need some variety.'

'You're still allowed to *buy* stuff from other shops,' I remind her, giggling. 'Just because you don't actually *work* there.'

'I know.' She nods. 'It just seems stupid to go elsewhere when you get discount at one shop, that's all.'

I put my hand on her arm. 'You're the best,' I tell her. I love how she doesn't waste money, even though she could if she wanted to.

'So are you.' She manages a smile.

'Are we going to try on those things, then?' I nod to the carrier bags stacked up in the corner.

She sighs, slumping onto my bed. 'I don't really feel like it now. Besides, you can't try anything on in that state. You look like you need to get some sleep.'

I have to admit she's right. I feel like shit. It's a good job I'm not on the late shift tonight. 'What will *you* do?'

'I thought I'd take a shower and pamper myself a bit. I tried Skyping Dad to see if he'd thought any more about getting me that job in one of his offices, but they're out of contact. Probably still flying.'

Cassie's parents have gone on holiday again. They do a lot of that. I love hearing about all the interesting places they've been to. Her mum's not like a tourist; she really likes to immerse herself in local culture – and she eats some really weird food – everywhere she goes. Cassie doesn't usually go with them – she likes shopping and sunbathing instead. I'm surprised how well she and her mum get along, actually, they're so different from each other.

'It's Africa, isn't it?'

She nods. 'Yeah. They said they might not be in touch for a few days as they're off on safari as soon as they land. I was also hoping to ask Dad for some kind of proof that he gave me that money as half of it was in cash – you know, in case anyone tries to accuse me of anything.'

My heart lurches at her sad face. 'You don't have to prove anything, love,' I tell her. 'We're all innocent until proven guilty, remember?'

She stands up with a shrug. 'I know, but you can't stop people *thinking* things, can you?'

I grab her arm again, and she turns back to face me. 'By 'people' you mean mad Margaret, I presume? No-one's going to listen to her. Besides...'

'What?'

'Well.' I go all hot and bothered as I remember losing my temper earlier. 'I may have...sort of...let slip that your family's a bit richer than most of us.' I screw my eyes shut but I can still feel her look of disappointment boring into me.

'You *what*?' She sounds calm but she's like a duck - all serene on the surface but feet paddling like mad beneath the water.

I slowly open my eyes. 'I just said you didn't *need* to steal money because you already had enough.' It sounded pretty reasonable in my head, but hearing myself say it aloud has put a totally different spin on it, I realise, all too late.

Cassie straightens up. 'So that's the only reason I wouldn't have stolen the money, is it? Nothing to do with the fact that I'm not a *thief* or anything? Just that I've already got enough money so I don't need to rob the damn hotel?' Cassie's never shouted at me before, and I cringe, wishing my bed could swallow me up. I hate this.

'That's not what I meant,' I tell her quickly, my voice coming out a bit squeakier than I expected.

'No, it's just what you *said*. To the whole staff.' She whizzes to the door and slams it on her way out.

Damn. I can hardly go after her – not that she'd want to see me now anyway. Besides, I'm finding it hard enough to keep my eyes open, and this pain in my leg just got ten times worse. Hot tears trickle down my cheeks and I pull a pillow around my face as I dissolve into sad, angry sobs.

Cassie's my best friend in the whole world and now I've not only betrayed her confidence, but made it look like I agree with the rest of them – which I don't. I'd never think that. But will she believe me? Will she just leave the hotel and never want to see me again? Oh God, what have I done?

5

It's been four days now and things just aren't the same without being able to talk properly to Cassie. She's not being horrid exactly, just a bit cold. She's saying things like 'it doesn't matter, honestly,' and 'don't worry about it', but she must know deep down that it *does* matter and that I *am* worried about it. She's just being nice. But not in a warm way.

She's helped me to move around a bit, too, but when I hold onto her arms her body's all stiff, not relaxed like it normally is.

I haven't been downstairs as Stan's sent food up for me. I haven't really been in the mood to eat a lot though. Well, apart from the secret stash of cakes, biscuits and chocolate Cassie and I keep in the bottom of the wardrobe for emergencies. Spraining your ankle and not being able to walk *is* a type of emergency, isn't it? Especially if it stops you going downstairs for normal meals.

Actually, it was a good job I have my own *secret* secret stash in the bedside cupboard, or I wouldn't have eaten much at all for the first couple of days when I couldn't even *get* to the bottom of the wardrobe. Although it was a help when Cassie realised I was struggling and pulled out the box of goodies and piled it all on top of the dressing table for me on the second day. She's thoughtful like that.

I've been off work since Tuesday and now it's Saturday I'm actually able to get my shoe on again and walk without hobbling around like an old lady. Mr Partington's really relieved, as weekends are always much busier than the rest of the week, and it would be really hard on the others if I didn't go into work today. I'm doing the late shift back in my own job and Cassie's doing the same hours on lunch and dinner in the restaurant.

We both had a bit of a lie-in this morning, so we won't be too tired later, and I got up first so Cassie's still in the shower now. I get straight into my uniform of blue suit and white blouse – a welcome change from the black skirt and white blouse with a little black waistcoat we wear for waiting-on. I've been practising walking in my Karen Millens so that I could wear them today, but I'm keeping my ballet pumps handy, just in case. It's nice to actually style my hair – well, it's only a mass of blonde waves that I sometimes tie in a ponytail or a really stylish chignon like I did the other day – and put on some make-up.

'You look nice.' Cassie comes out of the bathroom

with a towel around her body and another one turban-style around her head.

'Thanks, so do you.'

She narrows her eyes at me, clearly puzzled. Hmm, I get her point. It's hard to look nice wrapped up in towels, but at least I was trying to be friendly. Her mouth twitches a bit and I think, for one wonderful moment, that she's going to smile. Then she looks away and starts getting her clothes together.

The shopping bags disappeared a couple of days ago, and I wonder if it's worth asking her about them. I decide against it. I'm still dying to know what she bought, though. Maybe I'll have a bit of a snoop when she's not around. Just for the purpose of avoiding a row, of course. Not that I'm nosy or anything. I'm just...interested. It's good to take an interest in your friends. And their shopping.

'Are you going to chance the back stairs or are you using the lift still?' Cassie asks when we're both ready to go down.

'I think it'll be better to take the lift,' I say, frowning thoughtfully. 'After all, it would be awful if I fell now, just when I'm about to go back to work, wouldn't it?'

She nods. 'I'll accompany you – just to make sure. Like you said, it would be dreadful for anything to happen now, wouldn't it?'

Warmth trickles through my body. This is much more like the old Cassie. I wonder if she's missed working with me these past few days and is really pleased I'm coming back today. She hasn't spoken to me at all about work this week – well, she hasn't spoken to me full stop – apart from just being polite, of course. And asking if I'm okay. And if I needed anything. And whether... actually, come to think of it, she *has* spoken to me quite a bit during our non-speaking phase.

I follow her into the lift and she presses the button for the ground floor.

When the doors open again I'm overwhelmed by the smell of paint.

'Crikey!'

'Yeah, they've been doing a bit of a touch-up in the Remington Suite,' Cassie explains casually.

'Ooh, let's see.' I can't resist a quick look.

'Just follow your nose,' Cassie murmurs.

It gets even more overpowering as I get closer and I take a peek around the open door. 'They've changed the colour.' It's unthinkable.

'We can't get the old shade anymore, darlin',' a voice informs me from behind the door.

Stepping gingerly on some plastic floor-protector, I see a guy in overalls, painting the wall.

'Oh.'

'It's gone well out of fashion,' he continues, smiling at me. 'This is the nearest we could find. Buttermilk.'

'Buttermilk,' I repeat with a nod. 'That explains it.' It's only about two shades lighter than the cream, but they do say a change is as good as a rest.

'Party,' Cassie whispers to me, before disappearing around the corner.

'What?'

Then I hear the boss's voice coming up the corridor. *Shit.* I think Cassie's forgotten I can't move as quickly as she can.

'Er...well...very good. Carry on,' I say in my most businesslike voice just as Mr Partington arrives.

He frowns at me. 'Libby? What are you doing?'

'I was just reacquainting myself with the place, you know,' I say, straightening up as I walk towards him. 'I heard you were having some work done so I thought I'd take a look just in case...' My jaw drops as I notice someone standing behind him. And not just someone. *Him.*

Mr Partington smirks as he catches my gaze. 'Ah, yes. You remember Sergeant *Harper*, don't you? You served him a meal earlier in the week if I recall correctly.'

I'm gawping into the deep, dark eyes of none other than Mr Happy. *Oh God!* And to make matters worse, he looks even more handsome than I'd remembered in all the dreams I've been having about him. And to make them worse still, his mouth's twitching at the edges and his eyes are twinkling as though he's dying to burst out laughing but can't quite manage it.

'This is Liberty Lawrence, our junior manager,' Mr Partington says.

'Ah, Liberty. I do remember you, of course. But I didn't get your name the other day.' I stand there like a goldfish while his warm fingers encase mine in a firm handshake.

'What a coincidence. I don't think you quite got the

sergeant's name either, did you, Liberty?' Mr Partington gives me a very knowing look, and I wonder if he's ratted on me to the handsome copper.

'Well...um...' My face grows hotter by the second.

'Well, I'd like to see if the painters have time to finish off my office door today, so if you've finished your inspection, perhaps you could go and check on the restaurant?' Mr Partington has a great knack of making an order sound like a suggestion when he's got company.

'Yes. Um. Right...well...yes.' I nod several times before I can convince my legs to move.

'Good to see you back on your feet again, Liberty,' Sergeant Harper says with a hint of a smile, which may or may not have been more like a smirk.

I ARRIVE IN THE RESTAURANT TO FIND THAT Margaret's already seated the first couple of customers. She grimaces at me on her way through to the kitchen with their order.

'What's bit her bum?' I whisper to Cassie as I join her at the dumbwaiter, where she's folding napkins into bishops' mitres. I start to help. It's just force of habit, really. I never like to just watch the others work; it always feels like I'm pulling rank – which I would never do. The staff are my friends. Well, maybe not Moody Margaret, so much.

Cassie shakes her head. 'Don't worry about her. She's been like that all week. Ever since—'

I stop mid-mitre to stare at her. Cassie's not even looking at me, but I can see her face is turning red.

'Oh no.' I suddenly feel sick. 'Has she been off with you all week because of what I said in the meeting?'

'I don't think it's just because of what you said' she replies with a snort. 'She's been off with everyone. Don't worry about it.' She shrugs and continues to fold.

I frown. 'Why?'

She looks up at me then. 'You know that man you served in here the other night? The good-looking one with the bœuf bourguignon?'

I nod.

'He's a police sergeant.'

'I know.'

'What?'

'I know.'

'But you've only been back five minutes.' Her eyes widen as she gawps at me. 'You *knew*? That day, before—'

'No.' I shake my head. 'I just bumped into him in the corridor. He was with Party when they caught me in the Remington Suite.'

She frowns guiltily. 'Oh no – he caught you?'

'Yeah. He was going to see the painters with that guy, Mr. Happy. Although he's not Mr Happy, he's Sergeant Harper.'

'I know. I mean, I know that's who he is. But what was he doing with Party?'

'Hello again, ladies.'

We both look up as two men approach us. It's the reporters from the other day.

'You're back.' Ben smiles at me. 'Are you better?'

'Yes, thanks.' I nod.

'Usual place?' Cassie leads them over to the window table where they were last time I saw them. 'It's spring onion soup today and—'

'Don't tell me, the lamb's off?' Rob grins at her and she blushes.

'Yes. Just for a change.' She giggles. 'Give me a shout when you're ready to order.'

'Oh, we will,' Rob assures her with a dazzling smile.

Cassie slowly strolls back to where I'm still titivating napkins. My eyebrows are raised as I gaze at her expectantly.

She gives me a shy smile. 'They've been in here every day,' she confesses. 'Rob's asked me to go for a drink with him sometime.'

'And?'

'And as soon as I get a night off I will.'

I put my hand to my mouth. 'Oh no. You haven't been able to have a night off this week because of me being off sick, have you? I'm so sorry.' I feel dreadful. Although I can't help thinking that Fiona *must* be better by now. This is *her* job, after all.

'It's okay. In fact, it's been quite good that I couldn't go, in a way.'

'Really?' I raise my eyebrows in disbelief.

She turns so her back is towards them. 'I could have had a night off. Party said he'd get Cheryl to cover, but I thought it would just lead to more work for me when I got back as she always leaves the place in such a mess, so I declined. Besides...' she lowers her voice 'I'm playing hard to get.'

I gape at her. I've never seen her go on a date in the twelve months since we've met. Hard to get? Impossible, more like. And I know she hasn't had a boyfriend lurking in the background somewhere because we spend all our spare time together. Well, until this week, anyway.

'So, he's not um—'

'No.' She sounds defiant. Not to mention defensive.

'Well, I just thought with Ben being obviously, you know—'

'Yeah, *I* know. Pity Margaret doesn't. She keeps flirting with him and he just plays along. It's really funny to watch, but I'm sure she's taking it all seriously. I mean…as if!'

I stare at her and notice Margaret returning with two plates of hors d'œuvres just in time. She reaches the table but is too pre-occupied with frowning at us to serve her customers

Cassie puts her finger to her lips to shush me, then pretends to scratch her mouth as Margaret continues to peer at us curiously.

'Thank you.' The elderly woman she is serving is clearly becoming impatient, waiting for her to put the food on the table and Margaret suddenly looks around, takes the hint and plonks the plates – rather heavily to my mind - in front of her and her companion.

Rob looks over and waves to us.

'Do you want to take their order, or shall I?' I tease Cassie.

'Me,' she says, as if there was ever any doubt. 'You're not supposed to be working in here today, remember?'

Damn. I'd forgotten that. She goes over to serve them and I'm just about to go to my office when Margaret starts heading straight for me. If I leave now it'll look like I'm avoiding her, but if I stay put I'm right in her firing line.

'So, how are you? Settling in okay?' I ask in a friendly tone.

Her expression looks like thunder. 'Fine. Did Cassie tell you we all had to be interviewed by the police this week?' Her lips are tight as she speaks.

I gawp at her, then glance over at Cassie, who's giggling with the reporters. 'No, she didn't mention it.'

Margaret snorts. 'Hmm, I wonder why.'

'Probably because there was nothing to say,' I retort. I really don't like her insinuations. In fact, I've recently come to realise that I really don't like her, full stop.

'We were all questioned individually,' Margaret continues. 'About the *theft*.'

No shit, Sherlock!

I roll my eyes. 'And have they found out anything?'

'They haven't finished their investigations yet.' She shakes her head. 'Not everyone's been available for interview so far.'

Me. She means me. I can tell by the snide way she's

saying it. Now she thinks *I'm* guilty because I haven't been interviewed yet. But why not? I've been on the premises, even though I've been off duty. They could still have spoken to me. My mouth still worked, it was only my leg that couldn't.

Maybe Sergeant Harper doesn't want to interview me? Perhaps he feels too close – that we've got some kind of connection so it would be inappropriate for him to ask me about a theft. I did feel a sort of spark of electricity when I was with him that day. Although, it was more like a short circuit as he would hardly look at me at the time. Maybe that's why. Perhaps he knew he was falling for me and didn't want to let on. It wouldn't look professional. For either of us. And *I* was on duty, even if he wasn't. Or was he? Is that why he was here? No, surely he'd have been in the meeting if that was the case. What if he had the Remington Suite bugged so he could listen in to us, though? And Mr Partington was in on it. He would've heard me sticking up for Cassie. He'd know how horrid it all was. Surely he must have—

'Libby.'

I turn around and scream. Yes, *scream*. Mr Partington's standing there with Sergeant Harper right behind him. It's as though they've just leapt out of my thoughts and into the restaurant. I put my hand to my mouth, shocked at the sound that just escaped it. Everyone else appears shocked too. In fact, the old woman that Margaret was serving starts to choke on her hors d'œuvres and Cassie rushes over and puts her arms around her, presumably in an attempt to perform the Heimlich manoeuvre. The woman looks astounded as she waves her arms around, trying to get Cassie off her.

Mr. Partington and the sergeant look over in horror and rush to the table.

'Here.' Cassie relinquishes her hold on the old dear and Sergeant Harper takes over. He gives the woman a sharp thump on her back and the offending item comes shooting out of her mouth – followed swiftly by her teeth.

The elderly gent sitting opposite her rolls his eyes as though this is a daily occurrence, while the woman, who is now gasping for air, shrieks. Her high-pitched wail fills the restaurant while everyone just stares in her direction.

Stan and Adrian come rushing through from the kitchen and gawp at the scene, while Cassie very cautiously scoops up the set of dentures in a napkin which she silently offers to the woman who gapes at her in horror.

Sergeant Harper shakes his head, returning to his position by the dumbwaiter.

I wonder if I'm about to be arrested for nearly killing the woman, although to be fair, it wasn't actually my fault.

Mr Partington clears his throat. 'Would you come with us, please?'

I hear a snort and jerk my head around. Margaret's giving me a very knowing look as she nods her head.

Damn. She'd already guessed that they were here for me. I hate that she's right.

My legs turn to jelly as I attempt to follow them out, glancing back in dismay to Cassie. She gives me a pitying smile that says 'It'll be okay'. I give her a horrified one back that says 'You could have warned me'. My heart thumps hard against my ribs and I feel sick. I've no idea why. I know I haven't done anything wrong, but I feel like everyone's watching me, like I'm being led to the gallows or something. Except the gallows might be a bit easier to handle than this.

6

MY HEART THUMPS LIKE A DRUM AS I STEP INTO MR Partington's office. I stare down at the floor, and notice that those horrid marks are still on the carpet. He clearly didn't take my advice about the vinegar.

'Sit down, Liberty.'

The boss looks really officious as he sinks into the buttery leather of his swivel chair, while Sergeant Harper sits on a normal chair.

'This is Sergeant Harper, who is investigating the case of the missing money,' Mr Partington begins, peering over his Ted Bakers like an old schoolmaster.

You don't say!

I glance over at the handsome hunk and my heart starts pounding for a different reason. My stomach feels like I'm riding a rollercoaster. He really is gorgeous. It's just a shame he looks so serious. I'll bet if he smiled, he'd—

'Liberty, I need to ask if you know anything at all

about money going missing from the hotel.' His voice is deep and serious – *and so goddamn sexy!*

'Y-yes.' Damn! I could hardly speak and now I've said the wrong thing and they've both just sat forwards on their seats and are staring at me. 'Yes, I know,' I clarify. 'I mean, I thought that was what it would be about.'

They both look disappointed. *Did they actually expect a confession?*

'Mr Partington told us on Tuesday that some money had gone missing,' I continue, hoping I don't sound guilty. Not that I *am* guilty, of course, it's just that this sort of thing makes you feel like you are, somehow.

I straighten in my seat, trying to look a bit more confident – and *feel* a bit more confident. I'm a member of the management team. I should be *conducting* this interview, not answering the questions. And, to be honest, I'd ask much better questions than they're about to come up with, I can guarantee it.

I clear my throat.

'I take it that no-one has come forward to admit to anything?' I ask airily.

'No.' Mr Partington speaks very abruptly.

'Have you heard anything that might help the case?' Sergeant Harper asks, making my stomach roll over again.

'No. But I've been laid up all week. I've hardly spoken to any of the staff.' I want to add 'not even my roommate' but they don't need to know about that, even if it *was* because of the theft. I don't think it would help the case – and it certainly wouldn't help Cassie's case.

The sergeant glances down at my foot and his lips twitch a little. Hmm, he clearly remembers the incident that laid me up. *Not that he cared*, I remember, ruefully.

'A large amount of cash was stolen from that safe on Monday night,' Mr Partington begins, indicating the corner of the room. 'Unfortunately, owing to staff shortages, I hadn't yet banked the weekend's takings, so there was a significant amount in there.'

My eyes must be the size of saucers as I gawp at him. No wonder he's been so cagey about the whole thing! What on earth would possess him to delay banking the weekend's takings? There would have been thousands in there. No matter what else was going on, surely the banking would be the utmost priority? Mr Ainsworth's going to go mad when he hears about this.

'Did you know that the banking hadn't been done on Monday?' Sergeant Harper narrows his eyes at me.

'No,' I reply straight away. 'I was covering the restaurant on Sunday and Monday, so I haven't been working in the office.' *So there!*

He scribbles something into a little notebook.

'Libby's only junior management,' Mr Partington explains. 'She's not privy to that sort of information, anyway.'

I want to scowl at him for making me look so pathetic, but I have to admit he's helping prove my innocence, in a way. A rather patronising way, I know, but I'll take whatever I can get.

'Where were you on Monday night?' Sergeant Harper asks.

There's a thud in my stomach. Monday night. Why the hell did it have to be Monday night? Now I've got to rake it all up again. Just when I was beginning to forget about that scumbag Connor, too – though that's mainly because the dishy sergeant has been in my head all week. Although, of course, when he was in my head he wasn't a po-faced sergeant, he was a kind, loving man – one who cared about a girl almost breaking her leg while serving his lunch!

'I was at The Four Feathers,' I reply, suddenly realising they're both staring at me waiting for an answer.

Mr Partington's lips have gone thin and that vein's started up again on his neck. He thinks I've betrayed him. The Four Feathers is a pub down the road, and he's clearly miffed to think we've been patronising it instead of spending our money here. But who wants to stay at work when they don't have to? I live here, for goodness' sake; I have to get out *sometime*.

'What time was this?' Sergeant Harper's got his pencil poised.

'After I'd finished up here, about half ten.' My stomach churns as I remember bursting into the bar just in time to see Connor giving Bianca a lingering kiss. I'd told him I'd join him if I got away in time, but he obviously didn't hold out much hope. Or rather – he wasn't exactly hoping for the same thing as me. He was clearly banking on me not making it.

The sergeant flicks through his notebook before looking back up at me. 'Did you meet anyone there? Or see anyone you knew?'

It's obvious he's been speaking to Connor and Bianca, but I wonder just what they've told him. I swallow hard.

'I met my boyfriend there, Connor Worthington.'

The sergeant holds my gaze. 'Anyone else?'

'Yes.' I gulp again. 'Bianca Morrison-Wright.'

He gives a satisfied nod.

'They were kissing in the bar,' I continue. 'That's when I found out they'd been seeing each other behind my back.'

'I see.' Sergeant Harper scribbles something in his book. *It looks like the other two missed out that bit when they gave him their stories.* 'What happened?'

What the hell does he think happened?

'We had a row. They admitted they'd been seeing each other, so I walked out.' I shrug, trying to show them – and myself – that it doesn't bother me. The burn in my stomach tells a different story, unfortunately.

The sergeant raises his eyebrows. 'Is that all?'

All? I huff. *What more does he want? Blood?* I stare at him.

'Where did you go after you left The Four Feathers?'

'I came back here.'

'Did anyone see you?'

I think for a moment. Those of us that live-in have a key to the back door, so we come in through the kitchen and up the back stairs. We're not supposed to be seen by hotel guests unless we're on duty, so we're not allowed to use the front entrance. That night I'd had trouble with my key. I was sobbing so hard I'd fumbled and dropped it.

'One of the security guards helped me unlock the back door,' I explain. 'Frank Welch. He was doing his rounds when he heard me—' I was about to say crying, but thought better of it. I don't want him to think I've been affected by a cheating boyfriend, and certainly hadn't expected to have to tell Mr Partington about it. Especially not as it looked like he hadn't even read all about it on Facebook, like everyone else.

The sergeant glances up at me expectantly. Then a look of sympathy crosses his face and I realise he knows what I was about to say.

'I dropped my keys,' I add quickly. I can't stand that expression. I turn away and face the boss instead. 'They clattered onto the concrete and Frank heard and shone his torch on me.'

'Isn't there an outside light?' Mr Partington frowns.

'Yes. But, you know Frank. He was doing his rounds and came over to see if I was...er...if I needed any help. *With my keys.*' Actually, the sweet old guy had been really worried when he saw what a state I was in and offered me a cup of tea. I'd declined, just wanting to get to my room and bawl my eyes out properly, like any normal person would.

'So, you came inside?' Sergeant Harper has lost the sympathetic look, and is back to frowning again.

'Yes. I went straight to my room. Cassie was there. We share.'

The sergeant nods, consulting his notes again. 'Cassandra Beaumont.'

'Yes.'

'And you didn't hear anything at all in the night?'

'No.'

'Whose keys did Frank Welch use to let you in?'

I just gape at him, my mind whirling as I try to remember. 'Um... his, I think. Yes.'

'You're sure?'

I recall Frank putting an arm around me and helping me inside. 'Yes. He used his own keys. He carries a big bunch of them on a chain attached to his belt. I was in too much of a...er...' I trail off, feeling my face get hot again.

'I see,' says the sergeant softly.

I gaze at him. He actually sounds like he cares.

'So, what happened to your keys? Did you pick them up? Have you got them?'

My gaze quickly becomes a grimace. *Shit*. The whole scene plays out in front of my mind's eye once again, with Frank coming to my rescue and me scurrying off up to my room without a second thought for my keys.

Slowly, I shake my head. 'No.'

'You haven't got your keys?' Mr Partington looks furious.

'I'm sorry. I suppose I assumed Frank would pick them up. He just unlocked the door and I came in and went to my room. I heard him lock the door behind us and—'

'So he came inside?' Sergeant Harper asks.

'Yes. He was going to have a cup of tea. The back door leads straight into the kitchen so...'

'So he wouldn't have had time to look for your keys?'

I shake my head again, swallowing hard. *Shit!*

'I didn't think...'

'That's obvious.' The anger in the boss's voice is plain, so I keep my gaze firmly on the sergeant.

'I need you to show me exactly where you dropped your keys,' Sergeant Harper says, getting up.

Carefully, I put the weight back on my feet and head for the door—disappointed, though not surprised, that the boss is joining us.

Everyone stares at us as we walk through the kitchen. Cassie's standing by the still machine, and gives me a sympathetic smile as I pass her. I actually think we're okay again.

The staff have stopped talking and they're just watching us pass through like a royal parade. The smell of boiling cabbage and roast chicken fill my nostrils as my Karen Millens clip across the tiled floor. The radio crackles away quietly. It's a quiz. 'In what year did Meatloaf release *Bat Out of Hell*?' the DJ asks some poor guy who sounds like he's way too young to even know who Meatloaf is. Where do they find these contestants? I want to shout out 'Nineteen seventy-seven', and I would if it was any normal day. But it's not. So I keep quiet.

It's like Moses and the parting of the waves of the

Red Sea as the cooks stand aside to let us through to the back of the room and out the door.

'I was just here when I dropped it.' I point to the cracked step as the three of us crowd outside the back door. I'm secretly hoping to look down and see my key winking up at me from the concrete next to the plant pot full of weeds.

'Well, it's not here now.' Mr Partington channels Captain Obvious.

'Does anyone else know you've lost your key?' Sergeant Harper asks, after a quick search of the area.

'No. *I* didn't know until just now,' I admit.

'You haven't missed it since Monday?'

'No, I've been in my room all week with a sprained ankle. I didn't have any need of it.'

The sergeant nods. He takes a few snaps of the step and the concrete using his mobile phone – which, I notice, isn't the most up-to-date offering from Apple – then leads us around the outside of the building, checking the ground as if my key will magically appear. 'Were there any other keys with it?'

I shake my head. 'No. Just the one for the back door.' I'm actually relieved that I don't keep my office keys on the same key ring just in case I ever get drunk and lose the whole bunch. I roll my eyes at myself – I didn't even have one drink and I managed to lose my key.

'Well, thank heavens for small mercies,' Mr Partington mutters behind us.

'You'll have to get that lock changed right away,'

Sergeant Harper tells him. 'The place isn't secure while someone else could have a key.'

The boss huffs. I daren't look round at him.

'It'll come out of your wages, young lady.' Mr Partington's all heart.

'You must have insurance for this sort of thing,' Sergeant Harper says with a frown. He turns to face the boss, who suddenly looks flustered.

'Well...I...er...yes, I suppose.'

'Good.'

Warmth spreads through me at the thought that the handsome sergeant is actually sticking up for me. Well, in a way. Sort of.

'I take it you haven't noticed anyone seemingly richer than usual?' the sergeant asks me, back to his officious manner.

'No,' I say firmly. *And don't even bother to ask me about Cassie's shopping.* 'Not that I've seen much of anyone.'

'No, of course not.' He actually gives me a sympathetic smile. God, he's perfect. My insides start to burn at the sight, albeit fleeting.

We're at the front entrance to the hotel now.

'Well, I think I'd better have a word with the security guard again. Frank Welch,' the sergeant says after checking his notebook. 'Thanks for your co-operation, Miss Lawrence.'

I'm almost sad to leave him, as he nods pleasantly at me.

'Back to work, Libby,' Mr Partington says. I secretly suspect he just wants to assert his authority.

'Right...well...okay. Thank you.' I'm not sure if that's the right thing to say after a brutal police interrogation, but it's just about all I can manage. I walk as smartly as I can back to Reception, and my little office in the back of the stationery cupboard.

I hear muttering from the front desk and Frances, the receptionist, rings upstairs to ask Frank to go to the manager's office straight away. The security office is on the first floor – presumably so they get a better view of the grounds. Or, at least, the car park. We don't have that much in the way of grounds in central London, but that car park's worth its weight in gold. Not that any of the locals would bother to use a car, but quite a few of our wealthier residents drive here – or in the case of a select few, get driven by their chauffeurs.

I can't believe they hadn't had this conversation with Frank before now. What the hell did they talk about? Didn't it come up about him helping me in the other night? I sigh, putting my elbows on the desk and supporting my head. I feel like I've been through a mangle today – all that talk about catching Connor in the act on Monday night. I'm sure there's something in the rules about having to take the rest of the day off after an ordeal like that. And that sergeant might have been handsome but he hardly cracked a smile. Except that one. Almost. Kind of.

I'd have done a much better job if I'd been the one

asking the questions. Never mind all that crap about where I was and what I said when I found my boyfriend with his tongue down Bianca's throat. I'd ask proper questions like, 'Did you wear your Armani jeans on the night in question?' Because if I had worn mine, then I wouldn't have got to The Four Feathers before last orders – they're so tight it takes a good seven minutes of lying on the floor and pulling them on. I bought them second-hand from eBay and I'm sure they're labelled wrongly. I have trouble sitting up after wrestling my way into them, so I have to allow myself at least fifteen minutes to get into them and stand up again. If I'd have been doing all that, I probably wouldn't have arrived in time to see Connor and Bianca kissing. Connor always leaves a pub as soon as they call last orders to beat the rush at the end – unless, of course, they're having a lock-in. Although if we *had* been at a lock-in that night, it would have given us all a great alibi, even if it might have been a bit difficult to explain it away to the cops. (And Ken at The Four Feathers would be *spitting* feathers, as he'd probably lose his licence.)

'Were you wearing your red Ann Summers knickers with the black frill?' Another excellent question. Because if I had been, then it would have meant I was definitely not planning to come home that night – I won't go into detail, but Connor has a thing about those little beauties – and if I hadn't come back to the hotel I couldn't possibly have stolen the money.

'Did you, by any chance wear those pink strappy Ruby Shoos that you love to bits and want buried in your coffin with you when you die?' Now that *would* have been a good question. I don't know why, but those sandals always leave black marks wherever I walk – I must have trodden in some petrol or ink or something at one time. Anyway, if I'd worn them then it would have left marks all over Party's—

Shit - I know who stole the money!

7

I RUSH OUT OF THE STATIONERY CUPBOARD JUST AS Julie, one of the kitchen hands, plonks a tray of tea and biscuits on the reception desk.

Frances is on the phone, but puts a hand over the speaker. 'Can you take it to Mr Partington's office for me?' she asks her, gesturing to the phone by way of explanation.

'I'll do it.' Despite the throb in my ankle, I'm there like a shot. 'Is the copper still with him?'

Frances nods and Julie rolls her eyes. I ignore it and take the tray through. The sergeant's good looks clearly haven't gone unnoticed by the female members of staff, but that's the last thing on my mind right now.

'Come in,' Mr Partington calls after I've knocked on the door three-hundred and fifty-seven times. Well, maybe three, but it certainly felt like three-hundred and fifty-seven. He never replies on the first knock. I think it makes him feel important to keep people waiting.

'Your tea,' I announce, entering the room.

After two steps something soft and furry brushes against my right ankle. 'Aah!'

Mr Partington's eyes look bigger and bogglier than ever as I hurtle headlong into his desk, spilling the contents of the tray all over his paperwork, his suit, and his visitor.

The massive desk breaks my fall and I hold on to it for dear life, damned if I'm going to twist that ankle again – it hurts enough as it is.

The men both leap to their feet, yelling something incoherent – and, I suspect, totally unrepeatable – as the crockery smashes onto the cream carpet next to the lovely swivel chair.

There's a shriek from behind me and I jerk around to see a slightly familiar-looking old lady scoop her quivering Chihuahua into her arms. The dog's giving me the evil eye and I realise that it was him that I must have felt tickle my leg.

'I'm so sorry,' I murmur to no-one in particular and everyone in general.

'My poor Popsie! You've frightened him half to death.' The old lady scowls at me as she holds the little dog tightly to her.

'I'm sorry, but *he* frightened *me*.' It's clear my explanation is falling on deaf ears, as she resumes talking soothingly to the whimpering creature.

'Get this mess cleared up!' Mr Partington snaps. He and the sergeant have been trying to rescue the paperwork from the desk, but it's all drenched in water and milk, scattered with a generous helping of sugar.

I grab the tray and begin putting the remains of the crockery onto it.

'I don't know what you were thinking of, bursting in here and ruining all our hard work.' The boss is certainly in a foul mood, and I somehow get the impression my hopes of promotion may have been a little premature.

'I didn't mean to,' I protest. 'I tripped over that stupid—'

'How dare you?' The old woman's on her feet now, though judging at the way she's wobbling I don't think she will be for too long. 'My Popsie is traumatised because of you. I've only just bought him, and now he'll be wishing I hadn't!'

He's not the only one.

'You know full well we allow dogs at The Chalfont.' Mr Partington practically spits the words at me.

I gawp at him in amazement. 'Yes, but I didn't know—'

'Mrs Merrington-Smythe has just adopted Popsie from Battersea Dogs and Cats Home this morning,' he explains.

The penny drops. She's the woman from the restaurant who doesn't like congealed eggs and has a penchant for hideous jewellery. She didn't have a dog with her when I served her – I can't be blamed for not knowing she was going to go off and get one, can I?

'Oh.' I throw the old lady an apologetic smile. 'That's very commendable of you.'

'Don't you patronise me after scaring my dog like that!' She's a fierce old duck when she's riled.

'I didn't mean to—'

'Just get this cleared up!' Mr Partington scoops all the soggy papers from his desk straight into the bin, clearly having come to the conclusion none of it is salvageable. He turns to Sergeant Harper, who's now busy wiping milk from his suit with a handkerchief. 'I'm sorry, but it looks like we'll need to start all over again.' He shakes his head at the copper and then rolls his eyes at me.

'I'm sorry.' I'm beginning to sound like a broken record, but I really don't know what else to say.

'We'll adjourn to the Remington Suite,' Mr Partington announces with a disgruntled sigh. 'I do apologise for the inconvenience, Mrs. Merrington-Smythe.' He runs a hand through his hair. 'Liberty, as soon as you've finished here have some more tea brought through to us – *by someone else.*'

I gape at him. 'But I—'

'Just do it.' He waves a dismissive arm in my direction and ushers Mrs Merrington-Smythe out the door.

The sergeant shakes his head with a hint of a smirk and goes to follow them out.

'I know who did it, though,' I blurt out to the back of his head. 'I know who the thief is'.

He turns and stares at me with an incredulous expression. 'Really?'

I nod dumbly.

'I'll catch you up,' he calls down the corridor to the others before closing the door.

I've got a pile of broken crockery in my hand which I carefully place in the bin while the sergeant moves two chairs to the other side of the room, away from the mess. 'Sit down.'

My stomach lurches. He sounds so bossy; it makes me even more nervous.

We sit facing each other and immediately my face heats up. He's so near I can smell his subtle, spicy after-shave, and I notice that his mouth does actually turn up at the edges very slightly. God, he's even more heavenly close-up!

He takes out his notebook and then looks over at me questioningly. 'What do you know?'

My mouth has suddenly gone dry and I begin to tremble. This is it. I'm about to solve a real-life crime. I might even get a medal for this, or—

'Liberty?'

Okay, here goes...

'Well,' I begin. 'When I was in here on Tuesday morning I noticed these marks on the carpet.' I get up and point them out to him. 'They go from the filing cabinet to the safe.'

He narrows his eyes. 'Yes, I noticed them. What do you think they are?'

'Heel marks. From a stiletto heel.'

He moves next to me and kneels beside one of the

little brownish spots. I breathe in that fragrant aftershave again, and feel his warmth so close to me.

'I thought maybe some kind of footprints, but they looked a bit small for that. They could be stilettos, I suppose.' He nods thoughtfully and I feel a flush of pride. 'Does anyone wear stilettos for work?'

I nod. 'Just one person, Bianca Morrison-Wright.' I'm so proud of myself as I watch him scribble in his notebook, but then he pauses and flips back a few pages with a frown.

'This would be the woman who was kissing your boyfriend in The Four Feathers, I take it?' He gives me a really withering look as he quickly closes his book.

My whole body suddenly goes hot. 'Well, yes, but—'

'That's the best you can come up with?' He rolls his eyes and I just want the floor to swallow me up – dirty carpet and all.

'I can see how this looks,' I protest. 'But it makes sense. She's the only one that wears stilettos for work, and she was moaning on Tuesday about all the muck on the floor behind the bar. It's the same colour muck here as she got on herself then. You saw her in the bar - she fell in it. You can ask anyone...' Something tells me the sergeant isn't going to ask anyone anything. It's clear he doesn't believe a word I'm saying.

'Look, just because this woman kissed your boyfriend it doesn't mean she stole the money from the safe.' He shakes his head and my stomach roils with sickening embarrassment.

'It's not that...' I object, but it's no use.

'I should keep your theories to yourself from now on, Miss Lawrence.' He tucks his notebook back into his jacket pocket. 'Making false accusations can get you into a lot of trouble.'

My jaw drops as he shoots me a look of contempt and leaves the room. My heart beats a military tattoo against my ribs and I'm on the verge of tears. I was so sure he'd be pleased. That he'd believe me. I sink into the nearest chair and stare at the chaos surrounding the desk. I feel sick. And sore. And embarrassed. It hadn't occurred to me that anyone would think I was just making it all up because of what she did with Connor. I sigh heavily. I'm so stupid – of course it looks like sour grapes. I should have realized and kept my big mouth shut.

Big tears begin to trickle down my flushed cheeks and I rub them away. I get up, then grab the tray and head back to the kitchen. The lunchtime rush is over and there are only a few members of staff left, cleaning down surfaces and washing dishes. I dump the tray and grab a handful of disposable kitchen paper, as well as a dustpan and brush from the broom cupboard.

It takes ages to wipe down the desk, chairs and walls of Mr Partington's office, and vacuum up all the sugar. I'm surprised to find a sheet of paper on the floor —it must have flown off the desk and avoided the spillage in all the commotion. Mr Partington's scribble is difficult to read at the best of times, but this just looks like hieroglyphics. Apart from a few odd words. *Room*

109, Saturday 11.30am – 12.30pm, £650 cash, gold necklace.

Has there been another robbery? Is that what this meeting was all about? My mind races as I take a last look around the room. I think it'll pass Party's inspection. I'm still puzzled about those marks on the carpet, though. I whip out my mobile phone and take a few snaps of them, showing the trail from the filing cabinet to the safe. It can't just be a coincidence.

After a quick trip to the kitchen to return the equipment and get rid of the rubbish, I take the back stairs up to the first floor. As I approach room 109 I notice two security guards loitering in the doorway. They both look to be in their sixties, with grey hair. One must be new as I don't know his face – and I would remember him as he's wearing some really cheap-looking spectacles. I assume they don't get paid all that well in this job. I recognize the second man as Frank Welch, our longest-serving member of staff.

'Hi,' I say, throwing them my best, beaming smile. 'How's it going?'

Frank smiles, but the one with the specs frowns at me. 'You're the junior manager, aren't you? I didn't think you were part of this investigation.'

Damn! These guys have clearly done their homework.

I nod, trying to look efficient. 'Yes, Mr Partington's taken Mrs Merrington-Smythe into the Remington Suite for a chat with Sergeant Harper. He's asked me to check on things up here. Is there any news?'

'No.'

That wasn't the answer I was hoping for.

Both men look like they're about to leave the room, slowly moving towards me.

'Well...er...' I strain to see past them, but they're blocking the doorway. 'The old lady needs a cardigan. It's a bit draughty down there. Is it okay if I take it? Mr Partington said to just check with you guys if all the photos have been taken and everything.'

I've noticed something blue and woollen hanging on the back of a chair, and I'm hoping to goodness it's some kind of old-woman-cardi.

The men look at each other thoughtfully.

'I won't be a sec. You can watch me, of course.'

Frank turns and looks back into the room.

'You fetch it, I'll go get some coffee,' specky tells him, brushing past me.

I quickly pull out my phone and take several photos of the room while Frank bungles over to the chair and carefully peels the cardigan from the back of it. I even take another couple of surreptitious snaps without even looking, before tucking the mobile back into my pocket.

'Thank you.' I smile brightly as he hands me the thick, cable-knit cardigan in a vivid peacock-blue.

'That's okay. Are you all right now? I haven't seen you since the other night,' he says, following me out of the room.

'Yes. Thanks again for all your help.' My face feels hot as I remember the state I was in the last time he saw me, when he helped me into the building after I'd broken up with Connor.

I hear the door close and lock as Frank leaves, and he overtakes me as I slowly walk towards the lift.

As soon as he disappears into the security office I look back towards room 109. I'd love to take another good look around in there...hang on. Something catches my eye and I venture back towards the door with my heart thumping a deafening rhythm.

As I crouch down I can see the thing that caught my eye is something very small and red tucked just inside the fibres of the carpet. I pick it up. It's a flake of plaster – or paint. I stare at it for a second, my heart quickening even more. There are a few more pieces just a small way away from me and I collect them up, pull out my hanky and carefully place them onto the white cotton. They look like drops of blood on fresh snow.

A noise makes me jump and I hastily fold up the hanky, tuck it into my pocket and rush over to the lift. I step in just as the door to the security office opens.

'Mr Partington was looking for you,' Frances calls over from the reception desk, as I exit the lift on the ground floor and wander back to my office. 'He wanted to know what had happened to the tea you were supposed to have ordered for him.' She grimaces.

Oh no. I'd forgotten all about it.

'I'll get it now,' I promise and head off towards the kitchen. Julie's just removing her apron. 'Mr Partington's asked for a tray of tea for three,' I tell her apologetically. 'They're in the Remington Suite. Only...he...er...doesn't want me to take it in.'

Julie looks at me like I've just sprouted another couple of heads or something. 'What?'

'There was a bit of an incident earlier...'

She frowns. 'What sort of—?'

'Oh, and can you take this with you? He's got an old lady with him. One of the security guards saw it in her room and thought she might need it. It's a bit chilly in the Remington now that the painters have removed the curtains. Thanks ever so much. Must dash.' Despite my ankle – which is hurting like hell, to be honest – I scurry out of the kitchen and make for my little cupboard.

'Is everything okay?' Frances asks as I pass her behind the desk.

'Yes. Julie's just getting the tea.' I try to sound bright and efficient as I smile at her and dive into my sanctuary.

The first thing I do is sit down, remove my Karen Millens and put my leg up on a box of envelopes. It's at times like this that I wish I kept a bottle of whiskey in my filing cabinet. Well, actually, I wish I *had* a filing cabinet to keep one in. The desk drawers are tiny and the only storage I have is half of one of the shelves - the one they store the sick bags on for the first aid boxes.

I breathe in the scent of ink and plastic packaging. It looks like my chances of promotion have gone right out of the window. I fold my arms on the desk and bury my head in them, closing my eyes for a few minutes while I gather my thoughts. So much has happened today it's hard to get my brain around it all. I just wish some of it had been good.

A few minutes later the door opens and I look up to see Connor strutting in. He gives me a pitying look that does nothing to improve my mood and I swallow hard. *Just when I thought today couldn't get any worse.*

'Hey, babe. I've been wanting to speak to you all week, but Cassie wouldn't let me come to your room.'

'It's against the rules.' I tense my jaw as he casually perches on the corner of my desk.

'I also tried ringing your mobile but it wouldn't go through.'

That may have had something to do with the fact that I blocked his number.

I stare at him with disinterest oozing from my eyes – or, at least, that's what it was supposed to be. Unfortunately, I realise, it's actually tears. I'd been so miserable thinking about how it had all gone wrong today that I'd actually been crying. I can see from Connor's expression that he thinks I've been upset over him. *Yeah, right.*

I sniff and take a tissue from the box on the desk to wipe my eyes. 'What did you want?'

'I needed to explain about the other night.'

'When you were kissing Bianca in The Four Feathers?'

He sighs. 'Yeah. I was just consoling her. The family business is about to fold. Her dad's been having financial problems for a while now and it's all come to a head. He's got loan sharks baying for blood. He could lose everything. She's worried sick.'

Bianca's dad, Bob, owns a car mechanic company where her two older brothers work. It's a bit of a ramshackle outfit, despite its name: B M-W Car Repairs and Valeting. It's got absolutely nothing to do with high-end German cars, of course, it's just his initials – if you can count Bob as his real name. And their surname's only hyphenated because Bob never married Stella Morrison, the mother of his children, so they decided to join both their surnames.

I heard they named Bianca purposely something beginning with a 'B' so she could take on the firm when the time came, or, at least, they could name it after her in years to come. She's even got a middle name beginning with 'M' – Maureen or Maisie, I think, one of those nice old-fashioned names anyway – just in case her parents ever actually married and she became Bianca Maureen Wright or was it Mildred? Anyhow, they were determined to keep her initials right no matter what happened. Pity they hadn't thought of that when they named her older brothers, Kevin and Nigel.

They obviously never considered that their daughter would ever get married – unless they've made her promise to only marry a man whose surname begins with a 'W'. I seethe, remembering that Connor's surname is Worthington.

I frown at him. 'Kissing isn't consoling.'

'Well, I consoled her first. The kiss just sort of...happened.'

'Your tongue was practically down her throat.' Hurt rages inside me as I remember the humiliating scene.

He huffs. 'I tried to talk to you, but—'

'You said it wasn't what it looked like.' I know I sound all sneery, but that's just how I feel. 'Yeah, right.'

'If you'd just let me explain – I wasn't planning on leaving you for her. That wasn't meant to happen. In fact, I ran after you – didn't you hear me?'

I narrow my eyes. Come to think of it, I do remember him calling my name up the street, but I was too upset to care. I don't think I've ever moved so fast as I did to get home that night. I just wanted to get out of there. I shrug dismissively.

With a loud tut he makes a grab for my hands, but I pull them away just in time. My stomach lurches. I used to love it when he stroked my fingers, but right now I can't bear the thought. He made a fool of me and I can't forget that.

'Libby, I followed you all the way home, just to make sure you were safe. I knew you wouldn't want to see me, but I had to be sure you were okay. I saw Frank with you at the doorway, so I left it at that. I tried ringing you.'

I knew that already. I'd quickly rejected his call on my way up the back stairs when I saw who was calling. That's when I'd decided to block his number.

We hear some visitors checking in at the front desk.

'Why don't we go somewhere a bit more private to talk?' he suggests, looking over at the door. 'We can have a quick drink while it's quiet.'

I gape at him. 'Isn't your girlfriend on duty?'

He sighs. 'No. She's on a split shift so she's gone

home for an hour or two. There's no-one about. Even
Party's disappeared off the face of the earth.'

I know I shouldn't. It's the last thing any sane,
freshly-dumped person would do. But he's obviously
got something to say and I can't help wondering what it
is. Maybe he and Bianca have split up already?

'Okay.'

8

CONNOR'S RIGHT ABOUT THERE BEING NO-ONE ABOUT when we reach the bar. Cassie and Margaret have gone from the restaurant, too, and the place is deathly quiet except for the drone of background mood music. Unfortunately the mood the racket elicits is always a bad one as it's so monotonous. When I get promoted that's the first thing I'm going to change. And that's a very big *when.* I've already started compiling my own mixed album to play in its place, with Ed Sheeran, Queen and Dolly Parton. Something for everyone. That's bound to put all the customers – and staff – in a great mood, hearing some of their favourite tracks. People will flock to The Chalfont. It'll be the in-place. I wouldn't be surprised if we didn't start getting a few celebrities popping in, too. Everyone likes a great atmosphere.

'What do you fancy?' Connor's popped behind the bar and is looking at me in that dreamy way he always used to.

I *used* to reply 'you' and we'd laugh.

Not today, though. I'm already starting to think this was a bad idea. His dreaminess has turned into nightmarishness since the other night. 'Diet Coke, please.'

'Is that all?'

'I'm on duty.'

'Oh, okay.'

He pours my drink as I hop onto a bar stool. It's quite high up and I can see right over the bar from here. I can't help remembering the sight of Bianca sliding across the floor the other day, and I giggle at the thought, noting that the sticky mess has obviously been cleaned since then. Actually, the floor still needs a good sweep, as there are little red flakes dotted about the tiles. Looks like she was wearing those dodgy Louboutins again today. Whoever she buys them from must get any old pair of shoes they can find, paint the sole red and charge ten times the price for them. I really don't know how Bianca can think anyone's fooled by them.

'Are you two still seeing each other?' I ask, warily.

He sighs. I take that to mean they are.

'Then what do you want me to say?' I can hear the sharp edge in my own voice, but I'm damned if I'm going to let him bullshit me.

'I'm so sorry about what happened the other night. I still want to be with you. Can't we at least stay friends while we sort this out?' he whines.

I blink at him in disbelief. 'Friends?'

He huffs, taking a sip of his whiskey – despite the fact that he's actually on duty, too. 'Neither of us meant it to happen the way it did the other night. I don't want us to split up. But Bianca's going through a really tough time at the moment. Her dad's in so much trouble with these damn loan sharks, she's worried sick. She needs me.'

'You've been cheating on me. Why the hell should I care about what *she's* going through? What about what *I'm* going through, Connor? I thought we had a future and all along you were seeing her behind my back.' My lips are tight and I'm trying my hardest not to raise my voice. Or cry.

'I know I shouldn't have strung you along like that – I didn't mean to. I told you – Bianca's gone to pieces lately over her dad. He's got involved with some vicious bastards who are fleecing him for every penny he owns, and more. He's desperately trying to hold onto the family business, but it looks like he's not going to make it. She'll do anything to get him out of this mess. I just wanted to comfort her as well as be with you,' he says, reaching for my hand across the bar.

I flinch, spilling Coke down my clean, white blouse. *Shit!*

Connor's leaning towards me with a bar towel but there's no way I'm letting him touch me with a ten-foot barge-pole, let alone a thin sheet of cotton. I take the towel from his hand and start dabbing at my blouse irritably. It's no good, it's going to stain. *Why didn't I ask for lemonade?*

'I'm sorry,' he says in that super-smooth voice he always used to use to get round me.

'Good.' I fling the bar towel at him and climb down from the stool as quickly as I can.

I'm hoping I won't be missed for a few minutes while I hurry through the kitchen and up the back stairs to my room.

Cassie's lounging on her bed watching TV when I burst through the door.

'Are you okay?' She frowns, quickly sitting up.

'Yeah, I just need a clean blouse.'

I open the wardrobe and pull out a short-sleeved blouse that I don't usually wear for work, but I'm sure it'll be okay under my jacket. It'll have to do; I haven't got any more ironed yet.

'You look awful.'

I raise my eyebrows at Cassie, fastening the last of my buttons. I didn't think the blouse would look that bad. Once dressed, I peer over at the mirror. Oh no! My face is all flushed and my eyes are puffy. Most of my makeup's been rubbed off. No wonder Connor thought he'd have a chance to talk me round – he must have thought I was in a real state over losing him.

'Cassie, I really am sorry about the other day,' I tell her as I rush over to the dressing table to touch up my makeup. 'I didn't mean it the way it sounded, and I know I shouldn't have told anyone your family were rich. I just couldn't let them think—'

'That I'm a thief.'

I look over at her with fresh tears threatening the corners of my eyes.

'It's okay,' she says, coming over to the dressing

table. 'Here.' She picks up a fluffy brush and lightly dusts my face with powder.

'Was everyone horrid to you?' I say on a sigh.

'Not really. I got a few comments from Mad Margaret about being a 'poor little rich girl' and, of course, she wanted to know why I was working here when I didn't need to.'

'You didn't tell her about the bet with your dad, did you?'

She shakes her head. 'Nope. I just said I wanted some experience from the ground up. She actually looked quite impressed by that.' Cassie sniggers.

I give her a big hug and her body feels all soft and friendly against mine.

'The staff have mainly been speculating about who the thief is all week,' she tells me.

'Oh, I can tell you that,' I say airily, as I pick up my jacket.

Her eyes widen and she raises a querying eyebrow.

'It's Bianca,' I tell her matter-of-factly. 'But no-one's going to believe me now that she's just stolen my boyfriend as well.'

Cassie frowns at me. 'Are you sure it's her?'

I nod. 'Positive. I'll tell you all about it later,' I promise, heading out the door.

It feels so good knowing that Cassie's not mad at me anymore. I hated not being able to enjoy much time together this week, especially on top of the pain of this damn ankle.

I sigh as I reach Reception, where Frances is busy

jotting something down on a pad. She's really efficient and writes everything down.

'Mr Partington wants you,' she informs me with a grimace.

'Again? Where is he?'

'In his office. He said you're to go straight there as soon as you turn up.'

'Oh.'

'I said I thought you were in the loo. He thinks you've got a bad stomach.' Her eyes are big and she looks tentative, like she's trying to fathom whether she's said the right thing or not.

I nod. 'You're a lifesaver. Thanks.'

This time I reckon it's more like four hundred and fifty-nine times of knocking before Party actually answers the door, though it could only have been twice. I tremble as I wait for his reply, and take a deep breath before going in.

He's on his own.

'Come and sit down.'

I bite my lip. Hard.

'I'd like an explanation of the chaos which you caused in here earlier in front of my guests,' he says crossly.

I swallow hard before opening my mouth. 'I'm really sorry, sir.' I'm secretly hoping to have scored a few points by calling him that, but he doesn't seem to have noticed. 'I was bringing in your tea tray when I tripped on that stu...er...sweet little dog. I tried to steady myself on your desk but unfortunately I dropped the tray, and its contents went everywhere.' *As if he didn't know.* 'It was a complete accident and I'm really sorry.' I somehow feel that if I carry on speaking he won't be able to shout at me. 'I know you had a lot of important papers on your desk and I really didn't mean to ruin them all, but—'

'All right.' He puts a hand up to silence me.

It looks like my plan didn't work.

'Did you read any of the papers that were on my desk?'

I'm completely thrown by the question, and stare at him for a moment. 'No, sir.' Which is actually true, I only read the sheet that was on the floor – and only part of it was legible anyway. I'm also hoping he's noticed that I've called him 'sir' again, but he doesn't seem to have.

He nods slowly.

'Was Mrs Merrington-Smythe all right?' I ask, hoping he's going to spill the beans on the theft that I'm not supposed to know about. (I even tore up that piece of paper and threw it in the rubbish with all the rest, so no-one else could read it – though they'd have needed an interpreter anyway.)

He purses his lips and I suspect he's considering telling me what's going on.

'Yes, she's fine. She'd come to see me about the new dog she'd just acquired.'

He narrows his eyes and I know he's dying to say *the one you nearly killed with your big feet.*

'He looked very cute.' *What I saw of him from my bird's-eye view as I went flying over the top of him.*

'Yes.' He's still looking a little curiously at me and I wonder what he's thinking.

'I hope I cleaned up all right for you,' I say brightly.

'Beryl's going to give it a good going-over later,' he says. I take it that's his not-so-subtle way of telling me I didn't do a good enough job. I decide not to reply, but I just hope she remembers to bring the vinegar for those heel-marks.

'You need to be more careful, Liberty,' he says sternly.

'Yes, Mr Partington.' *Well, he didn't notice when I called him 'sir', did he?*

'Not only did you make an utter fool of yourself, but you caused me untold embarrassment. And that's without considering the amount of work I now have to repeat.'

'I'm sorry, Mr Partington. It was a complete accident.' I wonder if he's got any idea how much more of a fool I made of myself *after* he and the old dear had left. Sergeant Harper must think I'm a real idiot, blaming Bianca after telling him she's just gone off with my boyfriend. I'm glad he's left now. I hope he doesn't come back. My stomach roils with shame.

Mr Partington shakes his head, making me feel like a naughty schoolgirl. I hate it when he does that. He's not my dad.

'Get back to work,' he says with a tired sigh.

I stand up and leave the room without another word. There's nothing to say.

———

I'M GLAD WHEN IT'S THE END OF THE SHIFT AND CASSIE and I go back up to our room. It's been such a long and horrid day. I went to help in the restaurant towards the end of the night, and Bianca kept staring at me whenever I went past the bar. I know she thinks she's got one over on me now that Connor's with her. Luckily, he made himself scarce so I didn't have to see them together.

'Come on, spill!' Cassie's only just closed the bedroom door.

'What?' I feign innocence.

She's been whispering and nudging me for the past hour, trying to find out what I was talking about earlier. Her eyes are bright and hopeful now as she waits for me to explain.

'Hang on.' I quickly go through and clean my teeth before I start.

She's in her pyjamas in a flash and we remove our makeup together.

'You're sure it's her?' she asks, throwing a pile of dirty wet wipes in the bin.

'Yep. Even more so, now. But, of course, I can't say anything.'

'You have to. I mean, if she's guilty, they *have* to believe you.' Cassie looks incredulous.

She cleans her teeth with the bathroom door wide open, while I get undressed. I'm about to put my mobile phone on charge when a thought occurs to me and I quickly check through the photos I took of room 109 earlier. There's nothing to see except the standard hotel furniture, a few clothes and bags and a little doggy-bed in one corner. The last couple of snaps are just of the floor, where I was trying to take a few extra photos without the security guard noticing.

'What's that?' I frown at the picture of the floor. 'Look.' I show Cassie, who has just finished up in the bathroom and comes over to sit on my bed.

She peers closely, then rolls her eyes. 'Looks like Bianca's been there in those fake Louboutins,' she says with a grin. 'You can just see the red paint.'

'I found some outside the door, too,' I tell her, remembering the bits I rolled up in my hanky.

'So? She works here.' Cassie frowns. 'What does that prove?'

'Strap in,' I tell her excitedly. 'It's a long story.'

It's just like old times, the pair of us sitting on my bed in our pyjamas chatting, but it's the first time we've talked about anything like this. I explain about the heel-marks on Party's carpet and remind her of the other day when Bianca slipped on the muck behind the bar. I tell her how I'd tried to explain it to Sergeant Harper – who I've decided I really don't like anymore, by the way – and how he practically laughed at me. Cassie's really cross at him for that, and I'm glad she's backing me up.

When I divulge about the other theft, in room 109,

she looks like her eyes are about to pop out of her head – after having a good laugh at the idea of me tripping over Poopsie, or whatever his name was, and throwing the contents of the tea tray all over Party and the sergeant, of course. Then I explain that room 109 was where I took the photos, including the one of the red paint speckles on the carpet, and she stares at me.

'It has to be her,' she whispers, her eyes all wide and shocked.

I nod. 'And I've found her motive,' I say smugly.

She's gobsmacked when I tell her about Connor claiming he felt sorry for Bianca because of her dad's company collapsing.

'It would certainly give her a reason to try to steal the money if her dad's got loan sharks after him,' Cassie says thoughtfully. 'Those bastards can get really heavy if they need to – and if he's having trouble paying them, they're not going to be happy. That family must be worried sick.'

'Not if Bianca's just stolen the money to pay the loan sharks off,' I point out. 'I'd say they're probably celebrating right now.'

Cassie gives me a big, warm hug. 'I can't believe you've solved the mystery,' she says with a smile.

'Yeah, but I can't tell anyone. They'll just think it's sour grapes, like Sergeant Harper did.'

She frowns, shaking her head. 'But you've got the *proof*.'

I huff. 'And how do I explain knowing about the

second theft? I can hardly admit to reading confidential information, can I?'

As she leans back on my bed Cassie looks thoroughly deflated.

'Then we'll have to get Bianca to admit it,' she says after a few minutes.

'Yeah, right. And just how do we do that, Sherlock?'

'Watson. *You're* Sherlock, remember?' she says with a giggle. 'You're the one that solved all this.'

I feel a glow of pride inside me.

'Why don't we go and visit B. M-W tomorrow?' Cassie pipes up. 'Just to have a look around.'

'What for?'

'I dunno.' She shrugs. 'Clues, maybe.'

I beam. 'Okay. Oh, but – isn't it your day off? Aren't you doing anything?'

She smiles. 'I've got a date in the evening. Rob's taking me to a swanky restaurant for dinner. He said it'll be a chance for me to get all dressed up, but won't tell me where we're going. It's a surprise, apparently.' Her eyes are shining with excitement.

I give her another big hug. 'Ooh, your first proper date!'

'Yeah. He's working all day, unfortunately. They're still trying to find a good story. He said Ben's worried they'll be out of a job if they don't come up with something soon. It's been ages since they found anything worth the front page and their boss is getting tough with them.'

'But if there's nothing happening, what are they supposed to write about?' I frown.

'I know. I suppose that's why papers sometimes resort to making stories up or including fluff pieces.'

'I'd love to be a journalist,' I confess. 'I bet I could find interesting things to write about all the time.'

'You'd be really good at it,' Cassie says, smiling. 'You talk easily to people, you've always got something great to say, and... you can write poetry.'

I stare at her. '*Poetry*?'

She nods, a little unsurely. 'Yeah, you know. When you write in birthday cards and stuff you always make it rhyme. Remember Ivy's leaving card? You put 'I don't know what on earth we'll do, without you here to clean the loo'.'

Oh yeah. My mind wanders back to the elderly cleaner's leaving party. I'd even used a rhyme on the memo to the kitchen and waiting-on staff; 'On Friday the twenty-first service will finish at half past two, there's so much to prepare, so we need everyone there for Ivy's leaving do'.

Everyone said how clever it was – although Mr Partington *did* say it was a good job I only used the word 'loo' in her card and not on the official staff memo. I didn't tell him I'd originally written 'poo' but changed it at the last minute.

I'm not actually convinced how much use poetry would be to a journalist, but my mind's buzzing when Cassie finally goes back to her bed and switches off the light. Perhaps I should start thinking about becoming a reporter or something? I might see if Ben and Rob can give me any tips. On second thoughts, if they're about to lose their jobs for not finding anything interesting to write about, they might not be the best people to ask for guidance on the subject. Hmm, I'll have a good think about that...

9

DESPITE BEING ON THE LATE SHIFT THE NEXT DAY, I can't wait to get up and ready. I went to bed really excited last night and now I can't wait to go over to the garage to search for clues.

Cassie's brother arrives just as we're finishing breakfast. We rush out the back door as soon as we hear the roar of his motor. He's lending us – or, rather, Cassie – his E-type Jaguar for a couple of hours. She's promised him a slap-up breakfast in the hotel restaurant while we take his car for a full valet – not a bad deal in anyone's book. Although we didn't mention he'd be served by Mad Margaret.

'Be careful with it,' he warns her as we both clamber in. 'You pay for any damage, remember?'

Cassie rolls her eyes – she does that a lot when Piers is around. 'Don't worry, brother-dearest, I'll look after it as if it were my own.'

He suddenly looks panicked. 'Oh no. Don't do that!'

I giggle, remembering Cassie telling me how she managed to write off her state-of-the-art, cherry-red BMW on its maiden drive from the garage. She'd turned the wrong way up a one-way street and driven straight into a huge lorry. It was only two minutes after leaving the forecourt. Her dad had gone mad and banned her from having another car until she re-took her driving test. She manages on the Tube now.

'Remember, brake fast!' Piers yells as the engine screams.

'Yep. Enjoy your breakfast,' she calls as we drive off.

'Cassie, I think he might have meant brake fast,' I tell her as we approach the exit of the car park.

'What?'

'Brake *fast*. Now.'

'Oh.'

She suddenly stamps on the brake pedal, causing us both to lurch forwards in our seats, our heads almost hitting the windscreen. We've just reached the main road and the traffic is horrendous, considering it's Sunday morning. I really don't know where all these people go on Sundays but I wish they'd find a different route, just for today.

'This is fun,' Cassie announces when we finally get out of the car park and begin to speed up a little.

I'm not so sure, to be honest. I think I've got whiplash from that sudden halt as we left the hotel, and my heart's in my mouth as I see how close she gets to the other cars before slamming on the brakes. My nerves are in tatters and we're not even halfway there yet. I can't help wishing we'd taken the Tube instead – although, on second thoughts, I can see that the plan wouldn't have worked if we had.

'It's a lovely car,' I say, trying to think of something positive. 'I love the smell of the leather.'

'Piers cleans it every day. It's his pride and joy.'

I look around at the inside of the car, which is immaculate. I remember thinking how shiny the outside was when we got in, too. Piers really does take good care of it. 'So, do you think it'll look a bit odd that we're taking it for a valet when it's already gleaming inside and out?' I ask, biting my lip.

Cassie's jaw drops. 'I hadn't thought of that. Quick, make a mess.'

I stare at her. 'What with?' I've only got my little Lulu Guinness handbag—second-hand from eBay, but it looks admirable —which is only big enough for a small coin-purse, lipstick and a hanky. There's nothing in there that I can use to sabotage all Piers' hard work.

'We need sweet wrappers – and crisps.' Cassie puts her foot down and takes a right-turn - narrowly missing a little green Corsa with a loud horn – and pulls up in front of a newsagent's.

We run inside and fill a basket with popcorn, crisps and toffees. I go over to the freezer and find some ice-cream to smear all over the upholstery.

'This'll do for the outside,' Cassie calls over, waving a jar of Nutella at me, 'I'll grab a couple.'

The toffees are in our mouths before we've even left the shop, as we're so desperate for the wrappers. We throw two sticky papers onto the driver's seat.

'It'll take a lot more than that,' Cassie moans, chewing rapidly.

We start unwrapping the sweets and stuffing as many as we can into our mouths at once.

I feel sick as I open up the popcorn and start sprinkling it liberally throughout the car, stuffing it down the backs of the seats and under the mats, just for good measure. The smell reminds me of smelly feet and I start retching as it hits the back of my throat –almost making me spit out the toffees.

Cassie's already started smearing Nutella all over the bonnet and the sides of car, despite some weird looks from passers-by.

'Ugh, this gloopy mess is getting caught between my fingers,' she complains, between chewing, trying to wipe her hands over the metalwork. 'And the engine's so hot it's melting the chocolate.'

I roll my eyes. It's a warm day and as a result, the smells seem to be intensified, all sickly and smelly-socky. I open the crisps. *Who chose cheese and onion?* I pour them all over the inside of the car, even hiding a few in the glove compartment. I'm really feeling sick, and I still can't swallow any of these damn toffees. I thought they'd be quite easy to chew, but they're rock-hard on the outside.

Next, we open the boot and fill it with the food, making as much mess as we can.

'I can't eat any more of these,' Cassie announces, pulling a handful of toffees from the bag. 'Let's just open them and throw them in.'

She's already unwrapping a couple and she bombards the upholstery with sweets, followed by their wrappers, which fall like leaves onto the carpet. I wish we'd thought of that in the first place.

'I'm gonna throw up,' I mumble as my mouth waters around the toffees.

'Do it in the car. We need the mess.'

She practically pushes my head into the passenger side and I remember just in time that I have to sit there to get to the garage. I rush back around to the boot just in time and heave noisily as the whole of my breakfast, along with a few dozen toffees, and a bunch of carrots – where on earth do they come from? – splatter across the inside of the boot. The stench is diabolical and just makes me even more sick. People tut and complain as they walk past – rather hurriedly, I notice out of the corner of my eye – but I just can't stop.

'I'll get you some water,' Cassie offers, and dives into the shop, leaving me throwing up on my own. I can't really blame her, to be honest – it's disgusting!

She returns a few minutes later and opens a packet of wet wipes, offering me a few. Then she hands me a bottle of water.

'Just little sips,' she reminds me. 'You don't want to bring it all back up again.'

I nod, grateful of the coolness on the back of my burning throat. I feel weak and she helps me around to my seat, where I plonk myself down, taking deep breaths of fresh air – or, at least, as fresh I can get by leaning right out of the car to avoid the popcorn and cheesy fumes emanating from the seats.

Cassie's even bought me a couple of packets of mints. She opens one and hands me a sweet which I start sucking whole-heartedly as she closes the boot and then climbs into the driver's seat.

'Think you can make it to the garage, hon?' she asks kindly.

I nod gently and swing my legs into the car, then close the door. We open the windows and strap in.

'Drive slowly,' I plead, remembering how erratically we got here.

'As always.'

I give her the side-eye and realise she's actually being serious. *Heaven help us!*

'We didn't think this through,' I mutter a few minutes later, as I pull a sticky toffee off the sleeve of my silky top.

'The crisps are scratching my back,' she grumbles, 'and it stinks to high heaven, doesn't it?'

Tell me about it! I hang my head out the window to try to escape the stench, but it seems to be following me. It doesn't help that I got some sick down my front. I cleaned it off with the wipes, but the whiff is engrained in the fabric.

There are insects everywhere, inside the car and out.

'Ugh!' Cassie points to the bonnet.

It's swarming with wasps and flies, clearly enjoying the Nutella. Damn! I hurriedly duck back inside the vehicle, afraid of getting stung or bitten, which is only marginally better than being suffocated by the smell of cheesy feet.

Mercifully, we soon reach the garage and pull in. It's a scruffy-looking place, with old tyres and engine parts littering the forecourt. The doors to the workshop are wide open and someone's working on a battered old Toyota that looks fit for the scrap yard. Come to think of it, this whole place looks a lot like a scrap yard.

We clamber out of the car and Cassie saunters over to a man who's just come out of the building, wiping his hands on a piece of rag. He must be Toyota-guy. He's a bit older than us, with sandy-coloured hair and dirty overalls. His eyes light up when he sees the car – I presume they don't get many E-type Jaguars here.

His face falls slightly as they near the car and he obviously notices the state of it.

'Can I have a full valet?' she asks brightly. 'She needs a good clean inside and out.'

'Of course.' The guy grins at her, taking the keys she offers.

'Is it okay if we wait here while you do it?'

I've just caught up with her, and I'm already looking into the building for clues. It's good to have something to take my mind off my stomach.

'If you want.' The guy frowns. 'But there's a café just down the road. It might be more comfortable. It normally takes an hour or so. There's shops down that way, too. Some are open on a Sunday.'

'My friend's not feeling too well,' Cassie explains. 'She can't really walk and the smell of food would make her feel worse.'

I can't help thinking how much worse *he's* going to feel once he's opened the car and seen the state of it – especially the boot. What if he refuses to clean it? Oh my God! How on earth will we explain that to Piers? My stomach roils with worry.

'Here, you can use these.' An older man, who must be Bianca's dad, appears from the back of the building with a couple of manky-looking chairs. He's also brought some blankets, which look only marginally cleaner than the fabric of the seats.

'Thank you.' Cassie smiles at him as he plonks the chairs in front of a pile of tyres.

He smiles back, wiping a dirty hand through his thick, grey hair.

'I'll just fetch the Jag over. Are you okay with that one, Dad?' The younger guy gestures to the Toyota and the old guy nods and picks up a spanner.

'Jeesh!' There's a loud shout and I presume the younger guy has just opened the car door. He's probably wishing he'd stuck with the Toyota now. I can't wait 'til he flips the boot.

'We had a bit of a party on the way over.' Cassie offers the older guy a self-deprecating smile.

'That's all right, darlin'. You've come to the right place to get it all cleaned up. I'm Bob, by the way.'

'Thanks, Bob.' Cassie's still smiling.

I give her a nudge, nodding to some wooden, hand-written signs, half-hidden behind a stack of tyres. 'Closing Down Sale,' 'Everything Must Go.' They must be trying to sell off the spare parts.

'Does it get busy around here, Bob?' I ask as casually as I can manage while sucking on a mint.

'Sometimes.' He looks over from where he's been peering into the bonnet of the Toyota. 'We've even started opening on Sundays, as you can see.'

I can't help hoping that's because trade has risen since they started their sale, and not a sign of desperation. They certainly don't seem overstretched by their workload.

'Bloody hell!'

Cassie and I look over at the younger lad, fully expecting him to have opened the boot.

Glad of the distraction, I pull out my mobile and take a few snaps of the wooden signs, just in case we need them as evidence.

'Watch your bloody language, Nigel!' Bob barks.

'There's nuts in that!' He points at the bonnet.

Bob stops what he's doing and goes over to the Jag.

'What?' He takes a look, then draws his eyebrows together.

'Nuts!' Nigel points again and edges away from the car.

'Well, blow me!' Bob mutters. Then he shouts, 'Kevin, get out here.'

A good-looking blond guy in jeans and a black T-shirt appears from the side of the building.

'I'm on a break, Dad.'

'Sod your break. Your brother needs you. Something to do with nuts.' Bob waves his spanner in the direction of the Jag and walks back towards the Toyota, shaking his head.

'Is he all right?' I ask Bob as Nigel staggers away from the Jag, taking deep breaths.

'Allergic to nuts. Don't worry, he always carries an EpiPen. He'll be fine.' Bob doesn't seem at all concerned as Nigel disappears in the direction his brother just came from. 'Did you know you had nuts stuck to the bonnet of your car?'

'Umm...' Cassie says, giving me a look that says *Help!*

'There were some kids playing in the street earlier, when we were parked up,' I say, quickly. 'We saw them smearing something onto the car and we went out to stop them. We didn't know what it was, though. We assumed it was mud.'

Bob nods, rolling his eyes.

'The other guy isn't allergic, is he?' Cassie bites her lip and it suddenly occurs to me that we could be arrested for murder if both guys have a serious reaction to the Nutella. Or wasps. And here was me worried about their reaction to the contents of the boot!

'Nah, Kevin's fine,' Bob assures her. 'Strong as an ox.'

I hope he's got the constitution of an ox when he opens up the—

'Bloody Nora!'

Clearly not.

Bob throws down his spanner and stomps over to the Jag again. 'What now?' He puts his hands on his hips, frowning hard.

'Someone's barfed in the flaming boot!' Kevin backs off, his hand over his nose.

Bob turns and gives us an incredulous look. I'm beginning to think we should have gone to that little café Nigel told us about, after all.

'Oh, that must have been that man we saw,' Cassie improvises.

I gawp at her, my mind reeling. How do you follow that? 'Oh, yeah.' It's a feeble offering, I know, but what else can I say?

Cassie rolls her eyes at me. Then she turns back to Bob. 'I was having trouble getting the boot to close when this man came over and said he'd help. Then he threw up. It must have gone in there.' Her eyes are big as she feigns amazement.

He stares back at her.

I stare at her, too, expecting her nose to start growing like Pinocchio's.

Bob takes a deep breath and nods almost pityingly.

'Just get it cleaned up,' he calls over to his son. 'That's what the customer's paying you for.'

I sigh, though not as deeply as Kevin, who starts pulling on a set of blue overalls. We use that phrase at the hotel, too. It's a sort of code that means 'the customer will pay extra for this'. It's a good job Cassie's wealthy.

Watching the old man and his son working away, I can't help feeling sorry for them. Not only because of the boot situation, but for everything. They must have been terrified they were about to lose their business, their livelihood – maybe their homes. I wonder if they know where Bianca suddenly found the money to keep them afloat. Although I don't condone what she's done – far from it –I do feel sad that she felt it was her only option. She could go to prison for this.

'Could I possibly use your loo?' I ask Bob, desperate for a bit of a snoop around.

He raises his head from the bonnet of the Toyota. 'We don't actually have one for customers,' he says apologetically.

'I'm desperate.' I wince, wriggling in my seat for effect.

'We've got one *we* use,' he says, nodding. 'It's just through the office there.' He waves a wrench in the direction of a glass-fronted section and I eagerly go over. There are more sale signs leaning against the glass, and a small table inside, heaped with papers.

Bob's gone back to working on the car, so I sneak a few of the papers and dive through the door to the toilet. My heart's throbbing as I quickly examine them and discover they're overdue bills and final demands, just as I suspected. I use my phone to photograph them. I feel really sorry for the family, being so much in debt – it would terrify me to owe this much, and I'm sure this is only a small fraction of it.

I'd like to spend more time in the office searching through the paperwork – I might even find a threatening note from the loan sharks – but Bob's heading my way when I leave the loo. The sound of an engine distracts him, and I quickly slip the bills back onto the desk and leave the office.

'Thanks,' I say, as I pass him on my way back to where Cassie's waiting for me.

A car pulls up onto the forecourt. It's a grey Ford Focus that looks like it's seen better days.

'Can you give it a quick wash?' a man asks as Kevin goes over to him.

'Yep.' He nods. 'It hasn't got any nuts on it, has it?'

'No.' The man gets out, looking at Kevin slightly oddly as he hands him the keys.

Kevin grins. 'Great.' He calls Nigel, who comes back out to help, looking a lot better than he did a short while ago.

'There's a café down the road, if you want to wait there,' I hear Nigel tell the man.

My breath hitches as the man looks over to where we're sitting.

'It's okay. I'll wait here if that's all right.'

Nigel shrugs and the man walks towards us.

'Hello,' I say, stunned for a moment. What the hell's Sergeant Harper doing here?

'Hi, my name's James.' He offers me a hand which I shake dazedly. 'And you are?'

'Just waiting for our car to be valeted,' I reply curtly.

Cassie looks at me a little strangely, then smiles as James shakes her hand.

I assume he's trying to tell me he's undercover, as he would surely have said 'Sergeant Harper' otherwise – or just not have pretended we didn't know each other. I don't want to give away our names in front of Bianca's family, though, as she'll know we're on to her if she hears all about the Nutella and the sick that Libby and Cassie brought in on their E-type Jag. *Yes, Sergeant Smarty-Pants, we're undercover, too.*

'My car's just having a clean,' Sergeant Harper tells us, stating the obvious.

I notice him looking around. *Is he here for the same reason as us? Looks like it.* I furtively point to the wooden sale signs while Bob has his head beneath the bonnet of the Toyota. The sergeant nods discreetly.

'So, how's business?' he asks Bob brightly.

I roll my eyes.

'Can't complain,' Bob replies, not taking his head out from under the bonnet.

Sergeant Harper nods, and scans the rest of the building from where he's standing near to us. 'Good.'

'So, are you ladies off out somewhere nice?' Sergeant Harper's newly-found charm really matches his good looks and I wish I could believe he was actually asking because he was interested.

'No, just running a few errands,' Cassie responds with a smile.

'I'm working this afternoon,' I inform him, wondering if that was what he was actually getting at.

He nods again.

I'm certain that he can only be here for one reason – the same one as we are. He's checking up on my allegation that Bianca took the money. Maybe he did believe me after all.

10

It takes a lot longer than we'd hoped for Kevin to clean the vomit out of the boot of Piers's pride and joy, and he uses a whole can of sickly sweet-smelling spray to try to mask the smell.

'You might want to keep the boot open for a few days, if you can,' he advises Cassie, after she's parted with a huge wad of notes for the service – which must have gone above and beyond the call of duty in anyone's book.

'How are we going to explain that to Piers?' I ask, when we finally climb in.

'We won't,' Cassie shrugs, driving off.

'But we'll have to – it'll stink to high heaven if we keep it closed.'

'He won't notice until he comes to use it,' she says with a grin. 'He's hardly the type to do a load of shopping, is he? By the time he needs to open it up he'll have forgotten all about us and will think it's just stale or something. Don't worry about it.'

I'm not convinced. 'I'm really sorry it cost so much.' I feel incredibly guilty for being sick, and am relieved that the car smells much fresher now. Mind you, being able to drive with the top down's helping a lot, too.

'Don't worry. It was worth it. Odd that PC Plod turned up, though, don't you think? Considering he didn't believe you when you said Bianca had stolen the money.'

'Hmm.' I nod. Of course, cleaning his car hadn't taken half as long as ours so he hadn't hung around too long, but he certainly saw the sale boards that had been hidden behind the tyres, presumably no longer needed.

By the time we get back to The Chalfont it's almost time for me to start my shift. Piers is sitting in the bar, drinking orange juice and aimlessly flicking through the Sunday papers.

'You took your time,' he says, looking up as we approach.

'If a job's worth doing, it's worth doing well,' Cassie quips, tossing him the car keys.

'Thanks for the loan of your wheels, Piers,' I say hurriedly, glad that he's not annoyed at how long we took.

'No worries – as long as it's not dented or anything.' He shoots his sister a narrow-eyed look.

'No, nothing like that,' I promise, hoping he's not going to insist we watch him examine it for anything untoward – like a boot that reeks of vomit. 'Anyway, I have to get changed for work.'

'See you later.' Piers is a really good-looking guy – unlike my two older brothers - with the same dark hair and brown eyes as his sister, and he gives me a flash of those perfect, gleaming-white teeth of his just before I dive back through the restaurant and head up to our room.

Despite not having long to get ready, I can't resist a quick shower, and clean my teeth over and over to try to rid myself of the smell of sick. I've never understood how it lingers so long, and wonder whether Sergeant Harper detected it earlier. God, I hope not.

Once I'm dressed and ready, I spray copious amounts of body spray and perfume all over myself before heading downstairs for my shift.

Cassie's just coming through the back door into the kitchen when I arrive.

'Is everything okay?' I ask nervously. She's obviously just waved her brother off on the car park.

'Yep. He examined every inch of the bodywork,' she says, rolling her eyes, 'but didn't open the boot.'

I shake my head with relief.

'Stop worrying,' she says with a giggle.

'I owe you one.'

'Well someone owes *me*.' Connor's just come through from the back of the bar with a sheet of paper in his hand. 'Your brother ran up a tab while he was waiting,' he informs Cassie. 'He said you were going to settle it when you got back.'

'Flaming cheek!' Cassie's jaw almost hits the floor as she takes the bill from him. We'd settled his breakfast expenses between us when we booked his table. 'What the heck's he been drinking at this time in the morning?'

'Bucks Fizz,' Connor says casually.

Cassie frowns. 'Is he allowed to drink alcohol out of licensing hours? He's not a resident, you know? *And* he's driving.'

Connor shakes his head. 'I made an exception for him, being as he's your brother. And he said he'd eaten enough breakfast to soak up the champagne. I thought I was doing you a favour.'

'Some favour!' she grumbles, but follows him through to the bar, pulling out her purse.

'I'll settle up with you later,' I call to her before heading for my office.

'Don't worry,' Cassie shouts back.

I arrive at Reception where Frances is waiting for me. 'You've got a visitor.' She indicates someone reading one of the broadsheets at a small table by the window of the foyer.

'Oh?'

He lowers the newspaper and smiles at me.

'Sergeant Harper?' I keep my voice curt, after all, he really upset me with his self-righteous attitude yesterday and then pretending everything's okay when we saw him today.

He stands up, carefully folding the paper before

placing it on the table. 'Could I have a word? In private?'

'Mr Partington said you can use the Remington Suite,' Frances tells me.

I nod to her, and the sergeant hangs back, allowing me to lead the way. He's still dressed in the smart slacks and open-necked blue shirt from earlier, and I assume he wasn't really supposed to be working today.

'I'll send through some coffee,' Frances promises as we leave Reception.

'Thank you.' I smile at her.

The conference room has been laid out for a meeting, and we take our seats at the top of the table.

'It's nice to see you again,' Sergeant Harper offers as I pour out a couple of glasses of water. The acid from earlier is still burning my throat.

'I didn't expect to see you there,' I admit.

He shifts a little uncomfortably. 'No... well...I…'

The door suddenly opens and Julie arrives holding the tray of coffee. She looks a little surprised to see me.

'Thank you, Julie.' It feels so good to be treated like the manager I am, for a change. Albeit only *junior* manager.

She places the tray in front of me and I smile at her pleasantly. She leaves without saying a word. However, her look of disdain speaks volumes. She's never liked me much and will hate having to wait on me. I might have a word with her about that later – if I'm feeling brave enough.

I pour the drinks, careful not to spill any, conscious

of how closely the sergeant is watching me. Offering him a cup, I look up at him questioningly. God, he's gorgeous – but not as confident as usual.

'I thought about what you said.' He looks a little sheepish.

'About me making false accusations about people?' I raise my eyebrows, glad to see him squirm, even though I can't help feeling a little sorry for him.

He sighs, putting down his cup. 'I'm sorry. I might have been a bit presumptuous with that remark,' he admits.

'Really?' I'm not letting him off *that* lightly.

'I overheard part of a conversation in the bar,' he explains. 'It was about Bianca's family firm having difficulties.'

My face falls and a thud hits the pit of my stomach. 'That wouldn't be my conversation with Connor, by any chance, would it?' *Has he been watching me?*

'I'm not at liberty to say.' His blush tells me all I need to know.

'I see.' My mind is whirling. 'You just happened to be in the bar when this conversation was taking place, did you?'

He huffs. 'I was passing by on the way to the Gents, actually. I heard voices and, being a police detective, naturally checked to see if it was anything I needed to know about.'

'Naturally.' I nod knowingly.

'In this job people don't always give you information – you have to find it out for yourself.'

I gape, getting the message loud and clear. *He thinks I should have told him what Connor told me!* 'Maybe if you weren't so dismissive and patronising when people try to give you information, they might offer you more of it.' I can't resist the jibe.

His lips curl slightly. 'Touché, Miss Lawrence.' He raises his cup and tips it towards me, and I nod back at him.

We both take a couple of sips of our coffee before he speaks again.

'I presume you were at the garage this morning looking for more evidence to substantiate your claim?' he asks, slowly.

'Why would I need to do that? I was merely with my friend, who was having her brother's car valeted. There's no law against that, is there, Sergeant?'

He clears his throat, clearly miffed. 'No.'

'Is that why you were there? To find evidence?'

'Why would you think that?'

'Because you introduced yourself as James instead of Sergeant Harper.'

'It's my name. I was off duty.'

I nod, narrowing my eyes at him. 'So, you would have been quite happy for us to have addressed you by your title?'

He presses his lips together tightly. 'Well, no, actually. You're right. I was grateful to you for not divulging who I was. It might have made things a little... difficult.'

I can't stop the giggle that suddenly emanates from

my throat, and I'm pleasantly surprised to see his face completely relax as he watches me burst out laughing.

He chuckles, shaking his head as he puts his cup back down. 'Christ, you're good. I thought you were going to keep that up all day,' he confesses.

'I'm sure I don't know what you mean, Sergeant,' I reply with my best innocent expression.

It's great to see him laugh, and I feel mean for making him suffer – but, really, he *did* deserve it. He's even more handsome when he's smiling, though, and I hope to see him do more of it.

'So.' He pulls out his notebook when we both finally recover. 'The family firm was about to fold so Bianca stole the money from the hotel safe.'

'It looks that way.' I nod. 'Did you get the evidence this morning? Those 'Sale' signs I pointed out to you?'

'Yep. I wanted to take a photo but that old guy was too close. I might have to go back for that.'

'I got a couple,' I tell him, pulling my mobile from my jacket pocket, and scrolling to the photos. 'I also got some pictures of a couple of bills and final demands from their office. I don't know how good they are.'

He takes the phone from me and nods, clearly impressed. 'They're fine. Can you send them over to me?'

I flush with pride as I watch him slide through my pictures. Then his face falls and he frowns, swiping one way and then the other. 'Hang on...what's this?'

I swallow hard, looking over to see that he's found

the snaps I took in room 109 yesterday. *Oops!*
'I... erm—'

'You know about the second robbery?' He's staring
at me.

Well, I am management, I want to say, but I know
full well he's aware that I'm not privy to this case.

'Someone took some money and a necklace from
room 109,' I say with a slow nod.

'Yes, but how do you know? That was confidential.
Mrs Merrington-Smythe didn't want anyone to be told
about it.'

My heart pounds. I'm going to have to confess.
Damn! I place my cup on the table as my hands start to
tremble. I could lose my job over this. Maybe even get
arrested.

'Nobody told me,' I say quietly. 'I saw something
scribbled on one of the papers that must have got blown
off the desk when I had that accident with the tea tray.'

He sits forwards, swathing me in that heady aftershave he wears. 'I thought it was all destroyed. Did
anyone else see anything?' He furrows his eyebrows
anxiously.

'No,' I assure him. 'Only me.' I go on to explain
what I found, and – much to his apparent relief – what I
did with it.

'That was supposed to be private.' He's gone all
tight-lipped again.

'Please say it was that ghastly chunky gold necklace
she was wearing the other day,' I say, as the thought
occurs to me. 'I'd like to think the only reason she wore

it was because it was too valuable to leave lying around. Surely no-one could actually think it was attractive?'

'It doesn't have to be beautiful to be worth a lot,' he says coolly.

I take that to mean I'm right. I'm getting quite good at this detective-thing.

'But you know who did it, don't you?' I frown at him, puzzled. He can't keep it a secret once he's made the arrest.

He gawps at me. 'Not yet. Do *you*?'

I nod, but even as I do so I notice that supercilious expression cloud his face again.

'Did you see this?' I quickly take my phone from his hands and swipe back to the pictures of the bedroom floor, before he can say anything.

He squints at the photo. Then he enlarges it with his fingers. 'What is it?' He's certainly intrigued.

'Red paint,' I tell him matter-of-factly.

He looks at me as though I've just landed from Mars. I seem to get that look a lot.

'How much do you know about Christian Louboutins?' I ask with a sigh.

————

It takes another pot of coffee, much to Julie's disgust, as well as biscuits – which I was afraid were going to give her a coronary – before I've fully explained the implications of the fake shoes. At one point I was afraid he was going to go straight down to the market and try to find the vendor of the counterfeit footwear – or should that be 'counterfeet'?– but he has to concede there are more pressing matters to worry about.

We've established that if Connor had followed me home on Monday night he might well have found the key that I dropped by the back door, and could easily have given it to Bianca to let herself into the building without having to pass Reception and the night porter. If she had used Connor's key to get into Mr Partington's office, she could well have taken the safe key from the filing cabinet and stolen the cash.

It wouldn't have been too difficult for her to gain access to room 109 while Mrs Merrington-Smythe was out getting her new dog – any of the chambermaids would have let her in with a legitimate excuse, or she could have borrowed a key from Reception.

It all added up beautifully. I took the sergeant's number and messaged all the pictures I had through to his phone. I had suggested using Bluetooth but the bewildered look on his face told me that neither he nor his chunky mobile had caught up with modern technology yet.

'The only thing I don't understand is why there was no red paint in Party's office,' I admit. 'There were only the heel marks.'

'Could it have been cleaned up?' He frowns thoughtfully.

'Then why not clean it up in the bedroom, too?'

'Maybe she was disturbed. It's a shame there are no

security cameras up there. We could certainly do with some physical evidence.'

'I've got some of the paint upstairs, in my handkerchief,' I add, with a flash of inspiration.

'I'll need it,' he says with a grateful nod. 'We might be able to get it analysed, just in case anyone tries to claim it's the old lady's makeup or something.'

'I won't be a minute.'

'Take your time. I'll just have a word with your boss; let him know why I've detained you all afternoon.'

I hadn't realised it was so late as I go through to the bar and restaurant to see everyone getting ready for service. *Time flies when you're having fun.*

Giddy with excitement, I go through up to my room to fetch the handkerchief. I'm so glad that Sergeant Harper actually believes me now. He's so lovely, too, when he relaxes a bit – and much more fun than I'd first thought.

My phone buzzes and I worry for a second that the sergeant's getting impatient already, but it's just a text from Cassie. I smile, realising she's probably already on her date with Rob. He's got a whole, wonderful evening planned for her, apparently.

As I check the message my heart sinks.

Have told Rob they need to hold the front page – you've got a great story for them! He's really excited. See you in the morning ;)

Oh no – she knows this is all top secret. We can't possibly tell the press, it'll ruin everything!

I stuff the hanky in my pocket and rush back downstairs.

There's a loud clatter as I return to the kitchen and Stan yells at Esther to be more careful. She's just dropped a tray full of stainless steel coupe dishes which are now all over the serving area.

'It was only an accident,' I tell the chef.

Stan huffs. 'Just look at the mess!'

'Yes, but it's a mess the waitresses are dealing with – it doesn't affect you,' I point out calmly, as Esther and Margaret scrabble on the floor collecting up the dishes. Esther's part-time and is only covering for Fiona tonight. She won't want to fill in again at this rate.

Stan grunts, rolling his eyes.

I bend down to pick up a few of the dishes on my way through to the restaurant and the ladies mutter their thanks.

Connor's standing between the restaurant and the bar area, frowning.

'Is everything okay?' I ask, surprised to see him loitering.

He purses his lips. 'I was hoping one of the waitresses might come through,' he admits, seeming uncomfortable.

I raise my eyebrows. 'Will I do? What is it?'

He takes a deep breath, as though considering whether I will actually 'do' or not, which does nothing to boost my confidence. 'Well... it's Bianca.'

'What about her?' I can feel my jaw tighten already.

'She's upset. She arrived later than me tonight and

she's gone straight into the toilets, crying. I was going to ask one of the women to go in and see if she's okay. I know you won't want to—'

'Connor, it's my job,' I remind him, suddenly feeling very professional. It's time to pull up my big girl panties. Bianca is a member of staff and I'm one of the management team. It's my duty to ensure she's okay – even if she has just stolen my boyfriend, among other things - allegedly.

'Thanks,' he mutters as I pass him on my way to the Ladies'.

I open the door quietly, expecting to see Bianca in the vanity area – her usual haunt – but she's not there. I hear her voice from one of the cubicles and assume she's on the phone.

'But how can they do that?' She sobs. 'Daddy, you paid them *everything*. I know you did.'

She sniffs as she listens to his reply. I can't help feeling sorry for her. I hate it when anyone gets upset – even her. 'No, you can't owe them any more,' she insists between sniffles. 'You paid back every penny they asked for. They've got no right asking for more.'

My stomach roils. The loan sharks. It sounds like they're causing even more trouble. I sympathise with the family – even Bianca. Bob seemed so friendly and they were all so hard-working. Poor Kevin having to deal with all my puke just to earn his wage, and Nigel being made ill like that. It could have been really serious for him. It's probably not every day a customer brings in a car covered in nuts, but it must have been horrid for him to have to endure that – he looked quite poorly just before he disappeared indoors.

It's obvious they're a close family, and they certainly don't deserve this. What will they do if the loan sharks get violent? How will they cope if they go out of business? *Shit!* Why was I so keen to get Bianca arrested for the thefts?

11

I SNEAK OUT OF THE LOO, WONDERING HOW I CAN AVOID Sergeant Harper. Maybe I can claim I've suddenly been taken ill? Or lost my voice? No, he'll just want me to hand over the handkerchief; it's all he needs from me now.

I put my hand in my pocket and my heart skips a beat. It's gone. There's absolutely nothing there.

'Well, thanks so much, Sergeant.'

I can hear Party and James coming up the corridor. *Think, quick!* I dive back into the bathroom, just as Bianca emerges, red-faced from the cubicle. My heart sinks. I feel like a total bitch. How can I possibly go out there and make life any worse for her?

'Are you okay?' I ask.

She nods with a big sniff, tucking her phone into her pocket before running the cold tap and dabbing her swollen eyes with her hands.

'If there's anything I can do...' *Yeah, I could stop trying to get her arrested!*

She looks a little surprised, but nods gratefully and mumbles a thank you.

After a quick look around I'm satisfied that I haven't dropped my hanky here. I want to go, to get away from Bianca, and escape my guilt. But Sergeant Harper's probably right outside that door, waiting for me. *Shit!*

Bianca gives me a funny look, and I feel I've over-stayed my welcome. I give her a sympathetic smile, take a deep breath, and leave.

Luckily no-one's standing outside the toilets when I creep out, though familiar voices are coming from Reception. I need to retrace my steps but the restaurant's already getting quite busy. If anyone's seen my hanky they're more likely to have trodden on it than anything else – which means the speckles of red paint could be anywhere by now.

I saunter through the bar, trying to discreetly check the carpet. At least my ankle's feeling a bit better now.

'How is she?' Connor calls from his position by the optics, a concerned expression on his face. My stomach flips. He was never that bothered when *I* was upset. Still, I suppose this is a bit more serious than me crying because the tan Kurt Geigers that were in the Selfridges sale had all gone before I got there.

'She's just washing her face,' I tell him, leaning over the bar.

'Do you know what's upset her?' He asks quietly.

'Um...I didn't get to ask,' I reply. 'I think she'll be out in a minute, you can ask her yourself.'

'Thanks for that.' He smiles and I detect that he really is grateful to me – which only serves to make me feel even worse.

I resume my hanky-hunt in the restaurant where Margaret's scowling at me from the dumbwaiter. I'm sure she's dying to know what I'm doing, but probably won't want to ask – after all, I *am* in my management uniform tonight. Ignoring her, I quickly scour the floor. There are a couple of napkins that have been kicked under one of the tables, but nothing that looks anything like my little lacy handkerchief.

Passing swiftly through to the kitchen – I'm just not in the mood for Mad Margaret right now – I pin my hopes on having dropped it when I helped pick up those coupe dishes earlier.

'Are you okay?' Stan gives me an odd look – which isn't hard for him with those wonky eyes of his.

'I think I've dropped my hanky, that's all.' My attempt at sounding casual and airy fails, as my voice seems to have risen a couple of octaves for some reason.

'I think Margaret threw a dirty hanky in the bin a while ago,' Adrian offers. 'She said something about a snot-rag.'

My eyebrows shoot up with indignant rage. That was an Egyptian-cotton, hand-embroidered lace handkerchief, thank you very much. I hardly dare ask. 'Where did she put it?'

'The bin by the still machine, I think,' Adrian replies, gesturing to the corner of the room.

'I'll just see if it's handy.' I try to sound as though it doesn't really matter, but my heartbeat tells a totally different story. It's taken me all afternoon to impress Sergeant Harper – I don't want everything to fall apart now thanks to Mad bloody Margaret. Pity she's not as conscientious when it comes to napkins on the floor of the restaurant. Did she do it on purpose – or does that sound really paranoid? And even if it does, does that necessarily mean I'm wrong?

As I suspected, the bin is full of soggy teabags and wet coffee granules, as well as copious sheets of kitchen paper that have been used to wipe goodness-knows-what from the surfaces and floor of the surrounding area.

Rolling up the sleeves of my navy jacket, I then put my hand in the bin, tentatively moving odd bits of paper with the tips of my fingers in the vain hope that my hanky will be just lying there, staring back up at me, still containing the flakes of paint.

No such luck.

Amid titters from the kitchen staff, I plunge in a little deeper, stepping up the search with both hands, still convinced that it can't be that far down – it wasn't that long ago, for heaven's sake. Warm, squelchy teabags caress my palms, and coffee granules get stuck between my fingers, while filter-papers creep up my arms, plastering me in goo. I can't bear to imagine what these clumps of kitchen paper have been used to clean up, but they feel really disgusting and lumpy against my skin. I wish I'd thought to ask one of the kitchen staff if I could borrow a pair of latex gloves for this job, though I hadn't actually planned on having such a thorough rummage. Too late now.

My stomach roils with the stench of the bin. Even the aroma of fresh coffee can't mask the stink of sour milk, and I surmise that most of these paper towels I'm touching have been used to clean some up. I retch, hoping I'm not about to throw up all over the kitchen floor.

'Ah, there you are!'

I freeze as Mr Partington's dulcet tones fill the room, and slowly look around to see that he and Sergeant Harper have just come through from the bar. A second later, Margaret appears from the restaurant. Coincidence? I think not. She hoots with laughter, while the men just stare at me in disbelief.

'I dropped my hanky,' I explain, my face heating up. I'm actually up to my elbow in something quite inde-scribable, and notice that my arm's heating up, too. Some of those teabags clearly went in hot.

Jerking my arms out of the rubbish bin, I spot Sergeant Harper's mouth twitching at the edges, and his eyes twinkling. Despite the fact that he looks absolutely stunning, I'm more than a little peeved that he's smirking at me again.

'Is it this one?' Margaret walks over holding my beautiful, carefully folded, pristine handkerchief.

I gawp at her.

'It was on the floor. I put it on the shelf for safe-keeping,' she explains, sniggering at the state of my arms.

I put my hand out to take it from her – a hand that is totally covered in what can only be described as gunk.

'I'll take that.' The sergeant swoops in and places the Egyptian cotton into a plastic bag before I smear it in bin-detritus. *Thank God!* 'Thank you,' he says in his most charming voice, and Mad Margaret blushes. He tucks it straight into his pocket.

'Oh, so it's yours?' Margaret asks, giving me a supercilious look.

He smiles but says nothing and she practically melts onto the kitchen floor.

'I see.' She glances at me condescendingly, and I just know she now thinks I was hoping to keep the copper's hanky. *Great!* Though I can't help wondering why she would think a man like him would own a lace handkerchief. I wonder about a lot of things where that woman's concerned.

'Is that everything, Sergeant?' Mr Partington asks as I grimace at Margaret.

'Yes. Thanks again.' The men shake hands and then Sergeant Harper offers his hand out to me.

I reach my teabaggy, coffee-granuled, grot-covered hand out for his, but he catches sight of it and snatches his away at the last minute, smiling at me instead. 'Thanks for all your help.'

I open my mouth to tell him I need to speak to him, but just then Connor pokes his head through, asking for the progress on a bar meal he ordered half an hour ago. There's no way I can let him know that I've got something to discuss with the police.

The sergeant follows my boss out of the kitchen and through the bar entrance, while Adrian shouts something about the lamb being off, and how Connor should know that, he's worked here long enough.

'So, what was the copper thanking *you* for?' Mad Margaret looks quite put out.

I'm dying to tell her that I've been very useful to him, that I've practically solved a couple of crimes *and* supplied evidence to substantiate my claims, but I bite my tongue. 'I got his coffee for him earlier,' I reply with a shrug. I walk over to the nearest sink and start washing my hands and arms.

She snorts. 'Of course you did. I knew it wouldn't be anything important.'

I'M GLAD TO RETURN TO THE SANCTUARY OF THE stationery cupboard, and slump into my chair. I heard the kitchen staff – and Mad Margaret – erupt into raucous laughter as I left the kitchen, which only made the situation seem a hundred times worse. My mind's whirling with guilt and worry.

A short while later I pull my mobile from my pocket. The message from Cassie is taunting me. Will she tell Rob everything? I quickly text her a reply. *Don't say anything yet – it's a top secret police matter!*

Then I remember that I've now got the sergeant's

number in my phone and quickly call him. It rings a few times before there's a click and a very surprised voice says, 'Hello?'

'Hi, Sergeant Harper, it's Libby Lawrence from the hotel.'

His deep chuckle tells me he hasn't forgotten me. 'Hi, Miss Lawrence. Thanks for the handkerchief. The guys from Forensics are just verifying the paint now.' He sounds all officious again and I wonder if there's someone with him. 'I take it you got cleaned up okay?'

Trust him to bring that up. I roll my eyes, trying to focus on more important matters. 'Yes, thanks. Look... please don't arrest Bianca,' I blurt out, my voice quiet but clear.

'What?'

I sense his confusion, and imagine the bewildered look on his face.

'There's... there's more to this. Lots more. I need to speak to you about it, but just... don't arrest her – or speak to her, or anything just yet. Let me explain a few things first, okay? Please?'

He's quiet for a few awful seconds, and then that stern voice comes down the line – or through the waves, or whatever it is with mobile phones. 'Miss Lawrence, this is a very serious police investigation. I can't just ignore the evidence. We need to bring her in for questioning if nothing else at this stage. It would be negligent of me not to, now that I know about it.'

It's a good job the handsome sergeant is on the other end of the phone, as I suddenly feel the urge to strangle him right now. I take a calming breath. 'Look. I've just discovered there's a much bigger story here – one that might yield a much more fruitful arrest – or arrests. I'm not sure how many people are involved but there's bound to be more than one. And these people are much more important than a pilfering barmaid.'

I give him a minute to let the news sink in. 'Could we meet up and I'll tell you all about it?'

'All right.' His sigh tells me he's not actually convinced, but at least he's willing to humour me. Good. I'll take humour. I'll take whatever I can get at this stage.

'But please don't do anything about Bianca in the meantime. Or let any of your heavies do anything, okay?'

'This is the Metropolitan Police Force. We don't employ 'heavies', Miss Lawrence.'

I bristle. He's got that superior voice on again. I hate it when that tone is aimed at me. I know he thinks I'm just being stupid, but this is *really important*.

'Shall we meet for breakfast?' he goes on. 'Or will you be working tomorrow morning?'

My heart lurches. Is he asking me on a date?

'No... I mean yes. I mean no, it's my day off tomorrow so I can do breakfast,' I reply, trying to sound like someone who 'does' breakfast all the time.

'Good. Shall we say the Frimlington Way Cafe? That's not far from The Chalfont. About nine o'clock suit you?'

I gasp with delight. I love that place – they do the

most fantastic Italian coffee. 'Yes, that sounds fine.' I'm trying to sound businesslike, although I'm practically salivating already. 'But promise you won't do anything until we've spoken? With Bianca, I mean?'

'All right,' he concedes. 'I'll see you at nine.'

———

THE NEXT MORNING THE SUN SHINES AS I STROLL UP Haven Place to the white building with deep, red awnings. Cassie didn't come home last night – which is a first – and I just hope she's okay. I'll ring her later, but first I'm going to enjoy breakfast with the handsome sergeant. I'm a bit early and the place is still busy from the morning rush.

Little tables and chairs are dotted around the pavement outside, and there's a circle of paviours in the road in front of the building. A couple of bikes lean against one of the trees which looks like it's sprouted up through the flagstones, and people are chatting far too happily for a Monday morning, in my view.

I'm wearing a red dress and have left my hair down. I'm saving up for a pair of Christian Louboutin Follies Strass 'pumps' to go with this dress, with hand-placed red crystals all over the front, petering out towards the heel. The foot part of the shoe is made of transparent mesh, so it looks like the crystals are just sprinkled all over your toes – beautiful. I can't afford them yet, though, so instead I have on a really nice pair of strappy sandals from Top Shop.

My heels click across the café's wooden floor. To my surprise, Sergeant Harper has already arrived, and is sitting at a table towards the back. He stands up as I approach, his hand outstretched. My heart pounds. He looks almost edible and it makes me wish this was a real date.

'Hi, I'm James,' he says, smiling. He gives me a look that tells me he's undercover again, so I can't call him Sergeant Harper today. It's a good job I'm telepathic.

'Hi, James, I'm Libby.' I shake his hand, looking around to make sure everyone around us is being fooled by our act of only just meeting for the first time. Actually, there is no-one sitting near enough to listen, and the other customers are all minding their own business, anyway. What a waste of effort!

I'm trembling with nerves. He looks very dashing in blue chinos and a white Ralph Lauren polo shirt. The 'Dashing White Sergeant', you might say. *Well, my mum might say – she's into Scottish country dancing in a big way, so it's sort of worn off on me a bit.* Somehow, I can't quite see the gorgeous Sergeant James Harper attempting the Highland Fling at one of Mum's get-togethers, though the thought relaxes me a little.

'I hope you're hungry. They do a mean Full English here.' He sits back down and offers me the menu.

'Great. I'll have whatever you're having.' I smile, wondering if he's noticed that my lipstick is the exact same shade as my dress. Probably not.

Once we're settled with two huge plates of our

country's national fry-up in front of us, he lowers his voice. 'Forensics have verified that it *was* red paint that you picked up from the carpet.' he informs me. 'Now all we have to do is match it to the shoes in question.'

I take a large gulp of coffee, which is every bit as delicious as I remember, by the way. 'I know it was Bianca that took the money,' I explain quietly as we begin our meal, 'but the reason is because her dad's got into some trouble with a local loan shark, who's putting the pressure on him.'

James frowns hard. It feels really odd calling him that. I'm aware that he heard my conversation with Connor about the loan sharks, but he doesn't know the half of it.

'The thing is,' I continue, hoping to pique his interest. 'It looks like she stole the money because she was worried about what they'd do to her dad – I think they've threatened him or something. But now, even though they've got all the money, they still want more.'

He nods. 'That's the way these scum work.'

'So we have to stop them. I reckon if we can get Bianca to lead us to these bastards, we'll be able to uncover their whole operation. That's got to be a lot more important than a petty theft, surely?' I'm pleading with him now.

He stops eating and stares at me. I wonder if I'm actually getting through to him. 'We?'

'What?'

'*We?*'

No, it doesn't make any more sense the second time

around. I haven't a clue what the problem is, but he seems pretty rattled over something. I just give him a quizzical look, swallowing my mushrooms as quickly as I can in case he asks me something else.

'Since when are you in the police force?' he asks sharply.

I gawp at him. 'Sorry?'

He sighs, putting down his knife and fork. 'It's not a question of 'we', it's *me*. This is *my* job, remember?'

Oh, I get it. He's pulling rank now. He wants to get all the glory. I carefully place down my cutlery, shaking my head slowly.

'I don't think it's important who does what for a living,' I say, in my best headmistress-voice (which I've based on Margaret Thatcher, by the way). 'What's important is that we catch these bastards before they ruin any more lives. You have to look at the bigger picture here, James.' I'm loving it up here on the moral high ground. It certainly makes a change, especially where Sergeant Harper's concerned.

He looks stunned and says nothing for a few moments. Then he takes up his knife and fork and resumes his meal. 'All I'm saying is that you mustn't take the law into your own hands, Libby.' He's beginning to sound like my dad now. 'Leave the job to the professionals.'

'So, you *are* going to look into it?'

He looks thoughtful. 'How do you know all this? Have you got any proof?'

'Connor told me,' I admit. *As if he didn't know.*

'Your boyfriend?' He's frowning — not a good sign.

'Ex.'

'Right.'

I don't like the way he said that. 'He's really worried about her. And then I overheard her talking on the phone. She was dreadfully upset. Her dad was telling her that they were after more money, even though he's paid back everything he owed.'

James raises his eyebrows. 'You heard all this?'

'Well, I heard *her* side, but it was obvious what he was saying.' I sense all hope diminishing now. 'What sort of evidence do you need?' I'm hanging on by my fingernails here. There's got to be some way of convincing him this is a good idea.

He finishes his breakfast, clearly deep in thought. I, on the other hand, have just lost my appetite.

He places his cutlery neatly on the plate in front of him and then seems to spring into action. 'Who are these people? Where are they operating from? How many other victims have they conned out of their cash? Where's the contract Mr Wright signed with them? Is it legal?'

Blimey – he doesn't want much, does he?

'If I'm going to hold off arresting Bianca, I'm going to need a damn good reason to do so. Now, I'm willing to believe she's not going to leave the country or anything, not while she's so worried about her dad, but I need a hell of a lot more than hearsay to keep her out of a courtroom.'

I feel like I've just joined Police Academy, or something. I've got a sudden urge to reply 'right sir, yes sir.' I settle for 'Right,' and another cup of coffee.

There's got to be a way of proving all this. I never thought I'd say it, but I *have* to get Bianca off the hook.

12

My brain aches by the time I leave the café, and I surreptitiously watch James saunter in the opposite direction. He's gone to great lengths to emphasise that it's actually his duty to at least take Bianca in for questioning at this stage. I had to really plead with him not to; she was in such a state last night I can't bear to think what she'd do if the cops came knocking on her door right now.

I shake my head, surprised at myself for feeling any sort of sympathy for the woman who's been seeing my boyfriend behind my back, although it does take two to tango. Connor is the one who cheated on me.

I make my way up the Hills Gate Road and look around the market. It's busy for a Monday. I breathe in the scent of fresh fruit and flowers and try not to get distracted by the rails of beautiful clothes, as well as the tables of fascinating nick nacks which I know will tempt me and keep me browsing for hours if I let them.

It seems like I'll never find the stall I'm looking for, but then a small, wooden sign saying 'Shoes' catches my eye, further down the road. It's been perched well away from the market stalls and points to a side street. If I wasn't specifically looking for that particular stall, I might never have noticed the sign, as it was quite discreet, not like usual advertising boards. I feel like Alice in Wonderland, carefully following the sign into a foreign zone which I just know will be wonderful, but scares me a little at the same time. My heart thumps hard and I hold my breath as I walk up a couple of winding side streets and then turn a corner before finally reaching my goal. It's a makeshift stall, quite a way from the market. My guess is that they probably have a regular clientele who know where to look for them, so they can get away with being so far from the main street with its market and shops.

Pretty shoes with red soles line the shelves which have been created from old orange crates with strips of carpet laid across them, presumably to stop the paint scraping off the footwear. Although I know the shoes are fake, I have to admit they look lovely. Someone's gone to a lot of trouble to ensure that there are no maker's marks of any kind on the insole, and to the uninitiated they could easily pass for the real thing.

To those in the know, however, the absence of a brand name is a dead giveaway. And then there are those tattered brown boxes they're being sold in. Also, having studied the real thing in meticulous detail, I can tell just by looking that they're nowhere near the same quality. Still, they're nice shoes in their own right – just not Christian Louboutins, by any means.

A couple of girls push past me excitedly as I'm examining a beautiful black court shoe.

'I'm getting some more of these,' one of them tells the other, her face flushed with anticipation. 'They're real Christian Louboutins, and a fraction of the price!' She holds up a pair of beige shoes with five-inch heels.

'Are you sure?' her friend asks with a frown. 'Where does it say that?'

The first girl smirks. 'That's just the point. It's a brand new line, without the actual wording on, but you can tell the make by this.' She points to the red sole. 'Everyone knows the brand by the red sole, so they've now decided not to bother putting the name on them – they don't need to. I think it makes them look even classier not having writing on, don't you? It's like a sort of secret club. If you don't know your shoes, you won't know they're Louboutins and in that case you're not worth knowing anyway.'

Her friend looks suitably impressed as she picks up a bright red sandal.

'All right, ladies, what can I get yer?' The stallholder's finally finished his sale – three pairs of shoes and some sweet little ankle boots – and is nearing us. He's a good-looking guy, probably in his twenties, with tousled, curly hair and designer stubble on his chin — the only 'designer' thing around here. I imagine he probably uses his looks to full advantage while selling to the ladies.

'Hmm, I want these, but I don't think I can afford them,' the first girl says in a whiny voice, twirling her hair between her fingers.

The guy shakes his head. 'They're a bargain, they are. They'd be more than five times the price in any of the high-end shops – if you could get them, that is. These are the newest thing — no labels, just the sign we all know and love.' He taps the sole of one of the shoes with a knowing look on his face.

'Yeah, but they're still a hundred quid,' the girl replies with a shake of her head. She's quite pretty, with dark hair and big brown eyes, which she's putting to good use trying to get 'round the stallholder.

'Is this your stall?' her friend asks the guy. She's a little plainer, with big, round glasses that make her look a bit like a female Harry Potter.

The man eyes her suspiciously, a crease forming between his eyebrows. It's a shame because he's much more handsome when he smiles. 'Why do you ask?'

'Because if you're the organ-grinder then you can help her out a bit, can't you? Of course, if you're just the monkey...' She puts the sandal she's been examining back on the shelf.

'Well, as it happens I might be able to do something for you,' he says quickly. Clearly the chance of losing a sale is setting alarm bells ringing in his otherwise-empty-but-still-beautiful head.

'Can you reduce the price, then?' She's one hell of a good friend to the pretty girl, whose doe-eyes don't seem to be having any effect at all on the young guy.

'No, but I can offer you credit.' I strain to catch his words now, as he's lowered his voice. 'Pay me at least half now and the rest next week. I'll put them aside with your name on. If you're not here by five-thirty a week today they go back on the shelf and you've lost your deposit. Fair?'

The girls whisper to each other, and the guy looks around and smiles at me – obviously homing in on his next victim while letting the girls know this is a limited-time offer.

'All right,' the first girl says at last. 'Fifty today and fifty next week.' She hands him the beige shoes, which he quickly stuffs into a plain, brown cardboard box, then squeezes the box into the flimsiest plastic carrier bag I've ever seen.

'Fifty-five,' he counters, 'at least.'

The dark-haired girl, who had just counted out a couple of twenties and a ten-pound note, frowns at him. 'What?'

'A hundred quid, plus a tenner for credit. Half it – fifty-five quid.'

'You didn't say anything about paying more for credit.' Her friend rounds on him like a shot.

'Take it or leave it,' he says, slowly starting to pull the box back out of the bag.

'All right!' The first girl stares in wide-eyed panic, and quickly removes another note from her purse. 'Fifty-five. And it's Abigail.'

He stuffs the money into his pocket, then picks up a marker pen and scribbles her name on the bag.

'She wants a receipt,' the friend tells him defiantly.

He rolls his eyes, but pulls out a rather crumpled receipt book from his back pocket. It's the type you can pick up in any shop and there's nothing on it to identify who issued it – making it totally worthless.

'Won't be a second, darlin',' he assures me, making a big, huffy show of how much effort it is to scribble down the details.

'We'll go 'round the market after this,' the plainer girl tells her friend. 'I want to get some cheap make-up.'

'I can't even afford that now,' Abigail replies with a sigh.

'Actually, girls, I've got something here that might help ya.' He slowly takes a business card from his breast pocket, handing it to the customer as though it's the crown jewels. 'I don't mean anything by this, so don't take it the wrong way, but if you need a bit of a leg up – even just temporary – this guy can help ya. You just tell him Stu told you to call him, okay?' He gives her a wink as she takes the card and receipt and stuffs them into her bag.

'Okay, thanks.'

'All right, darlin'. I'll see you next week.' He blows her a kiss, while her friend scowls at him and they disappear around the corner.

My heart rate increases, and not only because of the beautiful shoes in front of me. I quickly replace the black court shoe I've been stroking lovingly.

'What can I tempt you with?' the man asks with a broad smile, gesturing to the display.

'Actually…I...er…'

He looks at me expectantly.

'Well... to tell the truth... I'd love to buy some of these, but I'm in a bit of financial bother right now.'

'Oh right.' If his face falls any further it will be down the bottom of a manhole any second now.

'I wondered if there was any way you could help me?' My gaze burns into his breast pocket, willing him to give me one of those business cards.

Unfortunately, he's looking down my dress and I can only imagine what he thinks *I'm* offering.

'Well... I think we might be able to come to some sort of... *arrangement.*' His eyes are practically on stalks now and I'm sure he's salivating. He reaches a hand out to me. This isn't going as well as I'd hoped.

'I meant... oh, it doesn't matter.' As his hand gets a little — or rather a *lot* — too close for comfort I decide to go for plan b, and run. Pity, because I really like those shoes.

I spend the next hour trawling the market trying to find Abigail, without being exactly sure what I'll say or do if I find her. Maybe she could lend me the card? I only need to take a photo of it — she can have it straight back afterwards. How do I actually ask a perfect stranger if I can see the business card for a loan shark that she just got from a guy selling fake shoes?

Eventually I give up and find the nearest Star-bucks. It's crowded and noisy and the coffee doesn't taste half as nice as the one I had earlier with Sergeant Harper. *James*. He wants me to call him James. Is that all the time, though, or just when we're working undercover? His name rolls around in my head. It really suits him; neat, tidy, to the point. No messing around with adding extra letters you don't need as in – I don't know – Keith (who needs an 'i'?) or Nicholas (that 'h' could go), and don't get me started on Frederick!

My phone rings, pulling me from my thoughts, and I dig in my handbag to find it.

'Libby? Where are you?' Cassie asks, her tone frantic.

'I'm just in town.'

'Look, I'm really sorry. I think I might have...'

My whole body heats up as a feeling of dread washes over me. 'What have you said?'

'Well...'

I knew it. As soon as I got that message telling me she'd spoken to Rob, I just *knew* she was going to blab! 'Where's Rob now?'

'I don't know. Look, Libby, I'm really sorry, I—'

'Where are you?'

'Still at work.'

I check my watch, relieved that she didn't call in sick this morning because she'd drunk too much last night. It's gone twelve. 'I'm coming back now,' I tell her, throwing my coffee cup in the recycling bin on my way out the door. 'I need to know exactly what you've told him, okay?'

'So do I.'

Her words stop me in my tracks. Literally. An old

woman on a mobility scooter rams into the back of my legs, almost knocking me off my feet.

'Ow!'

'Watch what you're doing!' The woman waves her fist at me but carries on driving down the pavement.

'Are you okay? Libby?'

'Yeah, I just got run over, that's all.' I stand outside a shop window, rubbing my aching legs.

'Oh my God! Do you need an ambulance? Can you breathe? Where exactly are you?'

'No, I'm fine. It wasn't a car. It was only a scooter.'

Cassie pants heavily down the phone, clearly panicking. Any other time I'd be making jokes about dirty phone calls, but she's obviously not in the mood right now – and neither am I.

'Even so...a scooter?'

'A *mobility* scooter,' I explain. 'I'm fine. I'm just worried about what you've told Rob, that's all.'

'So am I,' she replies, her voice laden with concern.

'But...what do you mean?'

'I got drunk, okay?' she snaps in a sudden turn of mood. 'I don't know what I said. I only know that he had to rush into work this morning. He said something about a great scoop and I haven't been able to get hold of him since.' She hangs up.

I suddenly feel a migraine coming on.

A woman tuts as she barges past me and I walk on, past a few more shops, not really taking anything in as my head floats in a cloud of doom. My legs really hurt and I make my way to a small antiques shop two doors up, which is recessed from the street. I'm hoping it'll be a bit safer there.

Stopping for a breather, I lean against the low windowsill while I rub the backs of my legs. I'm sure I'll have a couple of big bruises there by tomorrow. That's the least of my worries right now, though. I can't believe Cassie told Rob about the case. It'll be all over the papers this afternoon and Bianca will see it even before she gets arrested.

My whole body stiffens while coldness engulfs me to the core. James is going to be livid with me. This could wreck the whole case. Bianca might get away with it – which doesn't worry me so much – but so will the loan sharks who will come down even heavier on her dad if they suspect he might go to the papers, or even the cops. How could it all have gone so horribly—?

Something catches my eye. A gold object gleams at the back of the shop's window display. A necklace. *The* necklace. There can't be two of them. Surely no-one else could have such dreadful taste!

Quickly I pull out my mobile and call James. 'Hi, it's Libby.'

'I know.'

Of course he does.

'I've found the necklace.' I speak quietly so as not to draw attention to myself, but it doesn't work so well when I have to repeat the words three times before he actually hears me.

'Where?'

I give him the address and he promises to get here straight away.

In the meantime, I decide I may as well go in and have a look around – after all, it would seem pretty suspicious if I just loitered around outside, wouldn't it? There's a bell on the door that clangs as I step inside, and two old ladies leer over at me. They start whispering, presumably about the brown, cat-shaped teapot they're admiring. I wonder if they think I'm going to swoop in and try to buy it instead of them when they turn away from me, secreting the hideous object with their ample bosoms.

I try to avoid looking directly at the necklace in the window – although, now that I'm a bit closer I can see that it definitely *is* the same one that was stolen from Mrs Merrington-Smythe.

I take a sudden interest in a Toby jug featuring a policeman's head. It's even got a pair of handcuffs for the handle. Apart from being completely grotesque, it has a very macabre air to it. I wonder if James would like it.

Just then, the doorbell clangs and in walks the man himself. Talk of the devil. Not that I'd really call him the devil, exactly, but you know what I mean. Actually, that analogy, with this monstrosity in my hand makes me shudder. It could be James's taste, though, being a police— no. The look of horror on his face tells me it most definitely *isn't* his style at all.

I quickly put it back on the shelf, afraid that he might think it's *my* sort of thing. Unfortunately, in my haste I knock a tiny egg-cup which smashes onto the floor.

'Breakages must be paid for.' A booming voice comes from the back of the shop and I suddenly realise that there's a man sat at an old desk tucked away behind the counter.

James rolls his eyes – very unhelpfully, in my opinion.

'Yes, of course,' I reply. 'I'm awfully sorry. It was a complete accident.'

'Breakages must be paid for,' the man repeats as though I haven't said a word.

I can feel that migraine coming on again.

'How much?' I ask, pulling my purse from my bag.

'Twenty pounds.'

'*What?*' The word's out of my mouth before I can stop it. Luckily I manage to refrain from finishing the sentence with 'twenty quid for a manky little second-hand egg-cup – which I suspect was actually chipped *before* I knocked it over – by *accident.*'

The man stares at me expectantly and I can hear James sniggering as I go up to the counter and hand over the money. I'm surprised at the police sergeant just standing there, letting the shopkeeper get away with daylight robbery. I'll have a few words to say to him later – when we're no longer undercover.

'Bye,' James says pointedly to me as the man puts my hard-earned cash in his till and then picks up a dustpan and brush from a shelf under the counter.

I was rather hoping to stick around to see James in

action, but I can tell he doesn't want me here without even using my telepathic skills.

I leave the shop with a huff and walk slowly back towards The Chalfont. The fresh air, along with the relief that *something* has actually gone right today, seems to help my head and I feel a lot better by the time I get back to the hotel.

'Cassie's in the bar,' Julie informs me as soon as I get through the back door.

I frown. Cassie doesn't usually drink between shifts. Mind you, she doesn't usually get drunk and tell her reporter boyfriend about a top secret police case, either. 'Thanks.'

I go through the restaurant, which hasn't been left as tidy as I would have liked, but I understand that Cassie's got enough on her plate at the moment, so to speak.

When I enter the bar area, I spot Cassie at one of the little round tables drinking something that looks suspiciously like a rum and black. Her hands are trembling and she looks like she's about to burst out crying. 'What do you think you're doing?'

'She's been in a right state all day,' Connor tells me. 'I've given her that one to calm her down a bit but I daren't give her any more. It's lucky Party's not here or we'd both be sacked on the spot.'

'Okay, thanks, Connor.' It galls me to be grateful to him, under the circumstances, but I have to concede he probably did the right thing – 'hair of the dog' and all that.

He closes up the bar, as there are no residents around, and I'm glad to be left in private with Cassie.

'The early edition of the paper's going to be here soon,' she wails. 'I'm so sorry.'

'Can't you remember *anything* you said to him?' I'm trying to be sympathetic but I'm worried sick about this, too.

'He won't even talk to me. I've been leaving messages all day but he hasn't responded. I even tried Ben, but his phone goes to voicemail, too. They were doing the job together, Rob said before I left his flat. I'm sorry for not coming home, by the way. I was totally legless and Rob thought it best not to bring me back here in case I got into trouble with Party. The poor thing spent the night on his sofa. Anyway, he was really excited this morning but wouldn't tell me what it was about.'

The door to the bar opens and Frances brings through today's edition of the *Daily Chronicle*. She gives us an odd look but says nothing as she places it neatly on a little side table next to a vase of flowers. It's a courtesy copy for the guests. Cassie and I stare at each other, speechless for a second, before I stand and go to retrieve the paper.

My legs wobble as I try not to read the front page on my way over to Cassie. I place the paper ceremoniously on the table before us and we scour each page together, heaving a huge sigh of relief at the end of each one. By the time we reach the sports section at the back excitement begins to well inside me. There's absolutely nothing about the case.

Cassie bursts into tears as I turn the last page and fold up the offending item.

'I'm so sorry,' she tells me, over and over.

'It's fine. No harm done. Looks like you're not as much of a blabbermouth as you thought.'

She gives a small smile, the relief evident on her face. 'So, what have you been up to?' she asks.

I tell her about my day, and my discoveries, as she gradually starts to cheer up – with the help of the rum and black – and we kick off our shoes and relax for a while.

'I'm going to have a quick shower before my next shift,' Cassie says once we've put the world to rights. She gets up and gives me a hug before heading off.

Connor's already opening up the bar again, and James saunters in, smiling.

'Drink?' he asks. 'I take it you're still off duty?'

'I'll just have a Coke, thanks.'

The table I'm sitting at is right in the middle of the bar area. James buys our drinks and ushers me over to a more secluded corner.

'Was it the right necklace?' I know the answer but I ask anyway.

He nods. 'The guy gave me a good description of the man who brought it in and he had a CCTV tape that I've just dropped off at the station.'

'There's something else,' I say quietly. 'I think I know how to find the loan sharks.'

I explain about the guy at the market, and James frowns. 'You could have put yourself in danger,' he warns me. 'I told you; leave this sort of thing to the professionals.'

He's right, but I still don't like to admit it. I wasn't thinking about my safety, I just wanted to get the lowdown on those bastards.

'You did brilliantly today, though,' he says with a proud smile.

I feel all warm inside.

'Why don't we go somewhere a little quieter?' he suggests hesitantly, as a crowd of residents filter into the bar.

I don't need asking twice. We stand and head towards the door, just as Bianca walks in.

My gaze is instantly drawn towards her feet. She's wearing the most awesome black Christian Louboutin Scalopumps! *Shit!*

13

I QUICKLY AVERT MY EYES AND CONTINUE OUT OF THE bar, my heart hammering. James looks so relaxed, I don't want to tell him what I've seen, but he suddenly stops walking and faces me while we're in the corridor. 'Are you all right? You look pale.'

'Um...I need some air.'

He puts an arm around my shoulder - which I'd probably really enjoy if I wasn't so scared of throwing up all over him – and leads me out the front entrance. 'Take some deep breaths,' he says softly.

The cooler air on my flushed face feels heavenly, and I inhale as much of it as I can. My head's reeling and I almost want to cry. I can't believe this has happened. *Not now.*

'Come on, I know somewhere we can go,' he offers, his face full of concern as he pulls out his car keys.

I take his arm as he leads me over to the Ford Focus. He opens the door and helps me into the passenger seat.

Inside it smells of him and leather. It's very clean, although the upholstery shows signs of wear. I still can't believe a police sergeant doesn't have a nicer car, and make a mental note to ask him about it later.

'Are you okay?' he checks before starting the engine.

I nod, although I actually feel far from okay.

He starts to drive and I'm pleasantly surprised how smooth the ride is. He's a very careful driver. On the way, he calls the station and arranges for a female officer to go to the stall tomorrow to see if she can get the information from Stu, the guy with the shoes. Glancing at me, he adds: 'make sure she has back-up.'

He drives us to what can only be described as an 'old man's pub', The Fox and Duck, not too far from the hotel. I guess he's probably afraid of me being sick in his car, and has stopped at the first place we came to. Perhaps he detected the smell from Piers's Jag yesterday. Or maybe it was the whiff of my blouse where I'd tried to clean it off with a wet wipe? *Shit!*

'I know it's not much to look at but they do a great chicken supreme.'

He must have seen my expression as I took in the outside of the building. I give a weak smile and take his offered arm, allowing him to lead me inside. The thought of food makes my stomach churn again.

The interior of the pub's actually much nicer than I expected. It's bright and airy, and the decor's quite modern with clean lines and large expanses of carpeted floor.

We sit by the window with our drinks, away from the snooker table and the crowd of middle-aged men huddled around the dartboard. (I did mention it was an old man's pub, didn't I?)

'Is everything okay?'

I'm touched by his concern, and wish I could just say that everything's fine, but I can't lie. Something about James tells me I couldn't deceive him even if I wanted to – which I don't. I just wish things weren't so damn complicated.

'Did you see Bianca's shoes?' I ask after taking a long drink of my Perrier – the safest option under the circumstances, I thought.

His mouth twitches at the corners and his eyes shine a little more than usual. The bugger is laughing at me! I can't believe he honestly thinks I felt ill just because she's got nicer shoes than me.

'They're Christian Louboutins. *Real* ones. '

His face clouds over.

'And they're Scalopumps.'

When his expression doesn't change I realise that this guy - clever though he may be - knows nothing of women's fashion. What is it about men?

'Okay.' I place my glass down very precisely. 'Black, velour-textured leather, little corset-type lace-up front with scallop all around the foot?'

For a police sergeant, he's not all that observant, I notice.

'You can get designer shoes second-hand – or even new – from eBay and places, but these are the *Scalop-*

umps. This season's style. No-one's selling them off cheap because they've only just been released.'

'Are you sure?'

I can't believe he's just asked me that. I stare at him incredulously. He seems to read my expression and suddenly realise that he's dealing with an expert here. 'Right, well... we mustn't jump to conclusions. Just because we know that someone recently sold Mrs Merrington-Smythe's necklace for four-and-a-half thousand pounds, and Bianca's just turned up in the latest designer shoes doesn't *necessarily* mean there's a connection.'

How much?

I gape, desperate to hear his alternative explanation. At least we're both on the same page – neither of us wants to believe Bianca sold the necklace to buy shoes, but we can't deny the facts.

James purses his lips. Then he bites his lip, and frowns. Hard.

I raise my eyebrows expectantly.

His face colours and he takes a long swig of his Coke.

I send up a silent prayer for a miracle. It's one of those *'Hi God, I know you don't know me very well, but I've got a massive favour to ask...'* -type conversations. Anything's worth a try at this stage.

James sighs.

We're sitting opposite each other at a tiny table in a secluded corner. It should all be so romantic, but it's not. He's tense, still frowning thoughtfully. I grind my teeth

– I really didn't expect Bianca to turn up in a brand-new pair of six-hundred pound Louboutins – who would?

'I think we're going to have to face facts, Libby.' It's clear James doesn't relish telling me this at all.

'She could have borrowed them,' I blurt out, trying to block out his words before he says them.

He raises his eyebrows. 'Okay, does she have any rich friends?'

I shrug. 'She might have.'

He just looks incredulous now.

'You can't arrest someone just for wearing nice shoes.' I know it sounds childish but I just can't let him do it.

'We'd make sure of our facts first,' he assures me.

'Please, don't.' I grab his arm in desperation and he raises his eyebrows, clearly taken-aback. Not to mention annoyed that I've made him spill some of his Coke.

'I don't have much choice; it's my—'

'I'll get Cassie to talk to her.' Relinquishing his arm, I then pull out my phone. 'She owes me a favour – even though I did let the cat out of the bag about her being rich.'

James stares at me, bewildered. He does that a lot.

'Hey, Cassie, it's me.'

'You'll get me shot. Party's on the warpath over something,' she hisses back at me.

'I'll make it quick. Just ask Bianca about those shoes.'

'Her *shoes*?' She gasps down the phone. 'What shoes? I've hardly seen her all night. I've been rushed off my feet – Mad Margaret's totally useless, not to mention moody, and—'

'Scalopumps!'

The penny drops, I can tell by her squeaky voice as she replies. '*What*?'

'Check them out. We need to know where she got them and how she bloody well afforded them.'

'We?'

'I'm with James. Sergeant Harper. It'll look odd if I say something to her, but now she knows you're rich it'll seem more normal for you to ask about designer shoes. Besides,' I lower my voice, 'she hasn't just run off with *your* boyfriend.'

I feel James's eyes on me as I hang up. I know I should be more bothered about losing Connor, but somehow I've hardly missed him.

'I take it that was Cassandra Beaumont?' James asks.

'Yes. She's my best friend. And room-mate at the hotel. We both live in.' I take a sip of water to shut myself up. I know I'm rambling. I'm nervous about Bianca, plus it's so exciting to be here with him. On a date. Sort of.

He frowns. 'And she's rich? The hotel must pay well.'

'Ha. I wish,' I reply with a shake of my head. 'We're on a lousy wage. No, Cassie's from a rich family. She's only working there to prove a point to her parents – but don't tell anyone, it's a—' I break off, remembering only too well that I've already divulged her secret in front of the whole staff.

'I won't say anything.' James smiles reassuringly. 'So, what about you? Are you from a rich family, too?'

'You must be joking! No, not in the least.'

He raises his eyebrows in surprise. 'But you know a lot about designer shoes.'

A massive smile spreads across my face. He's brought up my favourite topic of conversation!

'I love them. I'm starting my own collection. I know it'll take forever on my wages, but it's what I want. I've already got some Kurt Geigers that were a present, and another pair I got second-hand off eBay, and some Stella McCartneys that I bought in a sale. And my Karen Millens – though they weren't as expensive as the others. Cassie's got all sorts; Louboutins, Jimmy Choos, Manolo Blahniks, you name it. She lets me borrow them sometimes.'

James has gone quiet. His face has fallen a little, as though he's disappointed. I wonder if he was hoping I was rich. He's obviously on a decent wage, being a police sergeant, and he might have hoped I was, too. After all, I am supposed to be management. I'm afraid I might have just blown any chance I may have had with him. *Damn.*

'I'm hoping for promotion at work,' I add quickly.

He raises his eyebrows. 'Really?'

I nod. 'I don't know when, but I'm hoping it'll be soon.'

'Do you enjoy working at the hotel?'

I think for a moment. 'Not especially. And once Cassie's gone, I don't think I'll like it at all.'

'She's leaving?'

'At the end of the month.' I nod again.

'So, will you start looking for a better job then?'

I raise my eyebrows. Doesn't he think my job's good enough?

He seems to read my mind and hurriedly adds, 'I mean... one where you're happier. Not that there's anything wrong with your current position.'

Thank goodness for that!

As we smile at each other I feel a funny tingling in my tummy that I've never had before. James is a bit old-fashioned in a lot of ways, but it's kind of cute. I love that he's such a gentleman and he's clearly quite sensitive, despite my first impression that he was miserable and self-centred. I wonder if he's shy.

'Do you enjoy your job?' I ask.

'Very much,' he says with a nod. 'Although my promotion to sergeant is only temporary at this stage. I have to prove myself in order to keep the rank.'

'By solving a really good crime?'

'There's no such thing as a good crime,' he says with a snigger. 'But yes, that sort of thing.'

Raucous laughter from the men at the dartboard makes us both look over. They seem like a friendly bunch, and one of them puts up a hand to acknowledge James.

'Do you know them?' I ask.

He nods and takes a sip of his Coke.

I'm surprised that his friends seem to be so much older than him.

He must be doing that mind reading thing again as he adds, 'They were good friends of my dad. This was his favourite pub. I used to bring him down here a lot.'

His sad expression and use of past tense deters me from asking anything else, but luckily his telepathic powers are firing on all cylinders and he fills in the blanks for me. 'He had cancer. I cared for him right up until the end. No way was I going to let him pass away surrounded by strangers.'

'I'm so sorry.'

He gives me a warm smile. 'Me, too.'

I don't know what to say, but James clearly senses my uneasiness as he continues, 'He'd have liked you.'

My face grows hot. 'Really?'

He nods. 'Yep. You seem like a genuine kind of girl. Not all false like so many of them these days.'

Now he just sounds old again. I suppose it's to be expected, if he spent so much time with his dad.

'I'll take that as a compliment.' I tilt my glass towards him and he chinks his against it with a smile.

'You should.'

He leans forwards and for one wonderful second I think he's about to kiss me, but his phone rings, totally ruining the moment. 'Damn.' He frowns at the screen. 'I need to take this. Excuse me.'

He mutters something incoherent into his mobile before disappearing outside.

I sip my drink – still not taking any chances with my

weak stomach – and try not to look too conspicuous, sitting alone in a strange pub with my water.

There's another burst of laughter from the dartboard and I flush and look out the window, positive they're all talking about me. It's getting dark outside, and I wonder where James went, half-hoping to spy him chatting on his phone. He's nowhere to be seen, though.

I look down at the table and let my mind wander. James mentioned food when we first arrived, and I carefully assess my stomach issue, hoping it might be safe to attempt the chicken supreme he'd recommended. Although it's not the most salubrious place he could have brought me to, it's not bad, and, anyway, it's the company that counts, right? I'm also touched that he's brought me somewhere that's obviously special to him.

I saunter over to the bar and order myself more water and another Coke for James. The barman, a grey-haired guy, probably in his sixties, smiles at me pleasantly. 'I haven't seen you in here before.'

I shake my head, smiling back. 'No. James recommended it.'

He raises his eyebrows. 'Yeah, I saw you come in with him.'

'He's just popped out to take a phone call,' I explain, handing over a tenner. I hope he doesn't think we've had a row and James has left me here.

'Ahh,' he says over his shoulder as he puts the money in the till and sorts out my change.

I can't mention anything about it being probably a work-related call, in case the guy asks about his job. He might not know that James is a cop, so I play it safe. 'Is he a regular here, then?'

The guy frowns. 'Fairly.' He hands me the change. 'Though I don't think I've seen him bring a woman in here before – apart from his wife, of course.'

A sharp thud hits the pit of my stomach, and I fight hard to keep my expression neutral as I thank him. I take the drinks back to the table in a daze.

James rushes in just as I sink back into my seat. 'Sorry about that. I'm afraid something's come up at the station.'

'Oh.' I don't know what else to say. My mind has gone to mush.

'They need me to go in. I'll drop you off first, of course.'

'I can get a taxi.'

'Don't be silly. Come on, it's on my way.'

'Right. Of course.' I grab my bag and follow him out of the pub, leaving the drinks untouched.

He hurriedly opens the car door for me to get in, and I pull my seatbelt on. He frowns thoughtfully as he starts the engine.

'I'm really sorry,' he reiterates, speeding down the lane. 'I didn't mean to—'

'It's fine.'

'Will you get something to eat at the hotel?'

'Probably.'

He's really tense, gripping the steering wheel and frowning at the road ahead. I wonder if it's really because of something happening at work, or whether his wife just rang, checking up on him.

'This doesn't mean you have to arrest Bianca, does it?' I'm trying to focus on the matter in hand to stop myself from crying, or yelling at him, as my face gets hotter by the second.

'I don't think so. Not tonight, anyway.' He glances at me just as I'm watching his reaction. He looks concerned. And apologetic. And downright gorgeous. *Damn him!*

'I do apologise,' he says hurriedly, as he pulls up in the guests' car park of The Chalfont.

I want to ask him exactly what he's apologising for; cutting our date short, or being married. I shake my head dismissively. Perhaps he didn't mean it to be a date, after all? Maybe it was just what he said – an excuse to go somewhere private to talk. About work. After all, that's what we did. Mostly.

'Well, goodnight then,' I murmur, starting to get out the second the wheels stop turning.

'Goodnight, Libby.' He leans towards me, but I'm not waiting around. Not now. I jump out of the vehicle and slam the door a little harder than I intended. I don't know my own strength sometimes. And I'm more upset than I care to admit.

His tail-lights disappear and I make my way around to the back of the building and let myself in through the kitchen. I'm confused and worried – and downright disappointed. The anger is already dissipating, leaving me feeling numb and miserable.

I don't even bother with the light when I reach our room, just flick on the TV and grab a box of Maltesers from my locker before slumping onto the bed. I could go down and get a meal if I want one, but I'm not up to having company right now, and the thought of Party in one of his moods is enough to keep me holed up here for the rest of the night. Besides, any appetite that might have been creeping back has vanished. I cram a handful of Maltesers into my mouth – chocolate doesn't actually count as food, does it? – just before the first deluge of tears streams down my cheeks.

―――――

'SORRY, I DIDN'T MEAN TO WAKE YOU.' CASSIE STARES at me, her big eyes full of concern. 'I wouldn't have put the light on if I'd known you were sleeping. How did it...?' She trails off as she gets a good look at me. 'Oh, hon, what happened?'

I sniff, my head thick and heavy, my nose bunged up to my eyeballs. My eyes hurt with the brightness of the overhead light. She quickly goes to switch it off, but I put a hand up to stop her.

'Leave it,' I tell her, my voice like a bullfrog's. 'I need to get undressed anyway.'

My lovely frock is a crumpled mess, splattered with melted Maltesers, and I can feel some of the little beggars wedged between my boobs where they must have rolled after I'd fallen asleep.

'What happened?' Her eyes are wide with worry as

she studies my face, which I suppose must be a mass of smudged makeup and swollen redness by now, adorned with the unflattering creases of someone who nodded off from the sheer exhaustion of crying.

'He's married,' I blurt out. Hearing the words only ignites another wave of fresh tears as I peel myself from the bed.

Cassie holds her arms out for a big hug, but I know it'll only make me feel even worse, and besides, I'm sure she'd rather not get the chocolate-sweat mixture all over her uniform, so I rush to the bathroom.

I CAN'T TELL WHAT'S WATER AND WHAT'S TEARS AS I stand under the shower letting everything wash over me. It's good to get the stickiness off my body, and I feel surprisingly calm as I face the showerhead with my eyes closed.

'Are you okay?' Cassie asks with a kind smile when I return to the bedroom, still red-faced but clean and composed.

I nod. 'Yeah. It was just a bit of a shock, that's all. It's no big deal, we hadn't got together or anything. I'm just a bit disappointed, you know?'

'Is that what he took you out for? To explain? Bianca told me you'd left together.'

I shake my head. 'He didn't tell me, exactly. I just sort of... heard.'

She frowns, but nods. 'That sucks, hon. I'm sorry, I know you liked him.'

I can't deny it, but another thought occurs to me. 'It might have just been a rebound thing.'

'It's only been a week.' Cassie frowns knowingly. 'It's all still a bit raw, I expect.' She trots over to the bathroom, leaving the door open, as usual, so we can carry on our conversation while she cleans her teeth.

'I'm not as upset over Connor as I thought I'd be,' I admit to the back of her head. 'I mean, we weren't together that long and it was never really that serious. I think what hurt more was knowing that he'd been cheating. And with Bianca Morrison-Wright, of all people.'

Cassie turns to face me, toothpaste framing her mouth, while her Sonicare DiamondClean toothbrush whirs around her perfect teeth. 'That reminds me,' she says – or at least, I *think* that's what she said, it's hard to tell with her mouth full – before she turns back to the sink for a quick rinse.

'Those shoes.' She zooms back into the room, as excited as a kid at Christmas, and pulls on her pink silk pyjamas.

I'd almost forgotten. 'I was right, wasn't I?' I suddenly feel a trickle of anticipation as she sits cross-legged on my bed, her eyes wide and shining almost as brightly as her teeth. 'Of course.' Cassie's expression says *was there ever any doubt?* 'The latest Christian Louboutin Scalopumps. Connor bought them for her.'

My jaw drops and, although a most unflattering look, I know, I can't do anything to stop it. 'The bastard! He never bought *me* Louboutins!'

Cassie draws her eyebrows together. 'But, don't you

see? He's probably in on all this. He and Bianca have arranged the whole thing together.'

I snap my mouth shut. My head spins with the implications and my stomach churns at the thought that I really didn't know my boyfriend half as well as I'd thought.

'If he followed me back here and picked up my key, he might have given it to her,' I concede, having previously assumed she'd taken it without his knowledge.

'Same as he probably gave her the key to the filing cabinet so she could get the safe key,' Cassie adds.

I roll my eyes. Why haven't I thought of that before? 'No wonder she looked so pleased with herself earlier,' I say with a grimace.

Cassie frowns. 'Pleased? I wouldn't exactly say that.'

Now it's my turn to frown. 'What? She's just managed to pay off the loan sharks – *again!* – and her boyfriend's bought her a brand new pair of Scalopumps. I think anyone would be happy with that, wouldn't they?'

'She and Connor had a massive row earlier,' Cassie replies. 'Everyone heard him calling her a stupid cow – even Party which is why he was in such a foul mood tonight. And when I spoke to her later she told me it was because she'd worn her new shoes – which, by the way, she assumed had come from that guy off the market.'

'She doesn't know they're real?' I gasp.

'I told her they looked pretty authentic to me and she was gobsmacked,' Cassie says with a shake of her head. 'She said she was going to ask Connor about them later. She didn't look pleased about it, although she said it might explain why they were pinching her toes – I assume the fake ones must be a more generous size.'

I stare at my best friend, speechless.

'She's still worried about her dad,' Cassie continues. 'She said she managed to borrow another thousand, but it's still not enough. Those bastards won't be happy until they close down the family business altogether, by my reckoning.'

'But that doesn't make sense.' I explain all about the necklace and how much they got for it.

Cassie's eyes widen. 'So, even with the cost of the shoes, she should have had more than enough to pay them off?'

The intensity of her expression tells me we've both had the same thought at exactly the same time. 'Connor's kept most of the money.'

14

THE NEXT MORNING, I AWAKE WITH A HUGE, HARD LUMP in my throat. Luckily, Cassie and I are both on the late shift, so neither of us needs to be up early.

Checking my phone, I see that James has already rung several times and has sent a text message.

Hi Libby. I'm really sorry about last night. I need to speak to you asap. J.x

I know I should be flattered that he's ended the message with a kiss, but somehow it just makes me even angrier. How dare he? I'm no home-wrecker, and I'm surprised he is, being as he seems so full of old-fashioned values. Unless it was all lies. Bile rises in my throat.

'Come on, let's pop into town for an hour,' Cassie coaxes as she clambers out of bed. 'A bit of retail therapy will do us both good.'

'I'm not really in the mood.'

She looks at me as though I'm an alien. Her wavy,

dark hair is all matted and sticking up at the back, and her expression is so comical I can't help but giggle.

'Are you feeling okay?' Then she suddenly crosses her eyes, making me burst out laughing.

'Okay,' I concede. 'You take the first shower.'

With a satisfied grin she bounds into the tiny bathroom, and I can hear her singing a Lady Gaga song as the shower hisses into action.

I peer at the screen of my mobile again. The message hasn't changed since I last looked.

Yeah, I'll bet you're sorry about last night. And I can imagine just what you need to speak to me about, but I'm not interested. He'll either want to tell me all about his wife and how she doesn't understand him, or tell me it was all a mistake and that he shouldn't have taken me out. Neither option is what I need to hear right now, so I'll give it a miss. I take a deep breath and throw the phone into the drawer of my bedside locker.

ONCE I'M SHOWERED AND DRESSED I FEEL MUCH BETTER – particularly as Cassie's lent me her navy Jimmy Choos to go with my skinny jeans. My ankle's actually a lot better now, and I admire my look in the full-length mirror on the back of the bedroom door. I've put on some makeup, and the deep blue of my top makes my eyes really stand out. My hair has actually behaved itself today and I've left it down.

'Wow!' Cassie smiles approvingly. 'Let's hope we bump into all the people we know.'

She's in Armani jeans and bright red Louboutins, looking as stunning as ever.

We both grab our leather jackets on our way out the door – well, hers is leather, but mine's a good imitation.

South Kensington's busy as usual, and we head to one of Cassie's favourite boutiques to try on some shoes. I love going in wearing designer shoes while I'm checking out other designer stuff, as the sales assistants always smile at you, as though you're part of the 'club'. Not like that scene out of *Pretty Woman* when Julia Roberts gets refused service.

'So, how are things with Rob?' I ask Cassie, who's admiring herself in a pair of Manolo Blahniks with five inch heels.

She grins. 'Great. He rang last night and apologised for not getting back to me. He and Ben had been in court all day, so hadn't been able to use their phones. We're going out again tomorrow night.'

I'm happy for her. 'What was that story he was so excited about?'

She rolls her eyes. 'Something to do with a local MP having an affair with a bored housewife. The wife had found out and was trying to sue the housewife for dragging the family's name through the mud. It was inconclusive though, so the case is continuing. It didn't make the front page because there was something more important about a local school being threatened with closure.'

I nod, vaguely recalling the picture on the front of the *Chronicle* yesterday as Cassie and I were skimming it for our story.

'Black or navy?' she asks with a pout.

'Depends what you want to wear them with.' Both colours look absolutely stunning.

She screws up her face in thought. 'I don't know.'

'You'll need to have a think about it,' I suggest, just as an assistant approaches us.

'Oh, those look fantastic on you!' the woman gushes, as though she's never seen the shoes before in her life.

'Thanks,' Cassie replies flippantly. 'We're going for a coffee to decide which colour.'

The assistant's face falls. 'Don't leave it too long. They're bound to be snapped up, being as they're so exquisite. And good value.' Her voice rises as she talks, betraying her horror at the thought of losing a sale.

'Well, I doubt both colours will sell out in my size in the next half an hour,' Cassie says with a shrug. 'And at least if one of them's sold out it makes my decision for me, doesn't it?' She's already slipping back into her Louboutins.

'If you leave a deposit I can put a pair aside for you – just for half an hour?' The woman's tenacious.

Cassie frowns. 'But I wouldn't know which colour to reserve, would I?'

The assistant purses her lips, her disappointment evident.

'Thanks, anyway,' Cassie goes on before the woman has time to reply.

I replace the shoes on the shelf, and Cassie slings an

arm around my shoulder as we leave the shop, rolling our eyes.

We're giggling as we reach Starbucks and order our coffees. I look around, remembering the last time I was here, just before I spotted the necklace in the antique shop down the road. The thought takes me straight back to James, and I realise that the lump in my throat has slid down to my stomach where it seems to have taken up permanent residence.

'Let's sit by the window,' Cassie suggests. 'We can play our favourite game.'

I follow her over to a small round table. We sit down and begin peering out into the street.

'Okay,' she says, grinning. 'The old lady with the blue hat.'

I look to where she's pointing. The thin, frail woman seems to be about eighty. Her white hair pokes out the sides of a large, felt hat, which she seems to be holding onto with one hand while walking with a stick in the other.

'Ooh, no. I hope the wind doesn't get any stronger,' I say in a silly voice. 'I won't know whether to save my hat or myself.'

Cassie bursts out laughing. 'Good one. She looks like she'd be blown over by a strong gust of wind, bless her.'

I nod, then take a sip of my cappuccino. 'That's what I thought.' It's great fun, trying to guess what people are thinking. 'Right. Your turn. The man running, in the black hoodie. Looks like he's in one hell of a hurry.'

'Where?'

'There, with his back to us, by the front of—'

The rest of my words are drowned out by the sound of emergency sirens as three squad cars and an ambulance hurtle past the window.

A shudder runs down my back and a feeling of dread envelopes me.

'It's all right, hon. We're safe,' Cassie assures me, clearly worried I'll have a panic attack or something. I've only ever had one in front of her, and it scared the life out of her – not to mention me.

I take deep breaths to steady my nerves as I watch people stare after the vehicles. Even though I know it doesn't affect me, I can't help feeling jittery.

'I'm fine.' I glance over at Cassie, who's studying me closely.

'You don't think Sergeant Harper will be involved in this, do you?' she asks warily.

I'm about to shrug, when it hits me. The market is down the road, and a few streets away is the stall with the fake shoes. I recall yesterday's conversation as James phoned one of his colleagues at the station. 'Oh, no.'

'Sorry, I shouldn't have said anything. I'm sure he'll be okay. He's a professional, after all.'

My whole body tenses up. 'He wouldn't, would he?'

'What?'

I explain about the shoes and how James had asked

for a female officer to investigate the stall today, with back up.

'You think they've arrested the guy?'

I nod. 'But surely they won't have had time to pick up the loan sharks as well? That was the whole point of the exercise.'

'They must know what they're doing,' Cassie says, shaking her head.

Just then her mobile rings and we both jump.

'It's Rob,' she says with a frown.

Another police car screeches past, and Cassie indicates that she'll take the call towards the back of the shop. I can't blame her, with all that racket going on outside.

I'm just finishing my coffee when she returns, looking gloomy.

'He said a big story's just broken out, so he might have to work over tonight.'

'I thought you were seeing him *tomorrow* night?'

'I am, but he was hoping to pop into The Chalfont in time for last orders just in case I got off a bit early, that's all.'

'Did he say what the story was about?'

She shakes her head. 'No, but he was really concerned when I told him where we are. He wants us to get away from the area as quickly as possible.'

I huff. 'It's probably time we were getting to work, anyway.'

I stand and follow her out the door.

'You haven't heard anything from Sergeant Harper, I

take it?' she asks as we head up the road in the opposite direction to where the action is.

'No. Actually, I left my phone behind.'

She lifts her eyebrows. 'He really has upset you, hasn't he?' She puts her arm around me and gives me a tight squeeze. 'We're not having much luck with our men at the moment, are we?'

'He's not exactly my man, though,' I reply sadly. I can't help wishing things were different. He seemed so charming last night, and I really wanted him to kiss me. It's a good job he didn't, though, with hindsight.

By the time we arrive back at The Chalfont it's almost time to start work. Everyone's chattering in the kitchen when we go in, but we still have to change, so we head straight up the back stairs.

'It's probably been on the news,' Cassie says as we hurry to our room.

'I don't think I want to know.' I'm hurt and upset. Has James done this on purpose? He knew I didn't want them to go in and arrest Stu, even if he can lead the police to the loan sharks. I recall the look on James's face last night when I told him I wanted to collect designer shoes. He clearly didn't approve.

I quickly get into my suit, then open my bedside drawer to take out my little stud earrings. My phone's flashing. I can guess who's left me a message, but I'm in no mood to speak to anyone right now, much less James flipping Harper.

'You're late.' Mr Partington's waiting for me when I arrive at Reception.

I glance at the clock. 'Two minutes. It's probably taken me that long to get here from the kitchen.'

'But you don't work in the kitchen. You work out here. Or in there, to be precise.' He points to the cupboard door where my office is. 'Which means you're even later.'

'Sorry. I'll leave early tonight to make up for it,' I respond dryly.

'Very funny.' He doesn't even crack a smile – not that I really expected him to. 'Sergeant Harper's been trying to reach you. And Bianca's not here, so you need to start setting up the bar. Connor will be here as soon as he can to take over from you.'

'Great.' I'm about to roll my eyes, but something tells me Party's ready to blow a fuse, so I quickly look away. It's just as well. I could so easily make a remark about being early if I'm working in the bar and not in my office, but I just paste on a smile and do an abrupt about-turn.

I start by polishing the tables and replacing the beer mats. There's no-one about, so I then go through and stack the mixers behind the bar. The smell of stale beer hits me and I notice that no-one cleaned the floor last night. I grimace as my shoes stick to the tiles. Why the hell can't Bianca do the job she's paid for? Where on earth is she, anyway? My stomach flips as I consider the possibilities.

If the cops have arrested Stu, there's a good chance they've taken Bianca in for questioning, too. Was that what James wanted to tell me? He's got a nerve, if that's the case. I pleaded with him not to arrest Bianca. Her dad will be worried sick – and if James's story about how close he was to his father's true then he would realise how devastating it could be.

I'm fuming as I finish setting up the bar and give the floor a quick once-over with a damp mop. Then I go off in search of Cassie while the floor dries – I'll be blowed if I'm going to slip on a wet floor.

'Any news from Rob?' I ask, joining my bestie at the dumbwaiter.

She shakes her head. 'Not yet. It must be serious. Stan said there's been nothing on the radio, either.'

I frown. 'It certainly looked like a big deal from where we sat.'

'What did?'

I jerk around to see that Mad Moody Margaret, as we've decided to call her, is eavesdropping again.

I roll my eyes at her but she just tuts.

'Liberty?' Mr Partington shouts out from the bar area.

I shake my head as I scuttle back to my post.

He's craning his head over the bar, as though he really thinks I'm hiding behind one of the barrels or something.

'Just checking on the menu while the floor dries,' I

tell him in a sing-song voice. 'I see the lamb's off again.'

He doesn't look convinced – possibly because it's not entirely true. I thought I'd subtly hint about Bianca not having cleaned the floor at the end of her shift, though, but he doesn't seem to be taking any notice. It's probably just as well, really – she's got enough to worry about right now.

'Sergeant Harper wants a word.' His voice is clipped.

'But I'm minding the bar. Can't it wait?' The words are out of my mouth before I notice James staring at me from the doorway.

'It's police business. Of course it can't wait,' Party spits furiously. 'Cassie can take over if we get any customers. You can use my office.'

With a sigh I turn to face James, and realise how worried he looks. Something's not right.

'Lead on, Macduff,' I mutter. I'm not looking forward to this one bit.

'*Lay* on, Macduff,' he corrects.

I roll my eyes. That doesn't even make sense. I won't start arguing about Shakespeare with the back of his head, though, particularly in the middle of the corridor.

He doesn't say another word until we're in the office with the door firmly shut. Then he explodes. 'Where the hell have you been? Why haven't you answered any of my calls?' he demands, his expression a mixture of

anger and something which I think looks like concern.
Surely not?

'In town. I had the morning off. And I didn't take
my mobile.' I shrug before taking the seat opposite
the desk.

I expected James to sink into the luxury of Mr Partington's big chair, but, instead, he pulls over a spare
chair from near the window and sits next to me, leaning
forwards. 'Libby, I'm sorry I had to cut our date short
last night—'

'Date? Is that what you call it?' I snap.

He sighs. 'Okay – maybe not a date, then. But I
enjoyed spending some time with you. I thought you
did, too, but—'

'I thought this was police business. If it's not then
I've got work to do.' I move to get up from my seat, but
he places a hand on my arm.

'Please, Libby.'

He pleads with me with eyes that are like two huge
pools of melted chocolate, and I almost feel like I could
dive right into them. His brow is furrowed and I can see
that he's really worried about something.

'What?'

'Were you in the vicinity of the market today?' He
swipes a hand through his hair. 'Your boss seemed to
think you must have gone out with Cassie. Shoe-shopping, he guessed.'

'Oh, did he?'

'Were you?' He sounds almost desperate, which
catches me off guard.

'Yes. We went to the shops and then for coffee at Starbucks.'

His face drops. 'The Starbucks by the market?'

With a frown, I reply, 'It's not exactly right by the market, but the road leads that way, yes.'

He swallows hard. 'Did you go to the market?'

I want to roll my eyes and tell him to mind his own business, but something about his demeanour tells me this is serious. Very serious. 'No.'

He takes a deep breath and sits back in his chair, though his hand remains on my arm.

'Did you arrest Stu?'

He looks shocked. 'Who?'

'The guy with the fake designer shoes. I told you about him last night and you said you'd get someone to go down there today.' I remind him.

'No.' He frowns.

'Then why were there loads of squad cars and an ambulance whizzing down that way just before eleven o'clock?' I stare at him obstinately, daring him to deny it.

Slowly, he leans forwards again. 'You were there at the time?' He looks horrified, his voice quiet.

'We were in Starbucks, like I said.'

'Did you see anything?'

'Apart from the emergency services hurtling towards the market, you mean?'

'Yes.'

'Like what?'

He chews his lip and I just know there's a lot he's

not telling me. It doesn't seem to make sense, though, given that I've already told him I know the cops were down there today. It doesn't take a genius to guess what they were doing there. 'Like anyone acting suspiciously.'

That wasn't the reply I was expecting. 'Suspiciously?'

He nods, then fixes me in his gaze. Under other circumstances I might be intrigued by that look, but I actually find it a little unnerving.

'But I didn't go to the market.'

'This was nothing to do with the market. Something happened near to where you were, though.'

I gape at him, remembering Cassie and I playing our game in Starbucks. 'There was a man running,' I say carefully. 'Black hoodie and jeans. He had his back to us so we didn't see his face.'

His eyes widen. 'Where?'

'In the opposite direction to all those emergency vehicles. It was just before they came screeching down the road.' I swallow hard. 'What did he do?'

He squeezes my arm reassuringly. 'It's not public knowledge yet. A woman was mugged. Her handbag was stolen. Unfortunately she was carrying a large amount of cash.'

I put my hand to my mouth, trying to decipher the look in his eyes. 'It's someone I know, isn't it?'

He lets out a long, slow breath. 'Yes.'

15

'BIANCA?'

'No.' He frowns. 'Why would you think that?'

'She didn't turn up for work. I thought—' I stop myself before divulging that I thought he'd betrayed me by arresting her, even though he'd said he wouldn't – or at least implied it.

He shakes his head. 'It was Mrs Merrington-Smythe.'

'Oh no!' I don't know which is worse.

'She's okay. Well, she's at the hospital being treated for shock. The man just came up from behind and snatched the bag right out of her hand. She put up a bit of a fight, mind you.'

My mind reels. 'And it was the guy I saw?'

'No. We suspect that he was involved, but he didn't actually take the bag. The guy who did it is already in a police cell. He's been treated for shock, too - who knew the old dear had such a strong left hook? We're just waiting for him to spill the beans on his accomplice. And he will. They always do.'

I balk. 'You caught him straight away?'

James gives a little smile. 'Thanks to you.'

'What?'

'I made sure the officer had plenty of back-up in case anything untoward happened when she approached the guy with the shoes. You never can tell. Sometimes, I don't know how, they seem to get a whiff that it's an undercover cop and they turn quite nasty. Anyway, when the attack on Mrs Merrington-Smythe happened the area was already swarming with cops. Some of the public called the uniforms in as well, so we were well covered. We're not sure what the guy in the hoodie was doing, but one of the witnesses said they saw someone matching that description flee the scene. It might be nothing, but we'll soon find out.' He nods, clearly quite satisfied with the result.

'So I helped, in a way?' I feel a warmth in my stomach, which alerts me to the fact that the big lump has dissipated at last.

'Yes…but…' His expression turns serious again. 'I was trying to get hold of you. I wanted to warn you not to go down there. I ended up ringing here to see if your boss knew where you were and he said someone had seen you go out with Cassie. He guessed you'd have gone shoe-shopping. Libby…I was worried.' He frowns with concern as his eyes plead with me to believe him.

And I do.

I want to throw my arms around him and tell him

I'm fine, but he already knows that. Besides, I can't. Not now.

'I'm sorry,' I whisper, and try to stand.

I'm pinned down by his grip on my arm, then treated to the scent of his aftershave as he leans towards me.

'What's wrong?' His eyebrows are drawn together. He really doesn't know.

'What do you think?' I try hard to put an edge back into my voice, because, quite honestly, what I really want to do is kiss him right now.

He shakes his head with a sigh. 'You didn't like the pub last night, did you?'

I stare at him.

'I'm sorry. I'm not used to taking women out. I hadn't planned to, either, it just sort of… seemed like a good opportunity to get to know you – and we needed to discuss the case somewhere private anyway. Look, next time we can—'

'*Next* time?' My voice is twice as loud and about ten times higher than I intended.

'You don't want to see me again?' He visibly deflates.

I'm confused. And sad. 'James, I'd love to go out with you again, but I can't.'

He nods slowly and removes his hand from my arm. 'I understand.'

'No,' I tell him, standing up. '*I* understand.'

'Is there someone else?' His voice is a little croaky and I can tell he's really upset. But then so am I.

'Yes, there is. Clearly.'

He gives a wry smile. 'Is it the barman? Have you taken him back?' He stands carefully.

It takes a second for the penny to drop and I freeze for a second. 'No!' I almost yell at him in frustration. 'Of course I haven't taken Connor back. And, anyway, this isn't about *me*.'

'What?' He's frowning again.

'It's about *your wife*.' I hurl the words at him just as the door opens and Mr Partington peers in, his eyes wide.

My whole body glows red-hot with a mixture of embarrassment, indignation and anger. My gaze flits from my boss to James, who is staring at me in bewilderment.

'Um…I'm sorry, I heard raised voices. Is everything all right?' Mr Partington asks in a very bumptious-sounding tone.

'*No*,' James and I bark in unison.

Slowly, my boss backs out of the room, closing the door quietly behind him.

'Great. I've probably just lost my job now, thanks to you,' I fire at James.

'I'm not married.' His voice is soft and his eyes narrowed slightly.

'Well, that's not what the barman at the Fox and Duck told me!' I snap back at him.

'We're divorced,' he says slowly. 'We didn't exactly shout it from the rooftops, especially as it was right after I lost my dad.'

The blood drains from my face. 'Oh no.' I put my

hands to my mouth, inwardly cursing myself for not making sure of my facts before yelling my head off.

'It's okay. You weren't to know. And I was hardly going to mention it in the Fox and Duck at the time. Dad's friends were upset enough about losing him, without hearing my woes as well. Not that any of them are that close to me – as I said, they were Dad's friends. I just pop in now and then to show my face. And eat the chicken supreme. Did I mention it's delicious, by the way?' His eyes twinkle as his mouth curves slightly.

'You did. Maybe I'll have to get you to prove it sometime,' I say in a small – but very relieved – voice.

'Tomorrow night?' His smile grows.

I take a deep breath, feeling like a complete fool. 'I think I've got an opening.'

'I'll pick you up at seven.'

'I look forward to it.'

'It's a date, then,' he says apprehensively.

'Oh, I hope so.' I smile.

'Until then, Miss Lawrence.'

I nod. 'Oh, and Sergeant. I'm really sor—'

His finger finds my lip just in time to stop my words. 'Tomorrow night, Libby. You can eat as much humble pie as you like – for dessert.'

He leans down, places a chaste kiss on my now-flushed cheek and leaves the room with a sexy wink.

I'm still hugging myself, smiling at the memory when Mr Partington bursts in. 'I take it you've finished?'

My mind says *I think we've only just got started*, but my mouth says, 'Yes, sir.'

'Good. And you do realise I gave you the use of my office to discuss police issues – not for personal arguments?'

God, he can be so pious at times I feel like yelling at him. But I won't. And neither will I allow him to ruin my new-found good mood. 'Yes, sir.'

'In that case, perhaps you'd like to explain the incident I walked in on earlier?'

'I'm afraid I can't, Mr Partington. Police business isn't for everyone's ears.'

'And what about personal disagreements?'

I widen my eyes innocently, putting on my best, fake shocked expression. 'I don't know what you're talking about, sir. Has the sergeant said something?'

He presses his lips together irritably. 'No.'

'Then, like I said, I'm not allowed to discuss any conversations I have with the police with you or anyone else.'

'Just get out.' He waves a dismissive hand in my direction and I scoot out the door, trying not to giggle until I'm far enough up the corridor for him not to hear.

THE REST OF MY SHIFT PASSES IN A ROSY HAZE. Connor's finally dragged himself into work – claiming a dental appointment held him up, of all things – and I'm actually allowed to get on with my own job, for a change.

I'm making good headway with the wedding fair, at last, and I actually feel excited chatting to the vendors about what styles of bridal wear and flowers they will be displaying. Trade space is selling quickly and I'm really looking forward to the event.

During my meal break I sneak up to our room and fetch my mobile. James had left several voicemail messages pleading with me to get in touch with him this morning. He sounded really worried, which only makes me feel even worse about the assumptions I made about him.

A while later I hear the boss's drone as he talks to Frances at Reception. I'm working away in my office and my first instinct is to pretend I'm not there, and hide behind a stack of copier paper. I suppose I'll have to face him sooner or later, though, so I bite the bullet and go through to join them.

It's only then that Mr Partington deigns to inform me that Mrs Merrington-Smythe is in hospital and won't be coming back tonight. He doesn't go into detail, and I feel a little smug, wondering if I know more about her situation than he does.

'Should I send some flowers?' I ask, glancing at the clock.

'You won't get anything delivered today, it's too late.' His tone is curt — he's still miffed with me. Probably more so now that I've mentioned the flowers – a gesture he should have arranged hours ago, in my opinion.

'I'll take some to her tomorrow, then. It's my day

off, so it's no problem. Have you contacted the hospital to ask how she is?' I'm thinking on my feet here, which is unusual for me as I'm usually thinking *of* my feet – and which shoes I'd like to put on them.

He gives me a withering look. 'They won't divulge any information to us; we're not her family. I only know this much because the sergeant told me.'

'No, but as a kind gesture, we could just ring and ask them to pass on our best wishes. She is a customer, after all, and we don't even know if she's got any family or friends in the area who can visit her.'

I can see he's mulling it over.

'I'll do it,' he says eventually. 'I think it'll sound better coming from me.'

Somehow, I thought he'd say that.

'What about her dog?' I ask, suddenly remembering the little pooch that nearly killed me. Well, maybe a slight exaggeration, but that's what it felt like.

Party frowns at me. *Nothing new there.*

'Where is he? Was he with her when they took her to hospital?'

'I don't know,' he admits, suddenly looking a little perturbed.

'I'll check her room. He might still be there.'

Frances hands me the key to room 109 and I scoot over to the lift and head up.

I can hear the dog whining as I open the door, and there's a squelch under my foot from a soggy patch in the plush carpet.

With a wagging tail he comes straight up to me. My

heart clenches. Poor little thing. He must be starving, let alone lonely, having been holed up in here all day.

A whiff of something unpleasant mingles with the floral scents of the old lady, and my heart sinks. There are no housekeeping staff on duty at this time of the evening, so no prizes for guessing who's going to have to clean up the poochie poo.

I scoop him up in my arms and notice he's trembling. 'Let's find you something to eat, shall we?' I murmur softly.

Stan is only too happy to find him some tidbits. I fill an old bowl with water and Popsie tucks in, oblivious as I tie him on a long leash to a drainpipe near to the back door.

'I need to clean the room,' I explain to Stan. 'I'll leave him out there for a bit, then take him to my office. He'll have to stay with me.'

'We'll keep an eye on him,' Adrian cuts in, eagerly.

Stan rolls his weird eyes, muttering something about hygiene, but Adrian ignores him.

IT TAKES THE BEST PART OF AN HOUR TO CLEAN THE room – or the worst part, depending on how you look at it - and I'm glad the hotel is prepared for this sort of eventuality with good, industrial-strength cleaner and air freshener. I change the bed linen, guessing Popsie probably spent a lot of time huddled up there, but luckily it looks like he only used the carpet as his toilet.

Mrs Merrington-Smythe is a very tidy old dear, as

everything is neat and uncluttered. An old black and white photo stands on her bedside locker and I can't help taking a peek. It looks like a large family, with one woman holding a tiny baby. I can make out a couple of ladies who vaguely resemble Mrs Merrington-Smythe – one of whom is holding the baby, but it's impossible to be sure if either is actually her in her youth, or just a relative of hers, as the photo must have been taken forty or fifty years ago, judging by the fashions.

I'm glad to think that the old lady might have a family somewhere. I can't help wondering where they all are now.

Replacing the photo, I then grab the dog's bed, which is now smelling much fresher than earlier, and head back down to my office. I'm not sure how Frances will feel about having the little pooch running about in the stationery cupboard, but I'm prepared to pull rank on this one if I need to.

'Oh, he's so cute!' She beams when I fetch him through, much to my relief, and I let her have a little cuddle with him before taking him into the cupboard with me and trying to settle him on his bed. I say *trying* because it actually turns out to be impossible to encourage such a young dog to go and lie down in a corner while I get on with my work. He wags his tail happily as he scampers about, sniffing at boxes of paper and knocking over my wastepaper basket, which gives him great joy when he realises that I screw my rubbish into balls, which he can play with quite happily – when he's not trying to eat them, that is.

I carefully move all the ink toners and adhesives to a top shelf – I'm not sure if dogs can get high on the smells of these things, but I'm certainly not taking any chances with Mrs Merrington-Smythe's pride and joy.

I don't get much work done for the rest of the night, and make a note to visit the florist's tomorrow instead. I'll be going that way anyway.

Party refuses to waive the rule about us not having pets in our rooms, so Popsie spends the night behind Reception, much to the night porter's delight. Mike has a couple of dogs of his own, and Popsie seems to pick up their scent on him as soon as he comes on duty, and clings to him like a limpet. It turns out that Mike's really good with animals, and, after making a big fuss of the little pooch, actually gets him to lie in his bed while we go through the handover.

Popsie hardly seems to notice me saying goodnight, much to my disappointment, as he's too busy watching Mike's every move, and I head off towards the kitchen.

Unfortunately I have to pass through the bar on my way and Connor hails me over. He's just polishing a few glasses as the last of the residents leave. 'I need a word,' he calls out, his voice smooth as caramel.

There was a time when that tone would have made my toes curl, but it doesn't have the same effect anymore. 'I'm tired,' I reply, but go over to him anyway.

'Look, I'm sorry about the whole Bianca thing. I really didn't mean it to jeopardise what we had.' He bites his lip and I can believe him. He honestly thought he could carry on seeing me while having a fling with her.

'You should have thought of that before you cheated.' I'm not giving him an inch. He's picked a bad time to have this conversation.

'But what if I tell you I don't feel anything for her? I want to be with you.' His puppy-dog eyes remind me a little of Popsie's, although I can't help thinking that the little pooch is a lot more sincere than this love-rat.

'I heard you'd had a tiff,' I tell him bluntly, remembering the conversation I had with Cassie. He was annoyed with Bianca for wearing her Louboutins to work, probably because he knew that we'd recognise them for what they were – real.

He tries to laugh it off, but his face doesn't relax like it should. 'Oh, that was nothing, really. Just a disagreement.'

'So, you're still with her? You haven't split up?'

His face falls as he realises that having denied the row he's now made the rift between us even wider. 'Well, I haven't actually said the words…'

'But you're going to?'

He fiddles with the cloth in his hand. 'Do you want me to? Would you like us to get back together?' His eyes are half-closed, his voice sultry and soft. I should be going weak at the knees, but somehow it's just my stomach that feels weak. I think I'm going to puke.

'Let's see. Her father's in trouble. The family business may have to fold. *Someone* in the hotel has been stealing money from the safe, and we're all under suspicion, although *some* have more of a motive than others. She's off work today - presumably ill - so must be feeling really rotten on all counts – oh, and you've had a row in front of everyone.'

His lips tighten, but he gives a shrug as though it doesn't affect him. If I was the violent type I might be tempted to slap him right now.

'Don't you think she's got *enough* on her plate without you cheating on her?' I snap, taking him by surprise.

'But it wouldn't be cheating. I'd just be getting back with you.' He's pulling a beer mat to pieces now, clearly flummoxed, and I wonder if he really believes what he's saying.

'No, you wouldn't. You'll never get back with me,' I tell him, my voice a little louder than I intended. 'Because you're a self-centred, conniving cheat, and I wouldn't go near you with a ten-foot barge-pole. You sicken me, Connor Worthington. I don't know what I ever saw in you, but I'm bloody glad I can see you for what you are, now. Just leave me alone and don't ever even think about asking me out again!'

I'm surprised to hear a small round of applause, and look around to see that Cassie, Stan, Adrian and even Mad, Moody Margaret are smiling at me from the restaurant entrance.

'Well said,' Cassie comments, coming over to me, beaming.

I let her lead me through the restaurant and into the kitchen, followed by the others.

'Good on you, girl,' Adrian chimes in, patting me on the back.

'I always knew you were too good for the likes of him,' Stan says from somewhere behind me.

I don't hear anything from Margaret, but it's good that she was there. Whether she's in a mood or just plain mad, I'm not sure, but either way it's probably just as well she hasn't voiced an opinion.

16

I'M GLAD OF A BIT OF A LIE-IN THE NEXT MORNING. IT'S only an extra half an hour but it feels so luxurious. Cassie got up earlier as she's serving breakfast, but I've got the whole day to myself, and, of course, I can't wait to see James tonight for our 'proper' date.

Popsie's pleased to see me when I reach Reception, and he starts jumping up at me. I recoil when I spot his muddy paws. How the hell did he get so dirty in here?

'Popsie!' Mike's voice sounds very stern and he seems too big and bossy to be shouting that name in the middle of a busy hotel foyer, but it stops the dog in his tracks. He immediately ceases bouncing and turns to face him.

'Good boy.' Mike's clearly satisfied, as am I – I'm wearing my Top Shop jeans and they were too expensive to get torn by the little mutt's sharp claws. I crouch down to reward the pooch with a gentle stroke.

'He's had breakfast,' Mike informs me. 'And Frank

took him on his rounds four times during the night, so he's been out and had some exercise, though he could do with more.'

That explains the muddy paws, then.

'Great. I'll take him into town with me,' I say, grabbing the lead.

Mike gives Popsie a cuddle before I attach the leash and head out the door, thanking the night porter for all his help. I had no idea he was so good with dogs. He's a big man, over six foot, and a little overweight, but he's kind and I think animals respond to that. He must be in his fifties and I know his children have all grown up, so his dogs are good company for him at home. His wife is a nurse and works shifts, too, so I think there's always at least one of them around to look after the pets. He was a gentle giant with Popsie this morning, and the dog clearly loves him.

'Come on, boy,' I say, gently tugging at the lead.

Popsie is interested in everything and everyone and I'm glad I've got all day to get my errands done, as he's certainly not in a hurry to go anywhere. He sniffs at every lamp-post and takes his time trotting down the pavement.

There's a bench a little further up and I intend to sit there and give us both a short break. As we near it I notice someone slumped over it, half-covered in newspaper. It looks like a homeless man as his clothes are all ragged and filthy. He's splayed out, hanging off the bench, with a whiskey-bottle cuddled close to his chest. He's fast asleep, snoring loudly, which seems to have alerted Popsie's attention as he sniffs around the man curiously.

My phone pings and I pull it from my pocket to see it's a message from Cassie.

Definitely seeing Rob tonight. Things are hotting up ;)

I smile. It's time she had a nice guy in her life – and Rob certainly seems like a *very* nice guy.

I glance down to see that Popsie has cocked his leg against the bench for a pee – and is squirting the man's coat. I'm amazed – not to mention relieved – that the man is still snoring away, quite oblivious to the fact that he's just become a human toilet.

'Oh no!'

I retrieve my notebook and a pen from my bag and scribble down a quick apology. *I'm sorry but my dog got your coat wet. Buy yourself another one.* It might be a little cowardly of me to miss out *how* Popsie wet the coat, but I'm sure the guy will soon realise, if he has any sense of smell, anyway. I wrap the message around a £20 note and tuck it into the breast pocket of the man's shirt. He flinches but doesn't wake so I pull on the lead and Popsie and I make good our escape.

Town's quite busy, as usual, and I'm concerned that the little fella's about to get trodden on, but he manages to hold his own with sharp yaps that warn people that he's there. It's a good job, as my instinct is to lift him up and carry him everywhere but I know he needs to stretch his legs after being cooped up yesterday, so I just dodge the crowds as best I can.

The florist's isn't far from us as we round a corner, and I'm already planning what I'm going to say. I want to get some really good displays in the conference room for the wedding fair, as it'll save me having to worry about decorating the place if the florists can do it for me. I'm going to offer them a little more trade space in return for a few extra flowers, which will also help advertise them.

'Hello.'

Warmth fills my stomach as the familiar voice greets us, and I look into the sultry, brown eyes of a certain police sergeant. 'James. I didn't expect to see you.' I feel myself blushing, and wish I'd put on a little more makeup this morning. It's wonderful to see him, though, and he looks as ravishing as ever.

'I see you've got company.' He crouches down and Popsie eagerly licks his hands while James fusses him.

'This is Popsie, Mrs Merrington-Smythe's dog.'

He looks surprised as he stands up. 'Really?'

'I'm looking after him while she's in hospital.'

'That's nice of you,' he says with a smile.

I shrug. 'Well, it's my day off so…'

'I didn't realise. What have you got planned?'

'I'm just going to get her some flowers and then I'm heading up to the hospital to see if I can give them to her. I'm not sure what time visiting hours are – or even if they're allowed flowers in hospitals these days – but I thought it would be a kind gesture.' I frown, wondering if flowers are such a good idea, after all.

'You don't have to worry. She's in a private ward. She can have whatever she wants,' he assures me.

'You've seen her, then? Is she okay?' I suddenly feel a little more optimistic.

'Last night. I called in on her to see if she'd remembered anything more. She seemed much better. Desperate to get back to her little man, here.'

I can't help wondering if Mr Partington would have informed her that I was taking care of Popsie, but I somehow doubt it. If it had been left to him, the poor dog would probably still be whining up in the room now, giving the cleaners a good excuse for some well-earned overtime.

We're walking together, now, his arm very lightly placed around me, his hand just touching the small of my back through my thin jacket.

'Is this the place?' he asks, looking up at the shop sign for Full Bloom Flowers.

'Yep.'

He follows me inside. The shop smells pungent, with a mixture of all sorts of flowers which I'll never know the names of, and beautiful displays everywhere. It's a little cramped because of all the stock, and it's quite busy, but there's a friendly atmosphere.

'If you need me to look after the dog while you're at the hospital, it's no trouble,' James offers with a smile.

'That would be great. I assumed I'd just tie him outside, but I'm not sure that's safe,' I admit.

'I'll take him for a walk in the park,' James says.

I beam at him. 'Thank you.'

He smiles at me and I get that gooey feeling in my stomach.

'Can I help you?' a young girl with a high ponytail and a green apron asks.

'I'd like some flowers for an old lady, please,' I tell her. 'Are those spoken for?' I point to a hand-tied bunch of roses and gypsophila with a few freesias mixed in, which is standing in a bucket near the counter.

'No, they're for sale.' She lifts them up and quickly dries the stems.

'She'll love them.' I whip out my purse.

'Do you want to write a card?' the girl chirps.

I nod. 'Get well soon, if you have one.'

James immediately reaches over and takes Popsie's lead from me.

The assistant hands me a tiny card and a cheap biro and I quickly scribble *To Mrs M-S with best wishes from all at The Chalfont Hotel* before handing them back.

'You're from The Chalfont?' the girl asks in surprise before attaching the card to a little stick which she tucks into the arrangement. 'You're not Libby, by any chance?'

'Yes.'

'Andrea's been trying to get hold of you – something to do with bridal flowers, she said. She's not in until later, but if you want to pop back, she can show you what sort of bouquets and displays she has in mind. She's got some brilliant ideas for you.'

'Thank you. I'm sorry I haven't been in my office

much lately. I'll either come back later today or give her a ring tomorrow,' I promise. 'I can't wait to see them.'

I pay for the flowers, then turn around to notice that James has already taken Popsie outside. I walk out of the shop and join them. 'Don't you have to work today?' I ask him curiously.

'Yes. I've just got an hour spare, that's all. My car's in the car park over there. Do you want a lift to the hospital?'

I smile at him. 'I was planning to take the bus.'

'No need. Come on.'

He's still got the dog and I follow him, disappointed that he hasn't put his arm around me again. I shudder as the wind springs up and I'm even more grateful for a lift to the other side of town.

'I'm looking forward to tonight,' I say once we're settled in the car, with Popsie safely secured in the boot – luckily it's an estate, we're not that mean!

James looks a little uneasy. My stomach roils uncomfortably.

'I've got something going down this afternoon,' he says slowly. 'I may not be able to make it, after all. Can I give you a ring later and confirm?'

I sigh. I suppose I'll have to get used to this if I'm going to date a copper. 'Of course.'

We hardly talk on the way to the hospital, and I guess he's as disappointed as I am. I know there's no point in asking him what exactly he's got on this after-noon, as he won't be able to tell me, and then I'll feel even more frustrated about the whole thing.

He drops me off outside the hospital. 'I'll park up and take the dog to the green over the road.'

'Great. I don't know how long I'll be, but I doubt I'll be too long.'

'I know what you women are like when you get talking,' he says with a smile that doesn't quite reach his eyes. 'We'll be having fun over there. You can come over when you're ready. Or ring if you want me to fetch you.'

'Thanks.'

I can tell he's in a hurry to move away from the dropping off point, so I just smile and close the door. Popsie looks quite happy in the boot of the car as James drives off, and I know he'll be fine while I'm inside.

I find the private wing of the hospital, and the receptionist quickly locates the ward I need for Mrs Merrington-Smythe.

'You can take them up,' she says in a pleasant tone. 'They'll be able to tell you on the ward if you can give them to her personally or not, it just depends what's going on with her at the moment.'

'Thank you.'

I head on up, impressed at how salubrious everything looks. It's nothing like the long, echoey corridors I'm used to, where you have to dodge porters who seem intent on ramming beds into you – patient and all. The tiles are actually springy under my feet, and there are beautiful paintings on the walls and curtains at the windows.

I reach the ward and explain why I'm there.

'Those are beautiful,' the ward clerk says, admiring the flowers. 'She'll be pleased to see someone. I think she's getting bored already.'

'Has she had any visitors?' I ask.

The woman stands up and comes out from behind the counter. 'No. I don't think she's local.'

She knocks on a door nearby. There's a weak reply before she opens it and peeks inside. 'Mrs Merrington-Smythe, there's a young lady to see you.' She stands back and allows me to go in.

'I'll just fetch a vase,' she offers before leaving us.

The poor lady looks much older and frailer than she did at the hotel, and she's rather pale. She's sitting up, her hair is a little matted and she has a bright pink shawl over a hospital gown. She reminds me a little of Barbara Cartland, only without the makeup

'Hello. I'm Libby from the hotel.'

She frowns at me, and I'm not sure if it's because she doesn't recognise me, or because she does. 'I know. You nearly killed my Popsie.'

Oh no – it was the latter!

I'm dying to reply 'actually *he* nearly killed *me*', but think better of it.

'I'm really sorry about that.' I say. 'I didn't know he was there and just tripped over him. I hope I didn't hurt him.'

She says nothing, but her eyes narrow a little.

'I've brought you some flowers.' I hope a change of subject might help. 'I thought you'd like them as I noticed a rosy scent in your room.' I hold them out to her.

Her eyes widen and she looks like she's about to yell at me, when the ward clerk reappears with a vase of water.

'Aren't these beautiful?' she remarks, seemingly oblivious to the fact that the patient looks like she's about to blow a fuse. 'You're a very lucky lady.' She takes the bouquet from me and gently places it in the water, smiling as she quickly straightens the flowers.

I glance back at Mrs Merrington-Smythe, who doesn't look like she's feeling particularly lucky.

'I smelled roses in her room when I went to take care of her dog yesterday,' I say, 'so I thought these would be a good choice.'

'How thoughtful—'

'Popsie? You looked after my Popsie?' Mrs Merrington-Smythe's words fire at me like bullets from a machine gun.

'I'll leave you to it,' the ward clerk says, backing out of the room.

'Yes.' I suddenly feel a little more confident about being left in the room with the old dear, now that I've clearly said something right. 'When Mr Partington said you wouldn't be back last night, as you were in hospital, I immediately asked about Popsie. I wasn't sure if you'd taken him with you.'

'Good job I hadn't. They might have hurt him as well as me.'

'Or he might have protected you,' I suggest, imagining the yappy little dog chewing at someone's leg.

'Ha! He's only a baby.'

I nod. 'He's lovely, isn't he? I moved his bed to my office yesterday and then today I brought him out with me. All the staff love him, and make a huge fuss of him.'

'Where is he now?' She frowns, looking around the room as if he's about to appear at any minute.

'Oh, he's fine. Ja – er – one of the policemen's taken him to the park while I'm in here.'

She nods slowly. 'This wouldn't be the policeman that was at the hotel the other day, would it? He came to see me last night. The handsome one with come-to-bed eyes?'

I stare at her, stunned. I would never have expected a comment like that from her. She gives me a conspiratorial smile. 'It's all right, dear. You don't have to answer that.'

'Well, yes. It *is* Sergeant Harper, actually,' I say, amazed that she'd been looking into his eyes, apart from anything else.

'Thought so.'

I can't help wondering what else the old dear thought, but I daren't ask – it's probably safer not to know. 'Do you have any idea how soon you'll be discharged?'

She smiles and it's obvious the change of subject hasn't gone unnoticed. 'Soon, I hope.' She sighs. 'Tomorrow, I think they said.'

'That's good. I'll look after Popsie until you're out, of course.'

'You're very kind.'

I'm sure that's not the word she would have used to describe me up until now, but I'm thankful for it.

'How are you feeling?' I hope it's better than she looks.

'Oh, I'm all right. They caught him, you know. But not before I'd given him a good hard thump.' Her expression is triumphant, though I can't help feeling that she still came off worse.

'Good for you.' I smile, warming to her. 'Do you have any family nearby?'

'No. Well…that's what I've told the hospital staff, anyway.'

I stare at her in surprise, and pull up a chair.

'I'm actually looking for my niece,' she says. 'That's why I'm here. I think she might be living nearby, but I've run out of places to look. I don't even know her name, which is making matters worse.' She scratches her head, her fingers curled with age. 'I'm on a fool's errand, really.'

'It's obviously important to you,' I reply, my heart-strings twanging with sympathy. 'What makes you think she lives around here?'

'I hired a private detective. He said she married a car salesman. Some hotshot, I believe. Sells high-end vehicles to wealthy businessmen. The only thing was, he wouldn't tell me her name, the name of the company, or the man – not without me paying an extortionate amount of money on top of the retainer I'd already paid him and the cash for the meagre bit of information he'd uncovered so far.' She narrows her eyes again. 'My late husband insisted I stop paying him right away. He was furious at how much I'd paid out already, without getting much back in return. I did as he said, but he passed away last year and now I'm desperate to find her.'

'I'm so sorry about your husband.' I don't know what else to say.

She nods, pursing her lips. 'So am I. He was a good man.' Her face takes on a thoughtful expression. 'He was all I had left after my sister died. Now the only relative I have is a woman I last saw when she was a baby. I kept telling her mother that she needed to make amends with her, but my sister was even more stubborn than me – and that's saying something.'

'I can imagine.' The words just fell out of my mouth, but she doesn't seem to have noticed.

'Me and Howard, my husband, spent all of our time abroad when little Madeleine was growing up, so we didn't get to see her, except in videos and photographs. Then, when she became an adult and wanted to marry this man, my sister forbade her to. Madeleine said she loved him and was going to be with him no matter what her mother thought, so Daisy, my sister, disowned her. Madeleine moved away and none of us heard from her after that.' She wrings her hands and it's not hard to imagine what a struggle she would have had coming to terms with all of it. 'That was nearly thirty years ago.'

'Do you know the name of the man she married?'
I ask.

She shakes her head slowly. 'No, which is why I
don't even know her name. All we knew was that he
was a car salesman. That's why Daisy was so set against
him – she thought Madeleine could do much better. I
tried to reason with her, to explain that we can't make
decisions for our children, but Daisy was having none of
it. In her book Madeleine was making the biggest
mistake of her life, and she was sure that by refusing to
accept the marriage, Madeleine would just have to think
again. You never got married without your parents'
consent back then, you see. She thought she was saving
her daughter from heartache.'

'That must have been awful.' A lump appears in my
throat.

'It was.' She nods, leaning back against her pillows.
She looks tired. And uncomfortable. And old.

I stand and plump up her pillows for her, noticing
the rosy scent she usually wears. I'm glad I chose those
flowers. 'You should get some rest,' I tell her, gently.

She takes a deep breath. 'Yes, maybe I should.'

'And don't worry about Madeleine. We'll find her.'
I'm suddenly determined to help.

She smiles kindly at me. 'Thank you, dear. You've
done enough already. Thank you for coming to see me –
and for the beautiful flowers.'

I beam at her. She's actually a lovely old lady once
you get to know her, and it's easy to see why she gets a
bit cranky sometimes with all this going on. 'You're

welcome. And I'll give Popsie a cuddle from you, too,' I promise, before leaving the room.

I feel a little sad leaving Mrs Merrington-Smythe on her own, knowing she won't have any more visitors today, but she did look tired, and hopefully she'll be going home tomorrow – or back to The Chalfont, anyway.

James is throwing a stick for Popsie as I cross the road and head into the park. He's so edible with his coppery hair glowing in the sunlight. His beard is shaved close to his face, giving him a sort of maverick appearance.

'Having fun?' I smile as I get nearer and he looks around in surprise.

'Yeah. He's a sweet little fella. Not quite getting the hang of coming back when I tell him to, and once he gets the sniff of a rabbit he can really give me a run for my money, but at least he's keeping me fit.' He seems more relaxed than earlier, and his eyes twinkle as he smiles back at me.

He whistles.

Popsie stops, looks at him, then scampers off again.

'Popsie. Heel, boy.'

It's no good. The mischievous pooch clearly has other ideas as he scoots off towards the trees.

James shakes his head. 'It wouldn't be so bad if he didn't have such a stupid name,' he grumbles. 'You should see some of the looks I've had shouting for him all the time.'

I giggle.

With a roll of his eyes, James runs off after the dog, while I admire his fit body. It doesn't take long for him to catch up with Popsie, attach the leash and jog back towards me. 'We'd best make a move. I've got work to do,' he says. He's not even panting – unlike Popsie.

'Thanks so much for doing this.' I nudge closer to him as we head for the car park, hoping he'll put an arm around me again, but he doesn't. 'No problem. Did she like the flowers?'

'Yeah.'

We climb into his car and are soon on our way back across town.

'James, how do you find someone?' I ask thoughtfully as we trundle through traffic.

'What, like a missing person, you mean?' He raises his eyebrows in surprise.

'Not exactly. Mrs Merrington-Smythe's trying to find a relative who she thinks moved around here somewhere. She's only got a name, Madeleine, and some really old photos of her. I want to help find her, but I'm not really sure how. It's all very sad.'

'Write down everything you know about the case and take it from there. Even the smallest snippet of information can lead to something big. Has this Madeleine ever been reported as missing? If so, there'll be a record of it somewhere.'

I shake my head. 'No, I don't think so. It was just a family argument when she got married, which is why we don't even have a surname as they can't track down a marriage certificate. All I know is that the man was a salesman for expensive cars.'

'There are plenty of high end showrooms about. It'll be like looking for a needle in a haystack without so much as a name.'

I sigh. I knew it was doubtful, but didn't realise it was going to be practically impossible. 'It was just a thought,' I say with a shrug.

James looks over at me. 'Has she tried an ad in the local paper? That can sometimes work.'

My heart leaps and I stare back at him. 'Great idea. I'll have a word with Cassie; she could mention it to Rob and Ben at the *Chronicle*.'

'You'd best make sure the old lady's up for it first, though. She might feel like she's hanging out her dirty washing in public.'

I pout. 'You're right,' I concede. 'I might just put out a few feelers, see what it would involve. If Mrs M-S comes home tomorrow I can talk to her properly.'

'Mrs M-S? Sounds painful,' he says with a cheeky grin.

I can't help but smile back at him.

'You will let me know about tonight, won't you?' I ask as we arrive at The Chalfont.

'Of course.' He looks a little more serious now.

We get out of his warm car and he goes around to the boot to fetch Popsie. 'I'm sorry if I need to work late tonight.'

'It's okay.' I shrug. 'It saves me finding a dog-sitter, anyway.' Something in his tone tells me he's not planning to keep our date, no matter what happens. I don't know why he's suddenly changed his mind, but I'm not going to let him know I'm bothered. Even though I am. *Very* bothered.

He brightens a little. 'Okay. Well, enjoy the rest of your day.'

'I will. And thanks again.'

For a second I actually think he's going to kiss me as he leans forwards slightly, but then he just taps my arm and smiles before going back around the car and climbing in.

Popsie whines as the old Ford drives away, and I know exactly how the little pooch feels.

17

'You can't mope around here all night,' Cassie remarks, touching up her makeup.

'I'm fine. Just tired.' I spent most of the afternoon walking Popsie around the streets near to the hotel. He's now fast asleep in his bed in my office. James texted me, but I wasn't surprised to hear he can't make tonight. It doesn't stop me feeling disappointed, though.

'Come out with us. There's a group of us going; you won't be a gooseberry or anything.'

I frown. 'I thought you had a date with Rob?'

'Well, it turns out that Ben's broken up with his fella, so Rob asked if it was okay for him to tag along. Then, because Ben didn't want to feel out of place, Rob asked a couple of others. They're all from the news-paper office. You might enjoy it.' She turns to beam at me.

It would be nice to go out and have some fun.

'What about Popsie? I'm supposed to be looking after him.'

'Frances was quite happy having him behind Reception earlier,' Cassie says.

She's right. When we returned to the hotel I took him around the back for something to eat and drink, and Frances came through to the kitchen and offered to keep an eye on him for me, provided we left his bed in my office. I reckon she's quite taken with that little pup, though she'd probably never admit it. By the time I left them Popsie was curled up fast asleep.

'Hmm,' I agree. 'He was dog-tired when I left him.'

Cassie rolls her eyes. 'Very funny. How about it, then? We're just going to the Feathers, so it's not far.'

'Okay.' I'm quite glad to have an excuse for a shower and to get changed and made-up. My hair's a bit unruly so I tie it up in a chic bun before we head out the door.

The Feathers is quite busy when we arrive, and there's raucous laughter from one corner where several people are gathered around a large table.

'That's them,' Cassie says, smiling. We head over.

Rob catches sight of us and stands up, reaching for Cassie as soon as we near them. He looks really handsome in black Armani trousers and a turquoise shirt.

'Come and meet everyone,' he says, after giving her a kiss hello. Then he looks over at me. 'Lovely to see you again, Libby.'

I blush, remembering the incident when I ended up flat on my face on the floor between his table and

James's. I just hope he hasn't told his friends about it. Judging by the way a couple of them are smirking I assume he has. *Damn!*

Ben looks a bit down, understandably, but everyone else is in high spirits. There's an older guy and two other girls, who all smile up at me, welcomingly.

'What are you girls drinking?' Rob asks.

'White wine spritzer for me, please,' Cassie tells him, giving him a little squeeze.

'Same here, thanks.' I smile.

Rob heads off to get a round of drinks and I take a seat next to Ben, who quickly introduces me to everyone.

'Are you okay?' I ask him quietly after all the 'hellos'.

He shrugs. 'I'll get over it. He cheated. I can't stand that.'

'Ouch. I know how that feels,' I say. 'I'm so sorry.'

'You're not going to go on about Daniel all night, are you?' The older guy — Geoff, I remember — scoffs. He's grey-haired and apparently quite blunt – though he'd probably describe himself as just honest. 'There's plenty more fish in the sea.'

'Well I can't see me angling any time, soon,' Ben retorts. 'I've had enough.' He sighs and his handsome face is quite drawn.

'Maybe if Daniel had kept his rod to himself you wouldn't be in this state now,' Siobhan says, chuckling. She's stunning, with a precise, shiny black bob, bright green eyes and a figure to die for.

The others giggle, including Rob, who's just returned with the drinks.

'Fish always makes me burp,' Tammy, the junior editor says, 'especially tuna.'

We all burst out laughing, except Ben, and she widens her eyes in amazement. She clearly doesn't know how funny she is. She's quite pretty, with long, wavy red hair and blue eyes which look huge behind her Prada glasses.

'Have you come up with a good story yet?' I ask Ben, thinking it best to change the subject.

'Nope. We thought we were on to something, but it turned out not to be as big a scoop as we'd hoped.' Ben looks even gloomier, and I'm already regretting asking the question.

I purse my lips and wrack my brain for something to say.

'I'm looking for a missing person,' I tell him, eventually. It's the best I can come up with.

'Ooh, where?' Tammy's eyes seem even bigger as she stares over at me.

'If she knew that, the person wouldn't be missing, would they?' Geoff says with a snort, and the others giggle again.

'I've only got a first name to go on, and the rest is a bit of a mystery,' I say. I go on to explain about Madeleine and the car salesman she married, leaving out all the personal stuff about her mum's disapproval.

'There used to be a massive showroom in Lime Tree Row, where the cinema is now,' Geoff pipes up. 'In its day it used to have all sorts of expensive cars; BMWs, Jags… I remember ogling a massive black Bentley there. I knew I'd never afford it, but I used to go down and drool over it whenever I got the chance.'

'What happened to it?' Tammy asks.

'It was sold, I suppose. There were always businessmen in smart suits going in there. I assume one of them must have bought it.' Geoff looks a little wistful. 'Superb, it was. A massive saloon. It shone under the bright lights, and the leather upholstery gleamed.'

'The showroom.' Tammy says, frowning hard. 'What happened to the *showroom*?'

Geoff bulges his eyes in surprise. 'They closed down. I don't know where it went. The place was empty for years before they decided to build the multiplex there.'

The building they've replaced it with is huge, with loads of different screens, a bar, a couple of restaurants and several fast food outlets to choose from. I could live in that place and never get bored.

'What happened to all the staff?' I ask.

'I'm pretty sure some of them were local guys, so I doubt they'd go far. I'm talking about thirty years ago, and in those days you stayed where your roots were. None of this gallivanting all over the country; you found another job nearby, even if it meant retraining to do something new.' He shakes his head, clearly happier with the way things used to be.

I glance over to see Cassie canoodling with Rob. They make a perfect couple and I feel a pang, wishing

James and I were like that. He seemed a bit frosty with me this afternoon, though, and I've got no idea why. I'm sure he was okay when we first bumped into him – I remember the feel of his arm around my back. A warm glow ignites in my stomach at the memory.

'How are you planning to find this missing person?' Siobhan, who's sitting on the other side of me, asks.

'Well, I need to gather up all the information I've got so far and scrutinise it,' I tell her, recalling James's advice. 'I might think about putting something in the paper.'

'Great idea.' Ben perks up all of a sudden. 'We could do a feature on it. Put in all the background stuff and print a picture of Madeleine with a 'Do you recognise this person?' headline. It might generate some interest, being local and all.'

'It might just save our jobs,' Rob pipes up. I wasn't even aware he'd been listening, as he certainly looked pre-occupied a moment ago. It's nice to see the return of his tongue, too, as I thought it might have been lost down my bestie's throat forever.

Everyone seems quite excited at the idea, but I can't help wondering if I shouldn't have run it past Mrs Merrington-Smythe before opening my big mouth. Come to think of it, I'm sure James mentioned something about checking with her first…

'Okay, well…I'll have a think about it. Check on a few things before I commit to anything,' I say, frantically searching my brain for a change of subject. 'Has everyone seen the latest from Christian Louboutin? Those Scalopumps?'

When in doubt as to what to talk about, there's *always* shoes.

'No.' Tammy and Siobhan stare at me blankly, and the guys seem to have gone back to drinking.

It was worth a try.

'I have.' I can always count on Cassie. 'They're expensive, but well worth every penny, from what I've seen.'

'I don't think any shoes are worth that much money,' Tammy says casually.

Cassie and I stare at her in disbelief. I take a surreptitious peek under the table at her footwear. Trainers. I might have known.

'You get what you pay for,' Cassie says.

'I don't see the point in splashing out for a pair of shoes which will be outdated by the end of the season, though.' Tammy is clearly unaware of the effect she's having on me and my best mate. Or how much we're both beginning to dislike her right now.

'Vintage is a big trend,' Siobhan states. I haven't met her before, but something tells me we're going to be good friends.

'Oh yes, everyone's getting into it,' Cassie agrees. I knew there was a reason she was my bestie.

'You've obviously got a good eye for fashion,' I compliment Siobhan with a smile. She's wearing a jade green cashmere jumper which brings out the colour of her eyes, and Victoria Beckham jeans. And I recognized her shoes as Karen Millens.

'It's all they ever write about in her department,' Geoff says scornfully.

'We mainly focus on women's issues,' Siobhan explains defensively. 'There's nothing wrong with that. After all, a recent survey showed that sixty-two percent of our readership is female. It makes sense to give the readers what they want.'

'Has it occurred to you that the majority of our readers are female *because* you concentrate so much on women's interests?' Geoff replies. 'If we gave the guys stuff to get excited about, maybe more of them would buy our papers.'

'What? There are four pages of sport every day. Not to mention all the medical issues, which affect men just as much as women. And there's the motoring section as well as—'

'Okay, okay.' Ben cuts off Siobhan's tirade by standing up, and I somehow get the feeling this is a well-worn argument. 'Is everyone having the same again?'

We all nod and he goes off to fetch the drinks, clearly desperate to get away from the bickering.

'Is he okay?' I ask Rob.

'Yeah, just licking his wounds. I thought it would do him good to get out and take his mind off every-thing.' He grins. 'Your story might be a great distraction.'

Damn! Although I'm happy to provide Ben with

something to take his mind off Daniel, I wish it didn't have to be that particular story. Not yet, anyway.

My phone vibrates in my bag and I fish it out. I frown at the unknown number flashing on the screen.

'Hello?' As everyone turns to look at me, I quickly get up and walk towards the exit. They're obviously good journalists, never missing the opportunity to pick up a story, but I really don't want my business brandished all over tomorrow's *Chronicle*.

'You bitch!'

'What? Who's this?' My whole body feels hot and I'm glad of the fresh air as I exit the pub. I recognise the man's voice and am already regretting answering the call.

'You heard me. You couldn't wait to accuse Bianca of something, could you? Well you'll be pleased to know the cops have just come round to the hotel and carted her off for questioning – and we all know what that means, don't we?' His tone drips with sarcasm.

A lump drops to my stomach. 'What? Connor? Is that you? Th-they've arrested her?'

'As if you didn't know. I suppose it was you who got that sergeant to send them here, wasn't it? You couldn't stand the thought of me and her being happy so you just had to ruin it. I never took you for a selfish cow, Libby, but that's exactly what you are.'

'I didn't—' He hangs up as I'm shaking my head down the phone at him.

I want to cry. And hit the wall.

I'm still staring at my mobile when it rings again.

It's James. I don't know if I want to talk to him right now. Is this why he cancelled our date tonight? And why he was a so cold with me earlier? He was planning this all along and didn't have the guts to tell me?

While I'm deciding whether to answer him or not, he rings off. *Damn!* My mind's full of all the things I should have said to him right then. But I'm not going to call him back. No way.

I feel sick. I always feel sick when I get stressed or anxious. Or even just upset. Like now. Actually, I think I'm all three at the moment. Which is probably why I feel three times as sick as normal. This is all so horrible.

Cassie comes outside, looking around until she sees me leaning against the wall. 'Hey, are you okay? What's happened?'

I nod, suddenly aware that tears are streaming down my face. I bury myself in her arms as she envelopes me in a big hug.

'Is it James?'

I take a loud sniff, nodding again.

'What's he done?'

She releases her grip a little, allowing me to look up at her.

'They've arrested Bianca,' I blurt out.

'What?' Her eyes are wide, like a Manga doll, as she stares at me. 'But I thought—'

'So did I. He said they wouldn't. He agreed that it was more important to get the loan sharks. Now he's cancelled our date and gone off and arrested her.' Fresh tears flood my eyes.

'But why?' she asks incredulously. 'What's the point in doing something like that?'

I shrug.

'Have you spoken to him? Has he got an explanation?' She frowns.

As if on cue, my mobile rings again.

'Are you going to speak to him?' Cassie knows me too well.

Rob appears in the doorway. 'Cass, I've been looking for you. Are you okay?' He frowns at me, and I feel even more stupid.

'You go in. I'll take this,' I tell her, quickly.

She squeezes my arm and goes back inside while I press the accept button on my mobile.

'Libby? Where are you?' James sounds worried.

'Why? What's it to you?'

'Don't be silly. I need to see you. Now. Something's happened and I need to—'

'Something like an arrest, you mean?' I bite back at him. 'An arrest you promised me you wouldn't make?'

He sighs down the phone. 'I didn't actually *say* that, and…besides, it wasn't me. I'm not even on duty. Look, where are you? I called the hotel and they said you'd gone out with your friends. Let me come and talk to you.'

'I don't think that's a good idea,' I tell him, suddenly realizing that this just isn't going to work. 'We've got nothing to say to each other.'

'Libby…' His tone smacks of desperation.

'If we haven't got trust, then we haven't got

anything. Goodbye, James.' I hang up, and switch off my phone in case he calls back, before sagging against the wall and letting the tears cascade down my flushed cheeks.

A few minutes later I'm aware of chattering as a group of girls comes piling out of the pub. They look over at me and then start whispering something I don't even want to hear.

I can't stand around here making a fool of myself all night, and I certainly can't go back inside looking like this, so I slowly start walking back to The Chalfont. After a short while I switch my phone back on for just enough time to quickly text Cassie to let her know I've gone home and I'm okay.

The only trouble, I realise as I press send, is The Chalfont isn't my home and right now I'm a long way from being okay.

18

AFTER A RESTLESS NIGHT, I GET UP EARLY THE NEXT morning.

Cassie's alarm goes off while I'm in the shower and she calls from outside the bathroom. 'Libby? Are you okay in there? It's only half six.'

I emerge wrapped in a huge bath sheet with a smaller towel wrapped around my head. 'I couldn't sleep,' I tell her, noticing the way she winces when she sees my face. 'I thought I may as well get up.'

'Oh, hon.' She throws her arms around me and gives me a big hug. 'Did you speak to James last night?'

'Yeah, but we didn't really talk. I've got nothing to say to him.'

She offers me a sympathetic smile. 'I told the others you weren't feeling well so had gone home.'

'Thanks, love.'

I get ready while she takes her shower. I'm not

working until nine, so decide to take Popsie for a good, long walk before then.

'Lucky you.' Cassie gestures to my jeans and Converse while she steps into her uniform and three-inch Jimmy Choos. Neither of us like working in flats, as the management recommend – they feel too frumpy. We wear good solid heels, though, not stilettos like Bianca.

'I'm in at nine, and then I'm here all day,' I remind her.

She pulls a face. 'Okay, *poor* you.'

I've done my best to disguise the redness and bags under my eyes from last night's crying, and eventually decide it will just have to do. Popsie won't notice, anyway, and by the time I get back to work I'm hoping to look – and feel – a lot better.

'Are you seeing Rob again later?' I ask her, as she ties her hair up in a ponytail.

She beams at me, and I remember feeling that happy about seeing James only yesterday. 'Yeah. Ben was quite interested in your missing person story. Rob's hoping it cheered him up enough that he won't have to come out with us tonight. We're planning a romantic soirée with—' She suddenly puts her hand to her mouth. 'I'm sorry, hon. That was really insensitive. I didn't mean—'

'It's fine.' I force a smile. 'Go on, you're going to be late.'

Cassie shrugs. 'I don't think Party's about to sack

me, do you? I've got less than a week to go. I think I've found a nice flat already.'

I purse my lips. I really don't think I could stand it here without her.

As if reading my thoughts, she comes over and gives me another hug. 'Don't worry, it'll be fine.'

I wish I had her confidence. Actually, right now, I wish a lot of things…

IT'S ANOTHER COLD DAY AND I'M GLAD THAT THERE aren't many people around as I walk Popsie through the dark streets. He was thrilled to see me, and even more so when I rattled his lead.

'Just you and me today,' I tell him as he sniffs at yet another lamp-post. I don't mind, I'm in no hurry. 'Hopefully your mummy will be coming home later.'

Is it right to refer to his owner as his mummy? I'm really not sure. Popsie's not bothered, anyway. He ignores me and lifts his leg against a tree which seems to have sprouted out of a paving slab. It hasn't really, but it's the way they look in this part of London.

'I wonder who Madeleine is,' I say aloud, as though Popsie's listening to me, which he isn't. He'd probably forget I was here altogether if I'd just stop tugging at his leash every few minutes to stop him going into the road.

We veer away from the traffic and onto a soft green where several other dog owners are exercising their pets. A huge German Shepherd bounds up to us and I immediately scoop Popsie up into the safety of my arms.

'Buster!' A man with a loud voice and an even louder Hawaiian shirt comes running over as the dog stops in his tracks and looks around for his master. 'Good boy.' The guy gives me an apologetic smile, grabs his dog's collar and leads it away.

I can't help wondering whether he was apologising for his dog, or his shirt.

I decide, on reflection, to keep Popsie on his lead. I think it would be safer all 'round, and I'm not really confident that I'd find him again if he went running off. I wish he was as well-trained as Buster, but then, I have to remember that Popsie is still only a puppy.

I run with him, to allow him to stretch his legs, and am surprised at how much better I feel for the exertion. Having a dog certainly is a good excuse to run around the green, something I wouldn't dream of doing on my own, although I notice that lots of people seem to like jogging around the perimeter.

The fresh morning air doesn't seem as cold after a while, and I sit on a bench to catch my breath. Popsie's panting like a steam engine, and I wonder if I'm wearing him out. I'm sure Mrs Merrington-Smythe won't be able to run with him like this. It'll be nice for her to have his company again, though. She must be very lonely, being the only person left in her family – apart from the elusive Madeleine, of course.

Once we've caught our breath we head back to The Chalfont. Popsie's a little subdued, probably because he's tired. Still, he'll be able to have a good sleep in my office – something I'm in danger of doing myself, come to think of it.

Last night was awful. I cried all the way back to the hotel and let myself in, avoiding Frank who was on his security patrol. I purposely waited for him to go around the front of the building so I wouldn't have to speak to him. Of course it meant avoiding Popsie, too, who was accompanying him, which made me feel even guiltier.

I was glad that Cassie was still out, as I was able to get all the misery out of my system and had actually fallen asleep by the time she got back. My phone remained switched off and tossed into my drawer, where it still is now. My stomach lurches at the thought of James trying to contact me. I really can't deal with him right now. I'm already dreading having to face Connor. It was sneaky of him to use another phone last night; I never would have answered it if I'd known it was him, which was clearly the point.

I deposit Popsie back behind Reception, where he goes straight into my office, while I rush upstairs to get another shower and change.

'HE'S GONE TO SLEEP,' FRANCES INFORMS ME WHEN I return a short while later. 'And he snores.'

I smile, peeping into the cupboard to see him curled up on his bed. There are a couple of sheets of paper tucked in there with him, and I wonder if he's picked them up from somewhere, or if Frances used them to wipe his paws. He really is very cute.

Although it's the last thing I feel like doing today, I get stuck into the wedding fair. I've finalised most of the traders and exhibitors now, so it's just a few ends that need tying up.

Andrea at Full Bloom Flowers is happy to hear from me when I ring and explain that I missed her yesterday.

'I've got some ideas for fresh and silk flowers,' she tells me. 'And I've got some foam ones on order, too. Shall I email you some pictures?'

'Actually, I could come down and take a look, if you're not too busy?' I offer, relishing the chance to get away from the hotel.

Frances is too professional to have gossiped about Bianca being arrested, but the kitchen staff aren't as discreet. I really don't want to hear about it right now, so I grab my jacket as soon as I finish up on the phone with Andrea.

'Leave him there while he's asleep,' Frances says. 'It'd be a shame to wake him.'

'Thanks.' I'm actually warming to the elderly receptionist. It's only taken two years. I'm not sure we'll ever be friends, exactly, but it's good of her to be so nice about Popsie.

'I'M SO SORRY TO HAVE MISSED YOU.' ANDREA GREETS me with a warm smile and an even warmer cup of coffee, both of which are very welcome after my stroll in the cold. I suppose I should have run here, as it certainly helped earlier, but I couldn't see my Kurt Geigers holding up to that kind of punishment – nor me, for that matter, there *is* a limit, after all!

She shows me into the back room where she's laid out some beautiful posies and bouquets.

'Would you be interested in decorating a couple of pedestals as well?' I ask, suitably impressed.

'Of course.'

'I thought we might have a couple of displays in the reception area to welcome everyone into the building, then some dotted around the conference room and restaurant. It would be a great way of showcasing what you can do for venues or churches or whatever, and would add to the atmosphere.' I don't mention that it would also save me worrying about décor. After all, what better way to decorate the room?

She nods. 'Let me know how many you can fit in and I'll have them ready. Are you having balloons?'

'Yes. There will be a balloon arch near the stage and some table arrangements with them.' I give her a rough plan of the exhibition.

'I'll avoid roses in those areas, then,' she says, scribbling in her notebook. 'Although we always remove the thorns for weddings, it's better to be safe than sorry.'

I take a sip of my coffee, thankful that she'd thought of that, as it hadn't even occurred to me.

'The weather forecast is good for Saturday, so we're hoping for a good turn out,' I say enthusiastically.

Andrea smiles. 'I'm really looking forward to it.

Lots of my customers have promised to pop in and support the event, too.'

We chat for a little longer before I notice the time and get up to go.

Before I leave the shop I buy a small bunch of lilies for Frances. I know she likes flowers as she often brings in some from her garden to decorate the reception desk.

'THESE ARE FOR YOU. JUST TO SAY THANK YOU FOR looking after Popsie,' I tell her, as soon as I arrive back at the hotel. She beams. I imagine she doesn't often receive gifts like this.

'You've been out buying flowers?' Mr Partington suddenly appears from the stationery cupboard and I can't help thinking it's not a coincidence that the tiny room also houses my office.

'*No*. I went to see the florist who's going to exhibit at the wedding fair,' I tell him. 'I just thought it was a nice gesture to buy Frances some flowers while I was there as she has been kind enough to look after Popsie for me while I was out.'

'You're organising a wedding fair?' a familiar voice pipes up. Mr Partington moves aside to allow James – or Sergeant Harper, as he seems to be on duty – to emerge from behind him.

I swallow hard. He looks as yummy as ever, although a little tired – and very sheepish.

'Yes.' I frown, annoyed that he's taken me by

surprise. I was hoping to avoid him today. And tomorrow. And forever, for that matter. *Fat chance!*

James nods slowly and I can practically see the cogs turning in his brain as he works something out. I'd give my eyeteeth to know what.

'Do you need to interview her?' Mr Partington asks, turning back to him.

My heart sinks.

'Yes, actually.' James's face is set in a determined expression, as though he knows he's the last person I want to speak to right now.

'Can it wait? Only I've got lots to do to get ready for the fair, and I need to call the hospital about Mrs Merrington-Smythe. She's hoping to come home today and I want to check that she's okay for transport. She *is* a very good client of ours, after all.' I take a step around the side of the reception desk, hoping to go into my office and slam the door shut.

Unfortunately, James takes a step towards me at the same time and I get a whiff of his heavenly aftershave.

'No.'

'What?' I stare at him.

'No, I'm sorry, but it can't wait. There have been certain…developments…in the case of the thefts and I need to interview you as soon as possible.' His eyes flash and I know there's no point in protesting. He's got the upper hand here, and there's not a damn thing I can do about it – *and doesn't he just love the fact!*

'You carry on. I'll keep an eye on the dog,' Frances says with a smile.

'Thanks.'

'You can use the Remington Suite.' Mr Partington gives me a warning look and I can tell he's not happy with the situation but, like me, doesn't have much choice in the matter.

A uniformed officer comes up to the desk just as we're about to leave. 'Sergeant Harper, I've finished my enquiries for now. Is there anything else you need?' she asks politely.

'No, thanks. I've got one more person to interview. I'll see you back at the station.' He sounds very professional and my tummy jolts.

'Thank you, sir.' She nods.

'Hang on. Isn't she going to sit in on my interview?' The words shoot out of my mouth before I can think them through.

James gapes.

'You're entitled to have a female chaperone if you want one,' the officer says, looking from me to the sergeant.

I swallow hard. 'Yes, please. I don't want to be accused of anything… *untoward*.' I stare pointedly at Mr Partington whose lips tighten as he seethes.

James glances over at my boss and nods slowly. 'Very well,' he says, narrowing his eyes.

The police officers stand back and let me lead the way, although I'm pretty sure they both know exactly where they're going. The conference room is set out with several smaller tables today, and I go to the one nearest the door. I intend to be in a position to make a quick getaway if necessary – not that I think I'll be arrested, I just don't want James to have the opportunity to speak to me privately at the end of the meeting.

The cops sit opposite me. There's an uneasy atmosphere in the room, and I squirm in my seat.

James clears his throat. 'This is Liberty Lawrence,' he tells his colleague. 'She's a junior manager here at The Chalfont.'

'I'm PC Kate Fitzpatrick,' she says, nodding at me. Her mousy-brown hair is swept tightly into an enviously neat bun and her fringe is cut quite short, giving her a slightly austere appearance.

James sits back in his chair, studying me closely. 'Miss Lawrence, you're aware of the money that went missing from the hotel safe recently?'

'Yes.'

'And you pointed out that the marks on the carpet in the manager's office looked like indentations from a stiletto heel.'

'Yes.' I clench my teeth, wondering just how many people he informed of my theory after telling me he wouldn't pursue the enquiry.

'We now have confirmation that the heels did, in fact, belong to Miss Bianca Morrison-Wright.'

'Really?' I try to sound as disinterested as I feel.

'Yes. Samples of the substance deposited on the carpet matched some of the dirt from the bar floor,' James goes on, as though oblivious to my attitude. 'This strongly suggests that Miss Morrison-Wright was connected with the theft.'

'You don't say.' I roll my eyes.

PC Fitzpatrick glances from me to James and back again, clearly curious as to what's going on.

I just wonder how much more time James is going to waste telling me things I already know – things *I* told *him*.

'You also know about the necklace that went missing from one of the hotel bedrooms?'

I nod and give a frustrated sigh. 'Room 109.'

'And you gave me some samples of paint which you found in the carpet in the hallway outside that room.'

'Yes.'

'Well, I can tell you that those flakes of paint *also* came from a pair of Bianca Morrison-Wright's shoes.'

I fold my arms. This is getting ridiculous. 'And your point is?'

He sits forwards. 'My point is, Miss Lawrence, that you also showed me photographs of the carpet *inside* room 109, which had specks of red paint in it. And those flakes *didn't* match any of Miss Morrison-Wright's shoes.'

I stare at him as a hard lump drops down to my stomach. 'What?'

'Our forensics team has also examined the keys which we believe were used in the safe robbery and Miss Morrison-Wright's prints aren't on any of them.'

'She could have worn gloves.'

He nods. 'Yes, she could have. However, no glove marks were found at the scene of either crime. And besides, in order to unlock the filing cabinet and safe, and to rifle through the bedroom drawer to pick out the necklace, very thin, possibly latex gloves would need to be worn. That sort of glove doesn't hide fingerprints, Miss Lawrence.'

I suddenly feel hot. Everything I had thought – everything I *assumed* – is wrong. How can that be?

'So… Bianca isn't the thief?' My throat feels dry and I have to force the words out of my mouth.

'We're still making investigations,' he says, slowly. 'But it doesn't look as though your theory is right, so I need you to forget about it.'

I stare at him. He thinks I *wanted* this to be Bianca's fault. He thinks I'm disappointed. All because she stole my boyfriend. How pathetic does he think I am?

'Good,' I say, trying my hardest to smile. 'I'm glad. It was only a suggestion. I did wonder why there was no red paint in Mr Partington's office, to be honest. Besides, Bianca's got enough problems with her dad without all this.'

'This would be his financial problems, I take it?' James is really playing it cool.

'Yes. So, if that's everything I'll get back to—'

'Not quite,' he says, just as I'm standing up.

I frown at him. 'Oh.' I sit back down, biting my lip in frustration.

'I need to ask you some questions.'

'Okay.'

He consults his notebook. 'How long did you date Connor Worthington?'

I balk at the question, wondering where on earth he's going with this.

'Miss Lawrence?' He gives me a pointed look.

'Er…six months.'

He writes it down. 'And during that time, did he ever mention wanting to buy a car?'

I automatically snigger at this. 'No.'

He narrows his eyes. 'You're sure?'

'Yes.'

'Why? What makes you so certain?'

He's studying me curiously and I get a whiff of that sexy aftershave again. God, he's so gorgeous. Infuriating, but gorgeous.

'Connor failed to get his driving license,' I inform him.

'I know.'

I raise my eyebrows. He's obviously looked into the matter. But why? 'Of course you do,' I nod slowly. 'And you might also know that he hated the whole driving experience and said he'd never do it again.'

'Couldn't he change his mind?' James asks, scribbling in his notebook.

'Why would he? He then moved to London so he wouldn't *need* to drive. Everyone gets around on the Tube or taxis. You don't need a car to live here, according to him.' I shrug, remembering the countless conversations we had on the subject. Connor said the people who drove here were mugs – they were putting themselves under too much stress just to show off. He even thought Bianca's dad was mad to have a mechanic business in London. He couldn't see how it would ever make any money.

James looks thoughtful. 'So, he didn't want a car. Was there anything else he said he wanted? Anything he dreamed of getting one day?'

I frown. 'Like what?'

James purses his lips. 'I don't know – I think most people are saving up for something, aren't they? Whether it's designer shoes, a car, a place of their own – or even something for someone else. There's usually something.'

I snort. I can't help it, it just comes out. The thought of Connor saving up to buy something for someone else is just so ludicrous. I'll never forget the Christian Louboutins he refused to get me for my birthday – and they were in the sale!

'No,' I assure the sergeant. 'He wasn't saving up to buy anyone anything.'

Flicking back through his notebook, James squints. 'What were Connor's interests while you were together? What did he spend his money on?'

'I've no idea. Certainly not me, anyway.'

'Think.'

'I'd rather not, actually,' I say firmly, sitting forwards. 'We were together until I found out he'd been cheating on me. Why would I want to think about the time I was with him? I'd rather forget all about it, thanks very much.'

James sighs, fidgeting a little in his seat. 'Look,

Libby. I know this is hard for you, but it's really important.'

'I don't see why. He cheated on me, okay? He really hurt me, and now he tells me he wants me back. Why the hell would I want to think about that?' I didn't mean to raise my voice, but I did. My whole body trembles and I'm not sure if it's through anger or upset.

James stares at me, his mouth gaping open.

I move to get up, but he grabs my arm so I stay put.

'Hang on. He said he wants you *back*?'

Even PC Fitzpatrick is gawping at me.

I frown. 'Yes. Is that so hard to believe? Someone thinks I'm worth dating.'

Pain immediately crosses his face and I regret being so cutting. With all this – whatever it is – going on, he obviously was too busy to take me out last night, but it still smarts. 'Are…are you going to take him back?' James's voice is a little croaky and I can't help wondering if the question is more personal than a part of the investigation.

I stare at him, biting my lip. I want to say 'yes, I'm going to go back out with him because at least he *wants* me,' but his eyes are begging me not to. And it wouldn't be true. My stomach roils with mixed emotions, and my trembling gets worse. I take a deep breath before answering, 'No.'

James closes his eyes and his whole body relaxes. I'm flattered at his reaction, but at the same time I want to cry.

'If there's one thing I've learned about relationships

it's that you should never go back,' I say. 'It just doesn't work.'

His eyes fly open.

I fight back tears and wrestle with a huge lump in my throat. 'And talking of work, I really need to get back,' I manage. 'Are we finished here?' I'm desperate to get out that door, which feels miles away, although it's only a couple of feet.

'I think so. Aren't we, Sergeant?' PC Fitzpatrick looks curiously at James, who is still staring at me.

He shakes his head slowly. 'No, Miss Lawrence, we're not finished. But if you need to go I can talk to you another time about the other issues.' His voice is quieter than normal and he looks sad.

His demeanour does nothing to help mine, and I quickly get up and leave the room as tears begin to escape my eyes and my mind whirls with 'other issues'.

19

BY THE TIME I'VE BEEN TO THE LADIES' ROOM AND composed myself, the police have left the hotel.

I dive into my office and double check I've got everything sorted for the wedding fair, trying to persuade myself that it's just another conference. When I can't bear to think of wedding flowers and dresses anymore, I put all the paperwork back in the drawer and tidy my desk.

Popsie's a great comfort, as he senses I'm feeling low and comes for a cuddle. I'm looking forward to taking him for a long walk later, to try to clear my head. He's great company, and I wish I could have a dog of my own, though I know Party would never allow it – even though it is a dog-friendly hotel. Clearly not *that* friendly.

Popsie suddenly tries to jump from my arms as we hear a commotion from Reception. 'Of *course* I can manage.'

I recognise that voice. Now I understand exactly what the little pup's up to. I head out into Reception before he goes out of his tiny canine mind. I can't help feeling guilty that I didn't get time to ring the hospital and organise the old lady's transport. 'Mrs Merrington-Smythe, how nice to see you again.' I greet her with a big smile, and put Popsie down. He immediately runs towards his owner with his tail wagging.

'Hello, dear. I hope you don't mind, but I left the flowers for another lady. Hip replacement, I think she said. Looked to be in a pretty bad way – and anyway, it's bad luck to take flowers home from hospital, isn't it?' She looks much perkier than yesterday and I'm genuinely happy to see her back on her feet.

'Of course that's all right. It was a kind gesture — I hope she appreciates them.' I nod, still smiling.

The old lady beams. 'She loved them. You'd think I'd handed her the crown jewels. Mind you, they were beautiful flowers. Thank you again for being so thoughtful. And for visiting me, too. I enjoyed it.'

Mrs Merrington-Smythe looks incredibly relaxed as she scoops Popsie up and cuddles him with one hand and takes her key from Frances with the other.

'I've got his bed in here,' I tell her, 'I'll bring it up, if you like?'

'Thank you, dear.'

I follow her over to the lift.

'I can't stand these things,' the old lady grumbles, holding Popsie tightly in her arms as we step in. 'If my legs were a bit younger I'd use the stairs.'

I smile. It's nice to see she's back to her old self again. 'Have you thought about putting a notice in the newspaper to find Madeleine?' I ask as we travel upwards.

'Oh, I don't know about that, dear,' she says thoughtfully. 'It might make me look very careless, losing my own niece. What would people think?'

I giggle, standing back as the doors open and she shuffles out. We make our way slowly to her room. 'People are always looking for lost relatives or friends,' I tell her. 'It's quite natural.'

She gives me a doubtful look.

'Well, it's an option,' I say, thankful that I didn't give any details to the reporters last night. 'Something to think about.'

'Yes, I'll do that,' she replies, her tone decisive. We arrive at room 109 and she opens the door. The scent of disinfectant hits us.

I had to work hard to get the place cleaned and freshened up following poor Popsie's unintentional imprisonment, but I hope I've done a good job.

'Ugh. I can't stand that smell,' Mrs Merrington-Smythe moans, reaching for her rose-scented perfume on the dressing table.

She sprays it around the room, and even on the dog, who looks most surprised. I can't mention that it's a lot better than the smell that was in here before, so I just say nothing.

I put Popsie's bed back where it was when I found it

and Mrs Merrington-Smythe lets him down to the floor. Straight away, he starts sniffing his surroundings.

'I think we'll have to go home soon,' she says sadly, sinking into the chair. 'It looks like I'll never find Madeleine. I was a fool to think I would, without her surname and everything.'

'What will you do?' I ask, perching on the corner of the bed.

'I really don't know, dear. I'd like to contact that private detective chappy and ask him for the rest of the information, but my poor Howard would turn in his grave. He forbade me to give that man any more money.' She shakes her head.

'How about a cup of tea?' I stand, pick up the kettle and take it into the bathroom with me. She certainly looks like she needs a nice, warm cuppa.

'You're very kind,' she says, as I return the kettle to the sideboard and switch it on.

I smile. She's such a lovely old dear – cantankerous, but lovely – and she reminds me of my gran. I wait for the water to boil, then make the tea.

'There's a big multiplex in town,' I tell her as I hand over her drink. 'It used to be a car dealership. High-end cars.'

Her eyes twinkle as she looks up at me. 'Really?'

I nod. 'The man that told me about it said that most of the employees probably stayed local after it shut down.'

She sits up straighter and her face shines with hope.

A thought occurs to me. 'Have you met our barmaid, Bianca?'

She shakes her head, her curls swaying slightly. 'I'm not a drinker, Liberty. Never have been.' She sounds quite definite about that and I hope I haven't offended her.

'It's just that her dad's a car mechanic. He owns his own garage. I could ask her if he might know anyone that worked there. It could give us a lead, if nothing else.' I'm actually quite excited at the thought, and I can see she is, too.

'That would be wonderful, dear.'

'I'm not sure if Bianca's on tonight, but I'll speak to her when I can, okay?'

'You're very kind. Thank you.'

I point at her. 'Just don't you go disappearing until we've found her. I won't have you going home empty-handed, got it?' I adopt a stern expression and she sniggers.

'Got it.'

I FEEL MUCH HAPPIER AS I RETURN TO MY OFFICE, though I'm surprised to see Mr Ainsworth, the Finance and Deputy Manager, standing at Reception. It's only Thursday so he must have returned early from his holiday, which I now realise was probably genuine - unless he's just spent the past week on a sun bed. I assume he's had to come back because of the takings being robbed.

I'd have loved to have been a fly on the wall when Party explained all that to him!

I don't know him very well as he's quite elusive, hiding away in his office down the corridor with his head full of figures. Gabby, one of the admin girls, helps out with the accounts, too, but I steer clear of anything like that.

'I'm covering the bar for a while,' he informs me with a sigh.

I know he hates anything that drags him out of his hidey-hole, and bar duty is one of his biggest bugbears. I find it odd, really, as the bar makes a lot of money, so you'd think he'd love it.

'Isn't Bianca in tonight?' I frown, disappointed.

'Nope. She might be in later.' He purses his lips.

Colin Ainsworth's quite an attractive guy if you're into silver foxes. He looks like a cross between George Clooney and Phillip Schofield, but without the smiles. Finance is obviously a very serious business. On the plus side, he's very efficient and organised – it's just that you seldom *see* him being efficient and organised because he's always hiding.

'Is she ill?' I ask, as casually as I can manage.

He looks around to ensure no-one is listening before saying quietly, 'No. She's at the police station.'

I stare at him. 'Still?'

He frowns. 'No. Again.'

'Has something happened?' I'm whispering now, my heart hammering.

'Not since last week. Just more questions, I believe.

Anyway, they shouldn't be keeping her too much longer, so I'm hoping she'll take over from me soon.'

I can see he's annoyed, though he's far too professional to admit it. Being dragged back from his holiday must have been bad enough, but having to fill in for the barmaid when he should be looking into the theft and all the financial implications must be really galling.

He marches off in the direction of the bar. I hope they've cleaned the floor today, as he won't tolerate getting his Kurt Geiger Santon lace-ups dirty – let alone his Armani suit!

I GRAB A SANDWICH FROM THE KITCHEN ON MY WAY UP to our room. Cassie's getting ready for her hot date with Rob, and looks stunning in a pink cashmere jumper and a white knee-length skirt. Her thick dark waves swathe her shoulders, framing her pretty face. She's done that smoky thing with her eyes and the effect is stunning.

'Where's he taking you?' I ask, slumping onto my bed to eat my sandwich.

'It's a surprise.' She's glowing with excitement.

'It's bound to be a really posh restaurant or something.'

'He just said it's somewhere nice, so that could mean anything, really. I hope I look okay for wherever he's chosen.'

'You look great. You could wear that outfit anywhere and not look out of place,' I assure her. I wish

I could pick out clothes like that. 'I assume Ben's not tagging along tonight, then?'

She giggles. 'Definitely not. It's just the two of us – Rob promised.'

I smile at her, really pleased that she's happy with him.

'Is that all you're having?' She frowns at my sandwich.

'Yeah. I'm not all that hungry.'

'Are things no better with James?'

I shake my head, not wanting to ruin her good mood. 'We haven't really spoken properly. Just police questions.'

'Hasn't he even phoned?' She opens her shoe-wardrobe, one of my favourite places in the whole world.

'I don't know. I haven't had my phone on me all day. I'll check it later.'

'You should.'

'I will.'

'Romys, I think,' she mutters, pulling out her pink 85s. I adore Jimmy Choos and these are a perfect match for her jumper.

I love watching Cassie put an outfit together. 'Which bag?'

She turns back to grin at me. 'You'll never guess,' she teases.

I frown. 'You've got a new one?'

She pulls out a beautiful, plush box, walks over and places it on my bed. Jimmy Choo.

I stare at her. 'You haven't?'

She nods excitedly. 'With some of the money Dad gave me. I thought I deserved a treat after working here for a year.'

I know exactly what it's going to be before she lifts the lid, but can't be sure which colour she'd choose.

'Meet my new friend, Charley.'

'Oh my God!' My jaw drops. It's just as lush as I remembered.

Cassie's wanted a 'Charley' bag for ages, and she's got it in the pink, which is the same shade as her shoes and jumper. It's so elegant and I can't resist putting out a hand just to confirm that it's every bit as luscious as it looks.

'You can borrow it, if you like,' she promises. 'Though not tonight.'

I smile. The bag cost almost £1000, so it's really generous of her to offer. 'I don't think I'll be going anywhere that posh for a while,' I tell her.

Her face falls and I immediately regret saying it. 'Oh, hon, I—'

'No, it's fine. I didn't mean it like that.'

I force myself to give her a big smile to reiterate my point about being fine, but I'm not sure if she's actually convinced. I even try concentrating hard to tell her telepathically that I'm fine – we're so well tuned in, it's worth a try – but then I realize I must be staring at her really hard because she looks quite perturbed.

She leans forwards and gives me a big hug. 'I hope things work out for you. James seems so nice.'

'He is,' I admit. 'And so's Rob.'

'Oh, yeah.' She looks like she just remembered that she's seeing him tonight and I giggle.

'Have a wonderful time.'

'Yes, Mum.' She gives me another hug and picks up the bag. 'I might be really late tonight,' she says, popping her lipstick and mobile into the Charley.

'I won't wait up.'

She gives me another smile and disappears out the door.

I immediately throw the rest of my ham and salad sandwich in the bin, peel off my uniform and head for the bathroom. I don't have any plans for tonight, so I take my time, pampering myself with some luxurious Neil George gel and body lotion that Cassie's parents brought me back from a holiday in Los Angeles. Apparently it's what Cameron Diaz and Renee Zellweger use all the time. I've had an affinity with Renee since the Bridget Jones movies, and Cameron Diaz is utterly stunning in anyone's book.

I put a deep conditioner through my hair and wrap it in an old towel, before slapping on a green face mask. Then I cover my body (well the necessary bits, anyway) in hair-removing cream before going back into the bedroom and finding one of Cassie's whale song CDs.

I desperately need to relax tonight, as the past couple of weeks have been so stressful. I'm in danger of getting wrinkles if this continues. In a flash of inspiration I fish my sandwich from the bin and pull out a couple of cucumber slices from the middle. Lying back on my bed, I place the cucumber over my closed eyes and try to find my happy place while the whale song washes over me.

My thoughts flit from Mrs Merrington-Smythe and her rose-scented perfume to breaking up with James, and then to Connor, who I'd almost forgotten about, to be honest. Apart from cheating on me, that phone call made me see him for the shithead that he is, and I'm actually glad to be rid of him.

I'm worried about Bianca – *I know, right?* – and intend to go and see if she's downstairs shortly. My mind keeps returning to James, though. The conversation in the Remington Suite earlier was really strange, like we were both talking in some kind of special code. He was obviously trying to explain to me why they'd taken Bianca in for questioning – despite our agreement, I might add – and I was telling him I wasn't bothered. At least, that's what I *think* we were saying, it's a bit hard to figure out.

SUDDENLY A LOUD HAMMERING INVADES MY tranquillity – well, *sleep*, actually. I must have nodded off. I sit up quickly, sending the cucumber flying and scream, wrapping my arms around myself as the cold hits my naked body.

The door bursts open. James stands in the opening, staring at me. I stare right back. Then I scream again.

'*Libby?*' He looks unsure.

That's when I remember that my whole, shivering

body is covered in an assortment of creams – and not the kind you'd like Jamie Dornan to lick off you – and they've all solidified into a hard, cracking, multi-coloured shell on my skin.

James's face is a picture of confusion - or is that horror? - and I can only hope he doesn't recognise me under all this gunk.

'No, no, not here,' I say, in my best Spanish accent – or is it Jamaican? - as I pull a towel over me. 'I do not know her.'

His lips twitch — he's not fooled for a second. *Damn!*

He quickly averts his eyes and I'm not sure whether to feel relieved or insulted.

The whale music's still playing but is doing nothing to steady my nerves. I spring off the bed and dive into the bathroom, slamming the door behind me. My heart races and my freezing cold body feels all hot on the inside. *How could this happen?*

I unwind the towel from my head and jump into the shower, hoping that when I go back out there he'll be gone and it'll be as if he was never here. Why *is* he here, anyway? What does he think he's doing bursting in to a girl's bedroom?

My embarrassment turns to anger as the warm water begins to melt the hardened creams from my body, and lead a muddy-looking trail of goo down the drain. Life creeps back into my face, which felt like it was tearing apart when I screamed, and the depilatory cream leaves certain parts of me feeling numb. On the plus side, my scalp feels refreshed and my hair's beautifully soft.

'Libby, you can't stay in there all night.'

Damn – he's still there. I must have been in here ages, though clearly not long enough. 'What are you doing here?' I yell, coming out of the shower and wrapping two towels around me, just to be on the safe side.

'I was worried about you.'

I roll my eyes, which I notice don't feel any better for having the cucumber treatment. Maybe the mayonnaise counteracted the effect. I know I should be flattered, but he really could've picked a better time to be concerned.

'Well, I'm fine,' I call back, 'as you could see.'

There's a silence and I remember just *what* he could see. Everything. *Shit!* I can't go out there. I'll never be able to face him. I'm going to have to stay here. Live in this bathroom forever. I look around at my surroundings. At least I've got a loo, and my toothbrush. But what about food? I'll starve! I quickly check the floor in case those slices of cucumber have somehow got stuck to my towel and found their way in here. They won't sustain me for long, but…

'Libby. Come out here.'

I detect a little mirth in his voice, which irks me. How dare he come into my bedroom when I'm naked and then laugh at my body? My back stiffens and if I were an animal my hackles would have well and truly risen by now.

As I stand in front of the mirror and pull a comb

through my probably over-conditioned hair, I jut my chin out stubbornly. We split up. Well, if you can split up when you're never actually together in the first place, that is. Either way, he's got no right coming in here and embarrassing me.

'Libby…'

I jump on the handle and fling the door open, glaring at him.

Of all the cheek! He's sitting on my bed, thumbing through the latest copy of *Cosmopolitan*, casual as you like.

He seems surprised to see me. I don't know who he expected to be in here – unless he *was* really fooled by my Spanish accent. *Damn*. Maybe I've just revealed myself when I could have got away with it. Then I remember he's been calling my name for the past twenty minutes or so, so maybe he wasn't taken in, after all.

I pull my towels a little tighter against my body and saunter into the bedroom. '*What* do you think you're doing?' I place one hand on my hip, trying to look defiant, and grip the towels tightly with the other, determined not to give him another peek at my body.

His eyes twinkle with amusement and I wonder if I look like a teapot or just rather camp, so I remove the offending hand and simply seethe at him instead.

'I've been learning all about flowers, and now I'm onto what a man's choice of tie says about him.' He purses his lips. 'I'll have to remember that next time I wear my yellow one.'

I gape at him as I wrack my brain to try to remember

what the yellow one meant. Was it trustworthiness or a good sense of humour? Or was that the one that meant he was in a sexy mood? I blush at the thought and look away quickly, making a mental note to look it up later. 'Why are you here, in my bedroom? My *private* bedroom, where visitors aren't allowed – particularly *male* visitors.' I narrow my eyes, looking in his direction but not at his face. That would be too awkward.

'I told you, I was worried about you.' He tosses my copy of *Cosmo* onto my pillow and I stare at it, wishing I had X-ray vision so I could see what a yellow tie signifies. Not that I've ever seen him in a yellow tie. Or any tie for that matter. He always looks smart, but tends to have an open neck, which I assume is a safety measure in case a criminal tries to strangle him with his own tie. I'm sure I've seen that once on an episode of *The Bill*.

He looks as scrummy as ever, dressed casually in a pair of black jeans and a Ralph Lauren shirt.

'That doesn't give you the right to come up here.'

He sighs irritably. 'I've been trying to contact you since I saw you earlier, but you won't answer your damn phone. I asked downstairs and the night porter came up to check on you. He said he heard some really strange noises coming from in here, so I thought I'd better check you were all right.' He glances at Cassie's music system, which, I realise has stopped playing.

'Oh.' I suppose whale song isn't for everybody. It's not even for me unless I'm in the mood. Which I was. But I'm not now. Any thoughts of relaxing and sailing off on my sea of tranquillity have long-since vanished.

'If you'd just let me explain things—'

'Things like what? Why you lied to me? Why you arrested Bianca after promising me you wouldn't? Which turned out to be the wrong move, since she's not even guilty.'

'There you go again. Going off half-cocked.' He waves his hand in exasperation.

'*Me*? I'm not the one who arrested a perfectly inno-cent barmaid because I didn't make sure of my facts beforehand,' I throw at him righteously.

'You're the one who thought she was guilty in the first place!' He looks really incredulous now. 'And, for your information, she wasn't arrested. She came into the station of her own accord and volunteered certain information.'

I frown. 'What information?'

He gives me a withering look. 'Since when were you a cop? I can't divulge every little thing to you.'

'Oh, here we go again.' I throw my arms up in the air. '*You* were the one pointing out earlier that I—' A sudden rush of cold air alerts me to the fact that my towels have just slid down my body and I shriek as they land in a crumpled heap at my feet. My hands automati-cally try to cover myself up, but there's a bit too much of me to hide, so I crouch down and grab the towels before scurrying back into the bathroom.

I'm sure I can hear James giggling as I slam the door and wrap myself up again. My skin's dry now, so there's no purchase of the towels against my body – especially as it's all silky-smooth and hair-free.

'Come on, Libby, it's not the end of the world.' He sounds like he's trying not to laugh. *Is this the effect my body has on him?*

'What's so funny?' I open the door, scowling at him.

'Nothing,' he says, looking all relaxed – unlike me.

'Were you laughing at my body again?'

His eyes are suddenly huge as he stares at me. 'No, Libby, I'm sorry…I didn't mean for you to think that. I was just amused at how embarrassed you get about me seeing you – which I didn't, by the way. I covered my eyes, in case you didn't notice. Don't ever think I'm laughing at you.' He looks really shocked, and I'm inclined to believe him.

I plonk myself on the end of my bed.

'I'm sure you've got a beautiful body,' he says softly, his eyes pleading with me to believe him.

'Well, *you* should know,' I reply dryly.

'Yeah, you've tried showing me enough of it tonight.' He bursts out laughing and I cringe.

'I knew it was too good to be true.' I stand up, gripping tightly to the towel. 'Why don't you just go?' I point to the door angrily.

'I'm joking,' he says, holding his hands up in a placating manner.

'Yeah, well *I'm* not. I'd like you to leave my room now, please, Sergeant.'

He looks mortified. 'Libby…I'm sorry. I meant what I said about you being beautiful. The thing is, I really like you.'

He stands and moves closer, his spicy aftershave

wafting over me. But I'm too angry to care, right now. Angry and indignant.

'Well, I don't like you very much, right now,' I retort. 'You've done nothing but embarrass and humiliate me since you came in here and I want you out. Or do I need to call Security?'

I can't bring myself to look at his face, and I'm holding my breath so I don't inhale any more of his scent. Unshed tears burn the back of my eyes and I just want to be left alone to cry.

Slowly he makes his way to the door. 'I *am* sorry,' he reiterates. 'I wouldn't hurt you for the world, you should know that. And as for humiliating you—'

'Just go!' I don't want to hear it. If I do, I might crumble. I can hear the sorrow in his voice and that's enough to open the floodgates.

As soon as the door clicks closed I crawl onto the bed and curl into a miserable ball. My head tells me I'm well rid of him, but somehow my heart reminds me that I really wanted him to stay.

20

I DON'T FEEL VERY FRIDAY-ISH WHEN I GET UP THE following morning. Cassie's fast asleep. I've no idea what time she got in last night, but she's not working until later so I try not to disturb her.

Luckily I've got a really busy day ahead, getting ready for tomorrow's wedding fair, so that should help keep my mind occupied – although I can't help wishing it was a different kind of event. One that didn't include lifelong vows and happily-ever-afters.

But I, Liberty Lawrence, am a professional so I will cope with this the best way I know how - *professionally.* My gran always used to tell me to put my best foot forward – though I was never quite sure which one she meant. One's a bit bigger than the other, which I hear is perfectly normal and everyone has it – but does that make it the best? I've got a wonky little toe on the other, which everyone said was really cute when I was a baby

– does that make *that* one the best? Anyway, whichever one it is, they both look great in designer shoes.

Mad Moody Margaret's serving breakfast this morning and I do my best to smile at her when I arrive in the kitchen. She doesn't even attempt to smile back at me, which I find a bit rude, to be honest. After all, if *I* can make an effort then why can't she? I turn away. If I want misery I'll look in a mirror, thanks very much.

'What can I get you?' Justin looks pleased to see me, which is a boon, and I breathe in the aroma of bacon and sausages.

'I'll just make myself some toast and coffee, thanks.'

He smiles, an expression which suddenly changes when Margaret gives him her next order, followed by the words 'and don't congeal the eggs.'

I smirk. That can only be one customer. I put my toast in to cook and pop into the restaurant to say good morning to Mrs Merrington-Smythe. Popsie leaps up to say hello as soon as he spies me and I crouch down to make a fuss of him.

'I've promised him a good walk today,' the old lady tells me with a smile. 'I just hope it doesn't rain.'

I look over to the window. The sky's as dull and gloomy as I feel. 'Doesn't look that promising,' I comment. 'But if you go up the High Street there are plenty of shops you can pop into if the heavens open. There's a dog-friendly café up there, too, just past the butcher's.'

She smiles at me and I realize that she's really quite pretty when she's not scowling.

'Good idea. I'll take a brolly – and a shopping basket to put Popsie into in case he gets wet.'

I smile. Most people around here would be looking at designer handbags to carry their tiny dogs in, but not Mrs Merrington-Smythe. She really is one of a kind.

'Well, I've got a wedding fair to organise,' I tell her. 'I hope it doesn't rain tomorrow.'

'It's good luck to have rain on your wedding day,' she says.

'It's even better luck to have a groom,' I mutter.

For an old lady she's got sharp hearing. 'Things not that good on the romance front, dear?'

'Nope. We had a row. He laughed at me.' I don't know why I'm telling her this, but she's really easy to speak to once you get to know her.

'Oh no.' She gapes at me. 'The dashing white sergeant?'

I nod, thinking how well she'd get along with my mum.

'Are you sure there's not a mistake? That doesn't sound like him — laughing at someone like that.'

'Quite sure.' I wonder how well she knows him to make that comment.

'Hmm.' She presses her lips tightly together and frowns thoughtfully. 'I can see I'll have to have words with that young man.'

I gasp. 'No, it's fine. You don't need to do that,' I assure her. 'I'm sure it'll all work out.'

'Hmm,' she says again, clearly not convinced.

Just then I notice Mad Moody Margaret walking towards us, her hands shaking as she carries Mrs Merrington-Smythe's full English.

'Here she comes, Mrs Overall,' Mrs Merrington-Smythe murmurs. 'If the eggs aren't congealed when they leave the kitchen, they will be by the time they get here.'

I snort loudly as I try not to laugh, startling poor Popsie. I didn't expect her to come out with something like that. Who knew she had such a wicked sense of humour?

'I'd better get back,' I say hurriedly. 'Enjoy your breakfast.'

Mrs Merrington-Smythe rolls her eyes. 'If it ever gets here I might.'

I give Popsie a little wave and head back for the kitchen, trying not to catch Margaret's eye on my way past.

'Cheryl stole your toast,' Justin informs me as soon as I return.

Cheryl looks up from a plate full of crumbs. 'I didn't know it was yours,' she says defensively – although she's still got her mouth full - and I can imagine Justin's been making her feel bad about it.

'It's fine. It would only have gone cold by now anyway.' I wash my hands, still imagining Margaret dressed as Mrs Overall, carrying a bowl of soup which sloshes everywhere as she shakes.

I make myself some fresh toast and take it, along with a large mug of coffee, to my office.

Tania's on the reception desk today, as it's Frances's day off, and she smiles as I pass her. She's a very tall girl in her late twenties, with gangly legs and a long nose. She wears square-framed glasses, and her mousy-brown hair in a grown-out bob.

'You've had a couple of calls already,' she tells me. 'A woman called Angela or Alexandria, or something, from Full Bloom Flowers said she'd email you. And Sergeant Harper said to switch your mobile on.'

I gape at her, taken aback by his audacity. I haven't turned my phone on since the day before yesterday, and don't relish the idea of doing so now.

'Thanks. I might do it later,' I say with a shrug.

'He said it's important.'

I'll bet he did.

My phone's still in the drawer of my bedside locker, and I'm sure I'll be too busy to go and fetch it today, so it'll just have to stay there. Besides, I really don't want to have to deal with him today. I can just imagine his first words when he sees me being something like 'I didn't recognise you with your clothes on.' Nope. I won't give him the satisfaction. Last night was humiliating enough.

Andrea's email is checking on how many pedestals we can squeeze in. She sounds really keen to do them, and even suggests some small displays on the reception desk and the corner table by the lift.

I've also had an email from the company supplying

chair covers, saying they want to come in at eleven-thirty this morning to set out the restaurant. I quickly reply telling them that we still need to serve lunch and dinner, as well as tomorrow's breakfast so they'll have to come tomorrow morning, as arranged. *Flipping cheek!*

I pop through for a quick word with Tania around mid-morning. It's actually nice to have some company – I'm missing Popsie already. 'I need to reserve a ground-floor bedroom for storage,' I tell her. 'All the luggage areas are full. Have we got any available at the moment?'

She looks on the computer system and finds one for me.

'Great. Anything that arrives today for the fair can go in there, ready for the morning.'

She nods, tapping at her keyboard.

The phone rings and she picks up the receiver, while still typing with one hand. 'Oh hi, Sergeant Harper.'

My body glows hot and I wait for her to ask if she can put him through to me. I'm looking forward to telling her I'm far too busy to take his call right now. I'm gutted when it turns out the call is for Party. She dials the manager's office. 'Mr Partington, I've got Sergeant Harper on the phone with some urgent news for you.'

'What was that all about?' I ask once the call's been patched through.

She shrugs. 'Police business, I assume.'

Seething, I go through to the bar. I dread facing

Connor since his nasty phone call the other night but I need to check that he's ordered enough champagne for tomorrow. I try not to think about this latest call. I'm convinced that James has done this on purpose. He's not speaking to me. Well, two can play at that game.

It's nearly midday and the bar hasn't even been opened up yet. What the hell is Connor playing at?

'Ah, Liberty, there you are.' Party suddenly appears at the doorway. 'Can you set up the bar, please? Connor can't make it so Bianca's on her way in.'

I'm glad to get the chance to speak to Bianca, but can't help wondering what on earth Connor's up to.

I go around and open up the bar, pleased to note that the floor's actually been cleaned for a change. The stench of stale beer tells me that the drip trays need emptying, though, and I immediately get onto it.

'Hi.' Bianca arrives once all the work's done, as usual, and I look up, ready to give her a piece of my mind until I see how pale she looks.

I frown. 'What's wrong?'

'I think this is my fault.'

Something tells me this has nothing do with a couple of jobs left to do behind the bar, and I feel a thud in my stomach. 'What's your fault?'

She bites her lip, looking around surreptitiously.

'I'll come 'round.'

Seconds later she's standing next to me, her eyes wide and worried. 'Do you know where Connor is?'

Right at this moment I don't give a damn where he is, but it's obviously important to her, so I just shake my head. 'Do you?'

'I think… I think he might have been arrested. And it's all because of me,' she whispers.

It's a good job I'm at the bar, because my mouth immediately goes dry. 'Why do you think that?' I'm dying to know what's been going on, and it suddenly occurs to me that if I checked my phone a bit more regularly I might find out.

'I spoke to the cops yesterday.' She looks as guilty as sin and I'd honestly think she was if James hadn't gone to such lengths to put me right on that score.

'I heard.'

She rolls her eyes. 'I know. They all said I'd been arrested, didn't they?'

'Something like that.'

'I wasn't. They wanted to speak to me here, but I didn't want anyone to know so I asked if I could talk to them privately, and we went down to the station. You know what this place is like.'

I nod. That makes sense.

'They wanted to examine my shoes. Someone used them to put marks on Party's office carpet after the robbery. They tried to *frame* me.' Her eyes are huge.

My heart pounds. 'Who would do that?'

'Well, at first, I obviously thought it was you.'

'*What*?'

'Well, you know. What with the Connor thing and all that. Anyway, when I spoke to the sergeant about it, he said he didn't think it *was* you, so I had no idea who else would do such a thing.'

My mouth drops open. I wish she could hear herself. 'Quite,' I manage.

'Anyway, it was the shoes I was wearing in the Four Feathers that night when you—'

'When I caught you snogging my boyfriend,' I finish for her.

She nods vehemently. 'Yes. I spent that night with Connor.'

I roll my eyes, not sure if she's boasting or just informing me. Either way, I'd rather not hear it. Then the penny drops. 'So Connor did it. He was the only one that had access to your shoes at the time.'

'Looks like it. I feel awful. I didn't mean to get him into trouble; I was just answering their questions.' She's very jittery and I can't help feeling sorry for her. It had never occurred to me that Connor was the thief and that she didn't know anything about it. She's clearly much more naïve than I'd given her credit for.

'Ah, two of my favourite ladies.'

We both look up to see Rob and Ben leaning over the bar.

'Hello,' I say, unable to keep the surprise from my voice.

Just then, Cassie comes through from the restaurant. 'What are you doing here?' She gives Rob a quick kiss, followed by a quizzical frown.

'And here's my favourite of them all,' Rob adds with a smile.

'We've been summoned,' Ben says mysteriously. 'A couple of pints please, Bianca.'

'Who by?' I ask eagerly.

'Sergeant Harper,' Rob replies. 'He's meeting us here in a few minutes with some news.'

Bianca and I exchange a look, and I hope mine doesn't match hers. I was going for surprise, but she looks downright bewildered.

Then Cassie throws me a look that says 'what the heck's going on?' and I reply with one that says 'I'm not really sure but it looks like things are kicking off'. (I'm not convinced she understood all of it, but she seemed to get the gist).

Mr Partington suddenly turns up and I cringe, knowing he'll be livid that I'm still here instead of working. Sergeant Harper's hot on his heels and I instantly wish I *wasn't* still here and that I *was* working.

'Right, well, if that's everything, I'll be off,' I say hurriedly, edging towards the back of the bar and the door that leads into the kitchen. I can sneak into my cupboard from there.

'You may as well stay for this, Liberty,' Party says sternly and I daren't argue.

I feel myself colouring up as James's eyes bore into me, but I stare resolutely at the counter.

'Connor Worthington's been arrested for both thefts here at the hotel,' Party tells us, his tone deadly serious.

Cassie gasps. Ben scribbles in a notebook. Rob pulls out his iPad and starts tapping away on the keyboard.

I chance a quick peep at James, who appears unimpressed that Mr Partington's told everyone his news. Jumping in before Party continues, James says, 'He's admitted everything, including trying to implicate Bianca in both instances.'

I can't meet his eyes. Those eyes saw me naked last night and I'll never forget that. Okay, so it was only for a few seconds – *twice* – and I *did* manage to cover up the important bits with my hands, sort of - but it's the principle that counts. And then he laughed. That's the unforgivable part. He *laughed.*

'Well, if that's all, I've got work to do,' I say, pretending to stifle a yawn.

'Yes, I think perhaps we should adjourn to my office for the details, gentlemen,' Party says, ushering the reporters and James out of the bar area, just as a couple of guests arrive.

Cassie throws me a look which says 'you knew?' and I reply by looking pointedly at Bianca. She nods and I imagine she'll be quizzing her as soon as the customers are served.

I, however, don't feel as excited as everyone else – possibly because I already knew, thanks to Bianca. I'm shocked that it was Connor who masterminded the whole operation, although, now that I know Bianca a little better, I can certainly believe it. It must take a certain amount of brains to be an opportunist – not that I'm saying she's thick or anything. What really galls me, though, is that he tried to frame Bianca for it all – *and I fell for it!*

As I return to the stationery cupboard I can't help

thinking it's a good job James is the cop and I'm just a junior manager. If it had been left to me, I'd have had poor Bianca hung, drawn and quartered just because of a few marks on the carpet.

I enter my office and sit at the desk with my face buried in my hands. I feel utterly useless. I seem to have done nothing but get everything wrong these past couple of weeks. Cassie's leaving next week and I'm still stuck here. My parents think I'm doing really well, but they've never even seen my office. They've mentioned visiting me a few times but I always put them off, telling them I'm really busy with important issues. I wear my Kurt Geigers or Karen Millens whenever I *do* see them, or borrow some of Cassie's shoes – as well as her clothes – so they think I'm really successful. Well, so Mum does. Dad wouldn't know a designer label if one jumped up and bit him on the nose.

One thing I'm grateful for is that I never took Connor home to meet my folks. Dad would go mad if he thought I'd been dating a common criminal! I can hardly believe it myself. I had no idea he was capable of something like this – and trying to frame Bianca just takes the biscuit. I suppose I should be thankful it wasn't *me* he tried to frame. I never realised I'm such a rotten judge of character.

The thought immediately takes me back to James. I had him wrong right from the start, thinking he was miserable and sullen when in fact he was just being professional. He must have been undercover that first time I met him, which was why he wasn't exactly making conversation. He was staying under the radar.

And I can't believe I thought he was married. I should have known better – he wouldn't string me along like that. My stomach lurches.

I was even offended that he didn't agree with me about Bianca being the thief – and look what a good job that turned out to be.

A thought suddenly occurs to me. If I was so wrong about him on all the other counts, why do I think I'm right in thinking he was poking fun at me last night? He even explained that he wasn't laughing *at me*, just at my reaction, so why didn't I believe him?

I know the answer to that one straight away. I lack confidence. I'd automatically assumed those men in the Fox and Duck were laughing at me when they were enjoying their game, because I was afraid that they would be making fun of me. And it would be my worst fear that James Harper would laugh at me because I really want him to like me. That's why I thought he was – because I was *afraid* that he was. Oh God, why am I so stupid? *(It's okay – you don't really have to answer that, by the way).*

21

BIANCA'S FRANTICALLY PICKING AT A BEER MAT WHEN I pass through the bar a few minutes later. It's really quiet for a Friday, and I assume the rubbish weather's keeping everyone away.

'What's up?' I thought she'd be happier now that everything's out in the open.

'You must hate me,' she says in a small voice.

I'm sure my eyebrows disappear into my hairline as I stare back at her. 'Me? Why?'

'Because I've just stolen your boyfriend and then got him arrested, of course.' She looks like she's about to cry.

I shake my head. 'No. You did me a favour. I'm glad to be rid of him – especially now I know he's a thief. As soon as I discovered he was cheating on me I knew it was over, but all these latest developments are just proof that he's not for me.'

'But I'm the one that got him arrested. They asked

me all these questions – about my dad and stuff – and I just sort of…told them.' She's frowning at me again. I'm used to people doing that. I get it a lot.

'How is your dad?'

She grimaces. 'He got taken in by some loan sharks. It was my fault. I'd got this card off a guy in town and Dad found it. I wouldn't have gone near that sort of thing with a ten-foot barge pole, but Dad was desperate. I didn't know anything about it, or the troubles he was having with the garage until it was too late. I feel so responsible. I should've known.'

'Why? Your dad's in charge of the family business. You don't even work there. How would you know that the place was in trouble?' I pull up a bar stool and perch on the edge of it, in order to be able to make a quick getaway if Party suddenly does one of his magical appearing acts.

She shrugs. 'I don't know. I just think I should have guessed, that's all.'

'And do you think it was your fault that Connor stole the money? Because he was doing it to help you out?'

She gawps at me. 'What?'

I narrow my eyes, a little disconcerted at her reaction. 'I didn't mean it *was* your fault he did it,' I assure her, 'I'm just asking if you *felt* that it was. Because it wasn't. It isn't. Connor's responsible for his own actions, as is your dad.'

I'm not sure if she understands what I'm saying, but her blank expression indicates there's a good chance she doesn't. Or maybe she does understand, she just doesn't agree with it. Which is fine. She's entitled to her own opinion, of course, but I don't think she needs to feel guilty.

'No.' She shakes her head slowly.

'No, what?' Now *I'm* the one who doesn't understand.

'No.'

'Oh, good. You shouldn't feel that you're to blame for someone else's actions. We're all adults; we make our own decisions what to do.' I *think* that's what she meant.

'No, not that.'

Oh. Maybe not.

'What then?'

She huffs. *She* huffs! How does she think *I* feel?

'Connor didn't steal anything to help me out.'

'Hang on. I don't understand.'

'Connor lent me some money to help my dad, but he didn't steal it. That was from his savings, to buy his car with.'

'His car? What car?'

'The one he's saving up for. He wants to buy a car. Dad said he'll help him find a really good one. He just needs to take his test.'

'O-kay,' I'm struggling to process all this.

'I've got to pay him back at the same rate of interest that the bank would be giving him on his savings – it's only fair. Otherwise he'll never have enough to get a good car.'

I narrow my eyes again. She totally believes all this. I could tell her the truth, but I really don't want to burst her bubble – or confuse her. I settle for 'Right,' and hop off the stool. This conversation's like wading through treacle and it's making my head ache.

'It's *you* that should feel guilty if anyone.'

Migraine alert!

'*What*?'

'You heard me.' She wipes down the bar nonchalantly. 'If anyone needs to feel guilty about Connor stealing money to get them what they want then it's you.'

'Me?' I grip the edge of the bar to stop myself from falling over as my legs feel a little weak – and not for a good reason.

She nods. 'Yeah. He didn't want to break up with you, you know. He wanted to carry on seeing you. So he thought the only way to get you back would be to buy you what you want.'

'Which is?' I hardly dare ask.

'Christian Louboutins. He said you wouldn't settle for the ones I get – even though they *are* genuine, by the way, the guy told me – so he was going to have to buy you a pair from a shop, just to keep you sweet. That's what the money was for.'

'*All* of it?'

She nods. 'Yep. The money from the safe wasn't enough, so he had to take that woman's necklace as well, to make it up.'

I balk. 'How much do you think Louboutins cost?'

'I dunno about the ones you get,' she says with a shrug. 'I pay for mine weekly.'

I shake my head, not sure whether it's worth enlightening her or not. It's possible she doesn't know how much money was in the safe, or how much he got for the necklace. And I'm pretty sure he won't have told her about the £650 he stole along *with* the necklace.

'Well, he certainly never bought me any,' I tell her, taking a step away from the bar.

'He did, actually,' she replies, matter-of-factly.

'What?'

'We had a huge row about it.'

'About him buying me shoes?'

'No. Well, yes. He left them at my place after he'd stayed the night, and I thought they were for me so I wore them. I wasn't too keen, though, they were really tight and hurt my feet.' She shrugs. 'Connor went mental. It's a good job you weren't here.'

'The Scalopumps!' Now it makes sense. I can't believe he bought them for me, although I wouldn't have touched them if they were bought with stolen money – even if they *were* Christian Louboutins!

I'm giddy with all these revelations, but still manage to feel sorry for Bianca having to squeeze her feet into shoes two sizes too small. She must have been in agony – what a horrid introduction to designer shoes. *Real* ones, that is.

'So, if he'd bought me a pair of shoes to get me back, had he split up with you?' She seems to have taken it very well if he had – I'd never have guessed. They even slept together afterwards.

She looks at me like I'm mad. *Me?* 'Of course not. He was going to see us both.'

'And you wouldn't have minded?' I can't believe her attitude.

She shrugs. 'We'd been doing it in secret long enough already– it didn't really make that much difference.'

My mind is well and truly boggled as I leave her and go through to the restaurant. Cassie is busy serving an elderly couple, so I decide to speak to her later, and make my way through the kitchen and up the back stairs.

I'm furious with Connor, and amazed that Bianca would allow him to two-time her. That girl must have lower self-esteem than me!

Once in the bedroom I fetch my phone from the drawer and head back downstairs before I'm missed.

I grab a pre-made salad on my way back through the kitchen and reach Reception just as Tania appears from the guests' corridor.

'There you are. I've just taken delivery of a load of hats for tomorrow. I put them in the bedroom.'

'Thanks, Tania. I might take a look later.'

'There are some really nice ones. I couldn't help noticing,' she says guiltily.

'Great.' I smile, wondering if she's the sort of girl who wears hats to weddings.

I wore a purple fascinator to my cousin's wedding

last year. I looked very out of place, to be honest, as it was only a tiny register office in Margate, and the feathers on my headpiece were rather large. And how was I to know that Uncle Cuthbert was allergic to feathers? He sneezed all the way through the service and his eyes watered so much that my Auntie Christine thought he was crying because my cousin, Amy, had written a poem which she read out during the vows. The poem almost made me cry, actually, but not for a good reason. It was dreadful – and didn't even rhyme! Unless you honestly think that 'happy' and 'marry' sound the same? No, I didn't think so, either.

What made matters worse was that no-one else wore so much as a flower in their hair. Mum cheated, too. She had a really nice navy hat to go with her suit, but she left it in the car when she noticed no-one else was wearing one. I felt utterly betrayed, but we never talk about it.

I'm just glad I didn't waste my Stella McCartneys on the occasion – I did think about it, but decided that red shoes with my purple and yellow outfit might be a step too far.

I take my salad into the stationery cupboard, still seething about the wedding. When *I* get married I'll make the dress code perfectly clear – no hat, no entry. You can't get plainer than that. I'll get bouncers – or, rather, ushers – to enforce the rule. I considered making the men wear hats, too, maybe top hats, but then they'd all have to wear morning suits or tails, and Uncle Cuthbert would go bonkers. He refused to hire a suit for

Amy's wedding, and she's his daughter! No way would he splash out for mine. I just hope he doesn't wear those pale blue chinos again — poor Amy was mortified!

I switch on my phone and it beeps and flashes like crazy to tell me I've got messages. My heart lurches at the thought that James was trying to get in touch and I didn't even take my phone with me, let alone switch it on.

Hi Libby, I'm so sorry, but I have to cancel our date tonight. I'm gutted as I was really looking forward to it, but this is urgent. I can't explain fully, but it's to do with the thefts at the hotel. I'm having a really hard time keeping Bianca out of it, as my superiors are asking questions. I'll do my best, though, I promise. Jx

Hey Libby, I was really hoping to talk to you. I hope you're not too upset with me. There have been more developments in the case. I'll try calling you again later, I need to explain. Hope you're having a good evening. Jx

I'm guessing he'd tried to ring me several times too, given the urgency of these messages, and feel guilty for not being there when he wanted to speak to me. There are also several more texts asking where I am, and if I can phone him just to let him know I'm okay.

He'd tried to keep his word, but he had a job to do. I should've understood that. I *do* understand that. What I *don't* understand is how I managed to ruin everything so royally!

I go back out to Reception, where Tania is just taking delivery of a beautiful bouquet of purple hyacinths. Their perfume fills the air and I can't resist going over for a closer look. 'Are these for the wedding fair? They're so pretty.'

Tania smiles. 'No, they're for you.'

My jaw drops as she hands them over, and I breathe in the luscious scent again.

'There's a note.' She points to a tiny envelope attached to a green stick which pokes out of the mass of tiny purple bells.

It's obvious she wants me to open it in front of her, but it's not going to happen. I go back into the stationery cupboard and place the flowers on the desk. Luckily, they're already in a water bubble, so I don't need to find a vase straight away, and I close the door before opening the little envelope. My hands shake and I hold my breath, despite wanting to keep smelling the flowers.

Libby, I hope you understand, Jx

My stomach lurches and I stare, disbelieving, at the note. He's telling me it's over. My legs tremble and I quickly sit down, glancing from the note to the flowers. They're so beautiful, but this is his way of saying good-bye. I've ruined everything.

Big, hot tears begin to stream down my face and I don't have the energy to wipe them away – or even worry about my makeup smudging. My heart aches as much as my head while I try to take it all in.

I haven't seen him since he and the reporters went into Party's office to discuss the news about Connor, and I assume he's still there. He must have ordered these last night after I threw him out of my room. Perhaps I can talk to him before he leaves? What would I say? What *could* I say? I got it all wrong and now I've spoiled it. He's had enough of me. All I've done is ignore him and take everything the wrong way. No wonder he's finished with me.

I bury my face in my hands and let the misery wash over me. I've brought all this on myself and there's nothing I can do about it.

IT'S A GOOD WHILE LATER WHEN I FINALLY EMERGE from my office. I just heard Tania offer to carry something for a guest, so figure it's safe to go out there without being seen.

The ladies' is mercifully empty when I creep in and start splashing copious handfuls of water over my face. I daren't look into the mirror until I've used at least ten gallons but I'm pretty sure I can't look as bad as I did when I arrived.

One glance is enough to convince me otherwise, though and I gasp at the horrific, bulgy-eyed monster that stares back at me. I look dreadful. I can't possibly go out in public with a face like this. All I really want to do is creep up to my room and hide.

The thought gains momentum the more I think of it. No-one will really miss me – in fact, Tania will probably assume I'm still hard at work in the stationery cupboard. Party's too busy with James Harper to worry about what I'm doing, I'm sure I heard the press leave a while ago. Besides, it must be nearly time for my shift to finish. There's no clock in here and I don't wear a watch as I usually rely on my phone for the time if I'm out and about. That reminds me, I've left my mobile on my desk. Typical! I won't need it tonight, though. Cassie's working and I've got no-one to call.

I can't hear any voices from the corridor, so I slowly open the door. No-one's about, so I quickly sneak out and run to the lift. I know I'm not supposed to use it really, but I can't possibly go through the kitchen looking like this.

Moments later I'm in the safety of our bedroom, and I sink onto the bed, face-down. It's a good job Cassie's working as I'd hate to have to explain everything to her. She's really happy with Rob, and I don't want to bring her down just because things aren't working out for me and James.

The thought sets me off on my road to misery once more and fresh tears start to soak my pillow. It's a good job I cried off all my makeup earlier, as I'd have a hard job explaining the filthy pillowcase to Housekeeping otherwise.

My head's throbbing and I know I've brought the headache on myself with my own stupidity – just like everything else.

22

My head doesn't feel much better the next morning. At some unearthly hour last night I'd got up and put on my pyjamas, without waking Cassie. I hadn't touched the salad I'd got for my dinner last night, and I'm pretty sure I missed lunch, too, so I raided the secret stash in the wardrobe, devouring a packet of Maryland Cookies and a couple of Mars bars. I hadn't realized just how hungry I was, and treated myself to some iced cupcakes Cassie must have bought, just to keep my strength up. Then I'd taken said strength and gone back to sleep.

Today I've got the delights of the wedding fair to contend with, so I get showered and dressed before putting on a little more makeup than normal, just to disguise my still-puffy eyes, and fix my hair into a chic chignon. It doesn't look as smart as it did the last time I put it up in this style, probably because it's still so silky from the deep conditioning incident that it keeps sliding out, so I add some extra hairspray and let a few more tendrils fall haphazardly around my cheeks. It's probably a good idea to cover my face a little more today, anyway.

I'd been looking forward to this event for months, but somehow I'm just not in the mood today. However, I remind myself that I'm a professional and paste on a big smile before stepping into my Kurt Geigers – it's a special occasion, after all – and heading downstairs, leaving Cassie still snoring (but don't tell her I told you as she swears she doesn't snore).

Justin's busy preparing vegetables for later and I quickly make some toast and pour myself a huge mug of tea as the smell of cabbage starts filtering up my nose. I hurry on through the empty restaurant – I can't help wondering if the customers have smelled the cabbage too and decided to eat out – and head for my office.

I know it's going to be a busy day and I really need to get rid of this headache, so I make a point of eating my breakfast before I start work. I'm surrounded by the sweet scent of hyacinths and gaze longingly at the flowers still on my desk. My mobile's sitting next to them, and the flashing light tells me I've got a message. I don't really want to read it, but have to concede it could be important, so I reach over and press the button.

Hi Libby. I just wondered if you received the flowers I sent you earlier, and if you got my message? Jx

I shake my head. I got the message all right. Does he really expect me to ring him up and thank him for sending it? I sigh. He must think I'm really adult if he expects me to send him a polite thank you message – it's clear he doesn't know me very well, isn't it?

I finish my breakfast and check my emails. A couple of today's exhibitors want to ensure that their deliveries arrived last night, so I grab the key to the ground-floor bedroom and go to see what's there.

Tania's right about the snazzy hats. I can't resist trying on a couple. I admire myself in the large full-length mirror behind the door, and have to admit I rather suit hats. I look really weddingy with my hair like this and a big, floppy red hat on. I try a little navy pillar-box hat which looks great with my suit, and a straw boater with cerise flowers around the rim.

There are a couple of tiaras in a box by the window so I try one of those on, too. I appear quite regal in one which is encrusted in diamonds. Not real ones, of course. At least, I *hope* they're not real when I notice that a few of them are missing. My heart lurches.

I hurriedly check the tissue paper it was wrapped in, but there's no sign of any tiny jewels. Getting down on my hands and knees, I frantically search the carpet, but there's nothing there, either.

I quickly wrap the tiara back up and replace it in the box with the other one. I know I should just back away and avoid tiaras altogether after that, but I can't resist a tiny peek at the other one. It's a little simpler, but sparkles magnificently in the overhead light. I place it on my head and look in the mirror. My breath hitches. This is the one. This is what I want for my own wedding. It looks amazing. Understated elegance. I love it.

Footsteps in the corridor outside alert me that residents are finally starting to get up and go for breakfast, so I really should get back to Reception. Although I'm rarely needed first thing, I'm supposed to be available in case the guests all decide to check out en masse and poor Frances can't cope.

I put the tiara back in its paper and check for the boxes of chair tie-backs and invitations I was supposed to be looking for in the first place. They all seem to be there, along with some pretty artificial bouquets Andrea from the florist's must have sent over.

My heart skips as I lock the door and head back to Reception. I'm worried sick about the missing stones in that tiara. Will people think I knocked them out? Did I? Or did Tania do it when she was in here trying on hats yesterday? She *did* look quite sheepish about it. I shake my head, determined not to accuse anyone of anything – I've learned my lesson in that regard recently.

'Good morning.' Frances is behind the reception desk when I arrive. She looks extra-smart today and I guess that she's trying to make a good impression because of the wedding fair. I'm glad the staff are taking it seriously. Although Mr Partington's the one in overall charge – as always – this event has sort of been my project. At least, I'm the one who's done all the work for it.

'Morning, Frances. We're using room five to store

all the deliveries for the wedding fair. I've just been to check on them.'

I don't know why I always feel I need to justify myself to the older lady, but I do. I hope I'm not blushing or looking guilty in any way, like someone who might have just tried on a priceless diamond tiara and lost half the stones out of it – because I didn't – I hope.

She nods and I realise Tania would have left that information in the handover book. I wonder if she also mentioned that there's a tiara in there with some of the stones missing. My heart lightens at the thought, and I make a mental note to sneak a peek in the book once Frances is out of the way.

I squeeze past her and go into my office, then reply to the emails to confirm that everything's arrived safely. I'm so glad the milliners haven't asked me to check *their* delivery – what would I say? *Yes, it's all fine except for some missing diamonds.*

I wonder if Ben and Rob have published the news of the thefts and Connor's subsequent arrest yet. Will anyone want to come to the wedding fair if they think the place is full of thieves? Is that why these people wanted confirmation that their goods had arrived? Did they think they might have been stolen? Oh no, this couldn't have come at a worse time.

'Have you seen the article in last night's paper?' Frances asks as I go back through with my clipboard. She must have read my mind.

'No, actually I didn't.'

She smiles at me. That's a first. 'You should have a look, Miss Marple. Seems like you practically solved the crime for them.'

But I was the one who got it all wrong! I frown. 'Is the guest copy still in the bar?'

'Probably. Beryl hasn't gone through there yet.'

A lady arrives at the desk, putting an end to our conversation. She's carrying some boxes and I assume she's here to start setting up for the wedding fair. I still haven't checked the Remington Suite, so I hurry down there to make sure it's all ready for the event while the woman's talking to Frances..

The room still smells of fresh paint and looks really light and airy. A man and a woman are already in there pumping up balloons from a large helium canister and the tables have all been set out exactly as I'd put on the plan. I'm glad Mike's so efficient.

'Is everything all right?'

'Yes, fine,' the man replies in a high-pitched squeak.

I refrain from rolling my eyes as the lady with him bursts out laughing. They've clearly been playing with the helium. I can't really blame them – I'd have probably done the same given half a chance.

The lady with the boxes arrives and looks around the room. 'I'm with the cake-making company,' she says with a smile. 'Where do you want me?'

'Is this okay for you?' I ask, pointing to a row of tables near the stage. They all have pristine, white cloths on.

'Great.' She dumps the boxes onto the first table with a sigh.

I hope those particular ones don't contain cakes, as they'll be in pieces by now if they do.

'Have you got much more to bring in?' I ask, secretly hoping she's going to reply that she has, but that she's also brought along an army of people to help carry them.

'Yes, there's loads.' She looks hopeful and I give up waiting for her to add the bit about the army.

'Can I help?' I try to sound willing.

She gives me a grateful smile. 'If you wouldn't mind, that would be great.'

I smile back. One of the good things about wedding fairs is that all the people are usually cheerful. I'm hoping that everyone who comes today will be happy – after all, weddings are supposed to be happy events, aren't they?

My thoughts turn back to my cousin Amy's wedding as I follow the lady to her van, which is blocking the entrance to the hotel. Uncle Cuthbert didn't seem very happy, coughing and sneezing all through the ceremony. Auntie Christine looked quite annoyed with him for making so much noise, and the people behind me kept tutting. Mum whispered to me that maybe I should remove my fascinator so that Uncle Cuthbert could breathe, and the people behind could see, but it had taken hours to put it on properly – not to mention a whole can of hairspray to keep it in place – and, besides, the idea of wearing any kind of hat to a wedding is that you wear it *at* the wedding, isn't it? Also, it would have caused much more commotion to try to take it off without a mirror, and I didn't want to make a fuss.

The lady plonks some heavy boxes in my arms and I turn and head back to the Remington Suite with them. I've arranged for one of the maintenance guys to come and help with any heavy lifting, but they're not on duty until nine, so it looks like I'm stuck with the job until then.

As I pass the entrance to the bar I can't help worrying that Beryl might arrive while I'm helping out and throw away the newspaper. I'm desperate to see what's been written about me. I'd have loved to be the one who got to write the article. How exciting to actually have a proper story to report for a change. Ben and Rob must get sick of writing about Tube delays and the rising price of milk.

We go back to the van to fetch more cakes and my heart sinks when I notice the security guard with the specs standing next to it.

'Is this your vehicle?' he asks the woman, who has just removed her coat and reveals a white apron with 'Kathy's Cakes' emblazoned on it, which matches the emblem on the side of the white van.

'Yes, I'm Kathy,' she tells him with a smile.

'You'll have to move,' he grunts. 'You're causing an obstruction. It's a fire hazard.'

I shoot him a dirty look. That sort of attitude will deter people from ever exhibiting here again. The event's going to be a disaster, I just know it. It's not even as if anyone else needs to park there, as it's still early and no-one else has arrived. I'm about to tell him to lay off when Kathy, still smiling, speaks up. 'Of course, I'll move it as soon as I can, which will be even sooner with your help. If you could just carry these for me?' She plonks a couple of large boxes in his arms while he gapes at her in disbelief.

'Absolutely. All hands to the pump. It's the only way to get the job done quickly,' I pipe up, enjoying the man's expression. 'Load me up, Kathy. We're always willing to help here at The Chalfont.' I beam at her as she plonks a pile of boxes in my arms and follow the security guard through to the Remington Suite.

I'm sure my Kurt Geigers weren't really intended for wearing while carrying heavy boxes, and I totter precariously as I struggle to see where I'm going around the mass of cardboard in front of me. I settle for following the sound of the old man's chuntering as he moans to himself about this not being part of his remit.

I put the pile of cakes down with a sigh of relief when I finally get to our destination, and wish I'd put Kathy's Cakes stall nearer to the door.

'There's just one more small cake left.' Her words are music to my ears. 'Would you be good enough to bring it through while I move the van?'

'Of course.'

I watch her thank the security guard for his help, and wish he could be a little more gracious about it. Or, at least, a little gracious. Or even gracious at all would be good. No chance. He heads for the lift as Kathy and I make our way back to the van, and I don't expect to see anything more of him today. He'll be sulking up there in his office for the rest of the day with a large cup of tea and an even larger chip on his shoulder.

'This is the top tier for the six-tier showstopper,' Kathy says proudly as she places a much-heavier-than-expected box in my hands.

'Ooh, I look forward to seeing it later,' I tell her with an excited smile. Or, at least, I hope it looks like an excited smile. I'm actually gritting my teeth and wondering what on earth is in the cake to make it so damned heavy. It feels like it's made of concrete.

She climbs into the van and starts the engine as I head back towards the conference suite. The corridor's getting quite busy now, as more people are arriving to set up, while the residents are coming and going for breakfast and check-out.

Out of the corner of my eye I notice Beryl in the bar, picking up the *Chronicle*. She's carrying a large rubbish sack in her other hand and I shout out to stop her mixing the two. 'Beryl. No!' I automatically put my hand up to wave to her, hoping to grab her attention over the hubbub of conversations, forgetting for just a second that I'm carrying the cake.

My left hand suddenly buckles under the weight of the concrete cake and I lurch forwards as I try to steady myself as well as the box. 'Aah!' The carpet looms up towards me as I hurl face-first onto the floor, the cake dragging me down like a huge anchor as it tips over and crashes onto the cream carpet.

I lie there, a little dazed, and a whole lot embarrassed. My chin hurts and I'm not sure whether I hit it on the floor, or on the cake on my way *to* the floor. People are muttering above me, and I delay looking up at them for as long as I dare.

A pair of shiny shoes stop right in front of me and a muscular arm reaches down to help me up. I take the attached hand and instantly feel a zing of electricity run through me. I chance a peep at the man who has come to my aid, although I don't really need confirmation. That tingling feeling and the scent of aftershave tell me it can only be one person. James Harper.

'Are you okay?'

'I'm fine,' I mutter, nodding.

'Liberty! Just look at this mess.' Mr Partington appears right behind him.

'She's had an accident,' James informs him irritably. 'Who's your first aider?'

Party fumes and the vein in his neck goes into overdrive. 'Adrian. Frances, go and fetch him, will you?'

I wasn't even aware that Frances was around. In fact, apart from Party I wasn't aware of anyone except James, who is still holding my hand.

Just then, Kathy returns from parking the van. 'Oh no! What happened? Are you all right?'

'Libby had an accident. She's just waiting for the first aider,' James tells her.

Adrian arrives, along with Julie and Cheryl, who immediately start clearing up the cake while Kathy salvages what she can from the decorations. We seem to have attracted quite an audience, so it's a relief when Adrian suggests taking me into the kitchen to get cleaned up.

I don't realise my chin is actually bleeding until he has to replace the swab with a clean one.

'You'll have a lovely bruise there,' Adrian informs me, 'but I wouldn't expect that cut to leave a scar.'

I roll my eyes. 'I bet Kathy's furious about the cake.'

'I think she's more worried about you. The sergeant definitely is,' he adds with a grin. 'He made it clear that you were the priority out there, not the mess or the cake or anything else. You were hurt and that was what counted, according to him.'

My heart lurches.

'How are you feeling?' Adrian asks, studying my face.

'A bit dizzy.'

'Sit here for a bit. I'll get you some water.'

He disappears and I don't have the heart to tell him I don't think the way I'm feeling is because of my fall, but is more down to the man who rescued me.

He returns and hands me a glass. 'Here you go.'

'Thanks.'

'I should be thanking you, actually,' Adrian confides. 'I swear if I see one more canapé today I'll go insane. Julie's stepping in while I see to you, so take as long as you like – I'm in no rush to get back to work.'

I smile at him. He's a nice guy and, apparently, a really good first aider.

BY THE TIME I GET BACK TO RECEPTION, MY CHIN adorned with a huge dressing, all the exhibitors have arrived and, Frances informs me, are getting on with setting up. There's no sign of James or Party, which is probably a good thing, and Frances is in her element titivating a display of hotel information she's laid out in the foyer.

'You've had a delivery,' she tells me with a smile. 'I put it on your desk.'

'Thanks. It's probably for one of the exhibitors.' I go through to my office. There's a large parcel next to the hyacinths. I'd expected it to be wrapped in brown paper, or maybe in a box with the name of a company and *Care of Liberty Lawrence* written on the label. No such thing. This squidgy, squarish package is wrapped in beautiful pink paper with a large ribbon and an oversized pink bow. It's not even my birthday.

I slowly unwrap the parcel and discover a pink, luxuriously soft towelling robe with the initial 'L' in a pretty swirly font on one side. It can only be from James. I can't stop cuddling it as it's so fluffy. Burying my face in it I can almost smell his aftershave. Tears trickle down my cheeks.

It's so kind of him. And so unexpected. He's more observant than I gave him credit for. I quickly wipe away the tears and breathe in the scent of hyacinths which are nodding at me from the desk. Even though he's split up with me, he obviously still cares, and I hope this means he still wants to be friends. The thought gives me an uncomfortable pang in my heart, but I know it's for the best. All I ever do is botch things up and get the wrong end of the stick when he's around – and I can't believe he saw me make a fool of myself yet again this morning.

Taking a deep breath I tidy the gift away under my desk and then go in search of my clipboard – taking a short detour to the ladies' to touch up my makeup, of course. I remember having the clipboard when I was in the Remington Suite earlier, before I went to help Kathy with the cakes. I don't relish the idea of facing her again, but it has to be done – after all, it would be unprofessional of me to avoid the suite all day when I'm supposed to be in charge of the event.

I thought she'd be really cross with me for ruining her cake, but it turns out Adrian was right — she looks more concerned than angry when she sees me and comes rushing over. 'Libby! Are you all right?'

'I'm fine. I'm just so sorry about your cake.'

'Oh, don't worry about that. As long as you're okay, that's what matters.'

I nod, detecting a little of James's influence here. I was sure she'd be angry when she saw the cake all over the floor of the hallway.

I'm grateful that Adrian put on such a large dressing, too. I'm sure it's helping me get the sympathy vote.

The conference room looks perfect, with the massive balloon arch and pedestals of flowers everywhere. There are bridal gowns up on the stage with the millinery on a separate stall to one side, followed by fine jewellery and someone offering personalised invitations and other stationery. There are also a couple of photography stands, one either side of the door, both with men behind them staring daggers at each other. To the other side of the stage the cakes look fantastic – and the five-tier one is every bit as impressive as the six-tier one would have been, I'm sure.

A DJ in the far corner is playing a *Take That* song, and near to him is a chocolate fountain surrounded by strawberries and marshmallows. I might take a closer look at that later.

I take my clipboard which, it turns out, I'd left on one of Kathy's tables, and stroll through to the restaurant. I came out through the bar entrance earlier so I haven't been in here since it was set up for the fair and I'm thrilled at how fabulous it looks. The chairs each have different coloured tie-backs, some with massive bows and some with roses. Flowers adorn every table and all the windowsills, and the scent is amazing.

Each table has been decorated in a different theme; some with classic, sleek decorations and a minimalist approach, while others are strewn with foiletti and have fancy name-cards and paper butterflies attached to all the glasses. There really is something for everyone. I love all the favours too, and can't wait to give them all a thorough inspection.

Andrea from Full Bloom Flowers doesn't look too happy and I venture over to where she's arranging some roses and gypsophila on a large pedestal.

'Is everything okay?' I ask.

Andrea shakes her head. 'I asked Chloe to send over some suitable flowers for this arrangement and this is what she's given me.' She holds up a beautiful bunch of bright yellow carnations, which look really sweet next to the pink roses.

'And those.' She points to some pink and white stripy carnations that tone beautifully with the display.

'I love carnations,' I tell her cheerfully, 'and the colours go so well together.'

She gives me a wide-eyed look. 'But these are yellow.' She waves them in the air. 'And we can't have stripes.'

I frown. 'Why? They're beautiful.'

She closes her eyes briefly, clearly sending up a silent prayer for patience. People often do that around me. I don't know why, but they do.

Opening her eyes again she says, 'It's not what they *look* like, it's what they *mean*. Do you know anything about floriography?'

I wrack my brain, trying to remember where I've heard of it. 'Yes. It's the language of flowers. There was an article about it in *Cosmopolitan* this month.'

Andrea looks suitably impressed, an expression I don't see very often. 'Then you'll understand what I'm talking about. Carnations are beautiful flowers, but only some of the colours are suitable for weddings. Yellow ones are a symbol of disappointment or rejection.'

I'm intrigued. 'What about the stripy ones?'

She shakes her head. 'They signify refusal. They

actually mean 'sorry, I can't be with you'. No-one wants that on their wedding day.'

'Oh no, of course not.'

'To be a good florist you have to understand the language of flowers or you can ruin everything,' Andrea informs me. 'I can see I'll have to go through it with Chloe yet again.'

My mind's reeling. A thought occurred to me when she said something about understanding. The message from James with the flowers. I tremble a little as I ask my next question, almost afraid of the answer. 'What do hyacinths mean?'

'It depends on the colour. Yellow ones are a sign of jealousy, whereas pink ones are playful.'

'What about purple?' I hold my breath.

'Oh, purple is a sign of sorrow. It means 'please forgive me'.'

I feel a massive surge of relief and my heart swells. James was apologising!

23

SOMEHOW THE WHOLE WORLD LOOKS A LOT BRIGHTER. The fair has now opened and crowds are flooding in, chattering excitedly. The traders are all smiling and offering their fliers – even the photographers. Cassie and Mad Moody Margaret are offering canapés to everyone and Bianca's handing out glasses of Buck's Fizz like it's going out of fashion – which it probably is, come to think of it.

Mr Partington has suddenly decided that *he's* in charge of the whole event – no big surprise there. Even Stan's emerged from the sanctity of his kitchen to speak to people about wedding menus.

Chloe arrived with different flowers, and she and Andrea managed to get the rest of their arrangements made up in the nick of time. Unfortunately, I haven't been able to find James, although I'm not really sure what to say to him when I do.

Ben and Rob have arrived with Tammy and a

photographer who's clicking away with his camera, and I notice lots of surreptitious smiles and winks between Rob and Cassie, who's with me.

'Well done, Hetty Wainthrop.' Ben beams as he approaches me in the bar area.

I roll my eyes. I'd rather be someone a bit more glamorous – not to mention younger – like Stella Gibson, if they must call me names.

'What happened?' He winces at my chin.

'Just a fall.' I heat up with embarrassment, remembering the incident when I fell between his table and James's in the restaurant.

He nods, knowingly. I guess he remembers it, too.

'I missed your article, I'm sorry,' I admit, eager to change the subject.

Ben clutches dramatically at his chest, doing a great impression of looking wounded. 'What? All our hard work and you didn't even *read* it?'

'Leave her alone,' Rob pipes up as he joins us.

'We're going to look around the conference room,' Tammy calls over, heading towards the door with the photographer.

Rob nods before turning back to me. 'We had a drink with Cassie last night – she was hoping you'd come down, but couldn't get an answer from your phone.'

'I went to bed with a migraine.' I miss out the bit about leaving my mobile in my office – which is where it still is now, come to think of it.

'We wanted to congratulate you. Sergeant Harper

said he couldn't have solved the case as quickly if it hadn't been for you,' Rob goes on.

I frown at them.

'It *was* you who identified the marks in the carpet as stiletto heels, wasn't it?' Rob asks.

'Well…yes…but…' My face grows hot as I glance over at Bianca who's pouring out even more glasses of Buck's Fizz.

'And you told the cops about losing your key and Connor following you home?' Ben adds.

I nod.

'And you knew all about the fake shoes and even found the old lady's necklace.' Rob looks impressed. 'You practically solved the crime for them, according to the sergeant.'

My tummy feels warm as I realise that I did, in fact, have a hand in solving the thefts – even if I *did* get the wrong culprit. At least I was close.

'Let's have a drink to celebrate,' Ben offers, as he and Bianca bring over some glasses of fizz from the tray on the bar.

'I'm on duty,' I remind them.

'Party's gone outside to look at some vintage cars,' Bianca says with a grin. 'If he does say anything I'll tell him it's just orange juice.'

'Well in that case, how can I resist?' I take the glass from Ben and have a sip, giggling as bubbles shoot up my nose.

'And talking of things you can't resist…' Cassie steps up next to me and points towards the doorway.

James is standing there wearing a smile that could light up the Blackpool Tower. Next to him is Mrs Merrington-Smythe, who is holding Popsie in her arms. She has a huge handbag looped around one elbow. The old dear waves to me with one of Popsie's paws. I wave back – with a hand, of course.

They come over to join us and my heart does a little flip.

'Thank you for the flowers and my present,' I whisper to him.

'You understood my message, then?'

I nod. 'Of course.'

'I knew you would.'

He gives me a squeeze before offering Mrs Merring-ton-Smythe a glass from the tray on the bar. I notice she's wearing that hideous necklace again. I'm glad she got it back, and assume Connor must have confessed to the theft or it might have been kept as evidence.

'What are we drinking to?' she asks with a smile.

'Solving crimes,' Ben announces, lifting his glass.

They all raise their glasses to me and shout in unison, 'To solving crimes!'

I giggle, wondering how much James must have omitted about me getting it all wrong.

'Look, I even got this back,' Mrs Merrington-Smythe says happily as she points out the necklace – as if I could've missed it!

I smile at her. 'I'm glad.'

'So am I. It may look grotesque, but it's worth a fortune,' she mutters in my ear. 'My husband bought it for our first wedding anniversary. I didn't have the heart to tell him I didn't like it.'

I burst out laughing. It hadn't occurred to me that she knew how hideous it is.

'That's the safest place for it,' James assures her with a wink.

'Oh, I think as long as Libby's working here, anywhere in this hotel's safe,' the old lady replies, 'and I'll be telling everyone that.'

'That's something we wanted to talk to you about,' Rob cuts in. 'Libby, our chief editor was impressed by the story in the paper and wants to talk to you about the possibility of a job in investigative journalism.'

I gape at him. 'Really?'

'You'd be perfect for the job,' James says, pressing a kiss on the top of my head.

'Say you'll think about it,' Ben urges.

'Yeah, you've got to go for it,' Cassie pipes up. 'James is right – you'd be great.'

I'm giddy at the thought. 'Okay.'

'Yeah!' They all raise their glasses again.

James leans in and his lips meet mine in a lingering kiss that I can feel right down to my toes. I don't want it to end and can sense that he feels the same. Never would be too soon for the outside world to invade our moment, as it does in the form of titters from the group around us. We reluctantly break apart, safe in the knowledge that this is only a temporary separation.

'Well, before you go rushing off to your new job,

I've got something here for you,' Mrs Merrington-Smythe says with a secretive smile.

James takes Popsie from her while she delves into her handbag, which reminds me of the one Mary Poppins carried. I'm half-expecting her to pull out a standard lamp, but instead she retrieves a Selfridges carrier and passes it over to me.

'This is a thank you from Popsie and me for all you've done for us. Not just finding my necklace, but also looking after Popsie and visiting me and... you know... everything.' She blushes and I hand Ben my glass so I can give her a hug.

'Thank you, but you really didn't need to,' I assure her, feeling a little embarrassed.

'You won't say that when you see what she's got you,' Cassie says with a snigger.

My heart leaps when I look into the bag and see a box. I pull it out. It's not just a box – it's a Christian Louboutin shoe box!

'Oh my God,' I whisper.

'Open it,' Cassie urges excitedly.

I carefully lift the lid. There's something sparkling through the tissue paper. I don't believe this. It can't be...

'I hope they're the right ones,' Mrs Merrington-Smythe says. 'Cassie sent a picture to James and he helped me get them.'

I'm stunned. Speechless. My heart pounds at my ribs as I slowly remove the paper and gaze at a pair of Follies Strass pumps. They're the ones with the red crystals which look like they've been scattered all over your toes. The ones I desperately wanted. They're perfect. And they're mine.

My jaw feels like it's about to hit the floor as I pass the box to Cassie – the only person I'd trust with my precious shoes - then lean over and squeeze the living daylights out of Mrs Merrington-Smythe. It's a good job she's not one of those thin, frail old biddies, as I think I would have broken her with that hug, but she just puts her arms around me and pulls me even closer to her.

'Thank you,' I whisper through tears of joy.

'Thank *you*, dear,' she replies, sounding a little choked up.

'Oh no, does this mean *we* have to buy her expensive shoes as well?' Ben moans.

'Yeah, this story's certainly saved our jobs,' Rob grins. 'Sergeant Harper, did you really have to arrest that guy from the market? We might have afforded the fake ones.'

I finally let go of Mrs Merrington-Smythe and turn to look at James. 'You arrested Stu?'

'We certainly did. He was breaking the law for one thing, passing those shoes off as designer, and besides, he's the one that mugged Dorothy... er... Mrs Merrington-Smythe.'

My stomach lurches. 'Is that the man in black who was running away? The one we saw from Starbucks?'

'Oh no, dear. The mugger wasn't capable of running anywhere once I'd finished with him,' Mrs Merrington-Smythe assures me, rubbing her fist. 'And do call me

Dorothy. After all this I hope we can call each other friends?'

I beam at her. 'Of course.'

'That was Connor,' James says. 'He pointed Dorothy out to Stu and then ran, letting his mate do the dirty work. Stu was also the one caught on camera taking the necklace into the antique shop. Connor was very good at covering himself.'

It sickens me to think I didn't have any inkling that Connor could be so awful. 'I had no idea he knew Stu.'

'Oh yes. They're best buddies,' James explains. 'Connor was taking a share of the stall money for recommending the shoes to anyone who'd listen – including customers from here. He also knows the loan sharks – in fact, it was him who encouraged them to lean on Bianca's dad to give her a motive for stealing from the hotel.'

'Which I didn't,' Bianca points out hurriedly. 'Connor used my shoes to dab marks in Party's carpet to make it look like I'd taken the money from the safe.'

I swallow hard.

'Actually, it was Libby who pointed out that it was odd that no red paint had been left with the heel marks. That's what alerted me to thinking there was something off about the whole thing,' James says.

I feel a swoosh of pride. *I got something right.*

James looks at me. 'Connor hadn't thought of that — he'd just used the heels thinking it would be enough to incriminate Bianca because of the muck on them. It was only later that he thought about using the paint, after overhearing you girls talking about it. He didn't have any of Bianca's shoes to hand that time, though, as she was wearing them, so he thought any red paint would do.'

'It's a good job you got it analysed,' Rob says, looking impressed.

'I only did that because Libby gave me some of the flakes she found on the carpet outside the room. We had to ensure it was the same as the flecks *inside* the room to substantiate our claim. When we found it wasn't we smelled a rat. We checked with security and they confirmed that Bianca had gone up there but hadn't entered the room.'

'Connor sent me up, saying that the lady wanted some orange juice,' Bianca says. 'I went up there but the security guard was in the corridor, on his rounds. He said he'd seen Mrs Merrington-Smythe go out a couple of hours ago, so Connor must have got the wrong room number. I thought nothing of it and came back down. Connor was really annoyed about it.'

'So he was trying to frame Bianca for that one as well.' Ben shakes his head.

Rob adds, 'It's a damn good job you've got him behind bars.'

'He wasn't going to go down on his own, though,' James says with a grimace. 'He gave us the names of everyone involved. We've picked up all those included in the manufacture and selling of the shoes as well as those damn loan sharks. I think a lot of people will be sleeping much more soundly with them off the streets.'

'It's a pity about the stall having to close, though,' Bianca says mournfully. 'Those shoes were much more comfortable than the ones Connor bought for you.' She looks accusingly at me.

'That's because I'm only a size seven.'

She gapes at me. 'I hadn't thought of that.'

Tammy rushes in from the Remington Suite. 'We need a couple of models for the photos,' she says. 'The woman with the dresses said they're short as some have gone outside to pose with the cars.'

'I'll do it,' Bianca says immediately. 'Cassie, can you mind the bar?'

'Oh no, I'll do the bar. Cassie, don't you want to go through?' I offer.

Cassie beams at me. 'Nah. You go and help them; I'll stay here with Rob.'

I'm a bit surprised as I know how much she loves dressing up, but I can tell by the way Rob's grinning at her that they're looking forward to some time together. She hands me back my precious shoes and we all follow Tammy, leaving Cassie and Rob at the bar.

The Remington Suite is heaving with happy-looking people, and the DJ's playing a song by *Ed Sheeran*.

'This is Maria from Brides and Beaux,' Tammy introduces us to a rather harassed-looking lady in a sharp lime-green suit. I remember speaking to her on the phone a few times.

'I need someone to model one of the gowns for me, and Paul needs a bride to show off some of the rings.' She looks a little dubiously at my chin.

'Who's got the smallest fingers?' Paul asks, peering at our hands.

Bianca has large hands, but her fingers are very slender. My fingers are ordinary-sized, but as hers are longer, she wins.

'You'll do,' he announces, pointing at her.

'I *think* I've got a dress that will fit you,' Maria says, bringing me back down to earth with a hefty thump.

I raise my eyebrows. I would certainly hope she had something in a *normal* woman's size. I've got my spanx on and everything.

'I'm not so sure about that chin, though,' Maria adds with a grimace.

'That can easily be airbrushed out,' Ben assures her.

'Oh, great. Turn me into a chinless wonder, why don't you?' I groan.

'The *dressing,* you idiot,' he clarifies with a laugh.

'In that case, come this way, girls.' We follow Maria through to a makeshift changing room beside the stage. They've slung a couple of curtains over some of the lighting poles and there really isn't enough room to swing a cat in there. Bianca and I are given a gown each. There's no way we'll manage to get into them on our own.

'Let's do you first, then you can help me,' I suggest.

She agrees, and we get to it.

She's got a really slim figure and looks radiant in the sleek white gown. The train's a bit of a challenge in the confines of the cubicle, but we get there in the end, though I have to admit to stepping on it a few times.

I, on the other hand, look more like a Southern belle. With the crinoline hoop on it's about as wide as the entire changing area, and it's a good job Bianca's got long arms or she'd never have got close enough to zip me up. It's a little fancier than I'd have chosen, with bows and frilly bits, but I love the style. We look lovely, all sparkly and white.

Maria pops in and hands me a couple of tiaras. *The* tiaras. 'I thought you could wear these.'

'They're beautiful,' I tell her, my mouth suddenly going dry.

'Yes, they are. One of them's missing a few stones but it won't be noticeable from a distance.'

My heart lifts. The *Hallelujah Chorus* rings out in my ears. She already knew about the stones. I didn't lose them after all.

'Don't worry about shoes. Just wear your own, or none, whatever suits you. They won't be taking pictures of your feet.'

The chorus suddenly sounds flat.

She swishes the curtain back over and I gape at it, outraged. Don't bother with *shoes*? For a *wedding*? Is she mad? They're the most important part of the whole outfit, and she expects us to not *bother* with them! I whip out my new Louboutins. They fit like a glove and sparkle beautifully, just as I knew they would.

As the one who took the tiaras from Maria I get first pick and immediately go for the understated one that I loved when I tried them on earlier. Bianca gets the one with the missing stones, but as she's so tall no-one will notice.

'Are you ready?' Maria's whipped the curtain back again before we can answer and we step out to a chorus of 'ooh's and 'aah's from James, Mrs Merrington-Smythe and everyone else who happens to be near us at the time.

I decide I quite fancy being a bride. All the attention makes you feel really good. And important. I'm not so keen on the idea of a double wedding, though. No offence to Bianca, but it would be nice to have all the praise lavished on me, and not have to share it.

The photographer's clicking away at us. I secretly hope that a photo of me makes it into the paper. Then I'll send a few copies to Mum and she can leave them lying around all over Kent. That'll show Jonathan Parker!

'We'll do Bianca first,' Maria announces, ushering her over to a small table with a register and a bouquet of flowers on it.

'You look beautiful,' James whispers to me as we follow them over. 'I can't wait to see you in one of those for real.'

My face heats up and I imagine I must be a lovely shade of red by now, matching the sparkles on my feet. There's something very special about a compliment from him, and I can't get enough of them – especially ones about wearing wedding dresses.

'Do we get to throw confetti?' Mrs Merrington-Smythe looks around hopefully, but is rewarded with a chorus of 'no's from a horrified-looking Maria and Paul. She looks disappointed and takes Popsie back from James.

Bianca sits at the table and picks up a rather elegant pen. She frowns at the book. 'Where do I sign?'

'You only *pretend* to write in the register,' Paul reminds her.

'It's just as well. You'd never get my whole name on that little line,' she scoffs. 'I mean, I wouldn't say I've got big writing, but by the time I've written Bianca Madeleine Morrison, there's no room for Wright. And then it wouldn't be legal, would it? How on earth's that supposed to work?'

She looks up at us.

James, Mrs Merrington-Smythe and I stare at her — I suspect the penny has dropped for them, too.

'What?'

'Did you say your middle name was Madeleine?' I ask slowly.

She sniggers. 'I know, it's awful, isn't it? It's my mum's proper first name, so it got handed down to me. Totally unfair, if you ask me. She doesn't even like it herself – that's why she's known as Stella – so why dump it on me? She must have hated me as a baby.' She rolls her eyes.

'So, your mother's name is Madeleine and she's married to a man who deals in cars?' Mrs Merrington-Smythe clarifies, her eyes shining.

'Oh no. Dad *used* to be a car dealer, but now he's got his own garage where he just mends them. I don't know how much longer he'll stay open for, though. Once they arrested the loan sharks we thought he'd be okay, but it seems he's still not doing as well as he should be. He needs new equipment or something.'

'Oh no, that's awful.' I remember how hard her dad and brothers worked while I was at the garage with Piers's car. They're real grafters, the men in that family.

'Oh, and they're not married,' Bianca adds, as though she hasn't heard me. 'Apparently my grand-mother wouldn't allow them to, and Mum didn't want to go against her wishes, so they just lived together.'

My heart pumps like a steam engine. I look over and see Mrs Merrington-Smythe is growing increasingly excited. James is grinning, too.

'Your grandmother wasn't called Daisy Morrison, by any chance?' The old lady can barely contain her enthusiasm.

Bianca nods. 'Yes, I think so.'

'Morrison?' I stare at Mrs Merrington-Smythe in amazement. 'I didn't know your sister's surname was Morrison.'

She looks unperturbed. 'I didn't think it was rele-vant, dear. Not only is Morrison quite a common... er... *popular* name, but I thought Madeleine had married and wouldn't be known as Morrison any longer.' It never occurred to me to look for her in her maiden name.

I hear James sniggering beside me, and just roll my eyes. I know he'll give me a long lecture later on estab-lishing all my facts, but I don't mind. As an investigative journalist I'll need lots of tips from him, and I'm sure he won't mind helping.

To my complete surprise – and Ben's – Mrs Merrington-Smythe hands Popsie to the reporter and then gives me a massive hug. 'Thank you, dear. You kept your promise. You said you'd find my family and you have.'

I give her a tight squeeze, although it's hard to get close enough in this dress. I'm so thrilled for her – for all of them.

'It looks like this is your Great Aunt Dorothy,' I explain to a very bewildered-looking Bianca when Mrs Merrington-Smythe and I part.

'Oh.' She still looks bewildered.

'Perhaps you could call your parents and ask them to come and meet up with her?' I suggest.

'Okay.' Bianca's just staring blankly at us now. I've got a feeling Mrs Merrington-Smythe will get used to that expression.

'This is all very fascinating, but what about the photo?' Paul says irritably. He's got a tray of engagement rings in one hand. He uses the other to pick out a ring and starts to place it on Bianca's finger.

'Not that finger, it's unlucky,' she says, snatching her hand back, inadvertently knocking the tray from Paul's hand.

The rings tumble to the floor, a mass of glitter and sparkle.

'Now look what you've done!' Paul yells, dropping to the carpet and scrabbling around. James and Maria help him pick up the rings, too, but I can't exactly bend down in this dress so I just watch them helplessly.

'How else am I going to get a photo of a bride in an engagement ring?' Paul huffs from his position on the floor. "I also need you to wear a wedding band – I suppose that's a problem, too?'

'I can use the other hand. It's just that the wedding finger's unlucky, isn't it? I'll never get married if I jinx it now.' Bianca looks incredulous as she watches them all crawl about at her feet.

I'm tempted to offer to do it in her place, but I don't want to cause myself any more bad luck – I've already had enough to last a lifetime.

I gaze at James, who's still kneeling on the floor, gathering up diamond rings. There are butterflies having a rave in my tummy and I feel a sort of calm excitement.

He said I look beautiful. I *feel* beautiful. I glance down at the dress, which billows out from my hips in a mass of sparkle. I always wanted to get married in this style of dress, just like a princess. I wonder if James will be my Prince Charming.

I glance at him again – it's hard to keep my eyes off him. He's every kind of gorgeous. And he's there, at my feet…kneeling…with a diamond ring in his hand…

THE END

TRADEMARK ACKNOWLEDGEMENT

The following trademarked items appear in *Best Foot Forward*. The author acknowledges the trademarked status and trademark owners of the following wordmark mentioned in this work of fiction:

Christian Louboutin: Christian Louboutin Ltd
Toyota: Toyota Motor Corporation
Ford: Ford Motor Company
BMW: BMW AG Group
Coke: The Coca-Cola Company
Nutella: Ferrero S.P.A
Maltesers: Mars Incorporated
Mars: Mars Incorporated
Pinocchio: Disney Enterprises, Inc
Facebook: Facebook, Inc
Gucci: Gucci Ltd
Ted Baker: Ted Baker plc

Prada: Prada S.P.A.

Spanx: Spanx , Inc

Bridget Jones: Fielding, Helen

Cosmopolitan: Hearst Corporation

Lulu Guinness: Lulu Guinness Ltd

eBay: eBay Inc

EpiPen: Mylan Inc

Corsa: Vauxhall Motors Ltd

Apple: Apple Inc

Ann Summers: Ann Summers Ltd

Ruby Shoos: Ruby Shoo & GH Warner Footwear plc

Armani: Giorgio Armani S.P.A.

Dior: Christian Dior Ltd

Jimmy Choo: Jimmy Choo Ltd

Stella McCartney: Stella McCartney Ltd

Kurt Geiger: Kurt Geiger Ltd

Bambi: Disney Enterprises, Inc

Mary Poppins: Disney Enterprises, Inc

Karen Millen: Karen Millen Ltd

Happy Meal: McDonald's Corporation

Mr. Happy: THOIP

Sherlock Holmes: The Sir Arthur Conan Doyle Literary Estate

Jaguar: Jaguar Land Rover Ltd

Selfridges: Selfridges Retail Ltd

Harvey Nichols: Harvey Nichols & Co Ltd

Sonicare DiamondClean : Philips Electronics Ltd

Pretty Woman: Touchstone Pictures (Walt Disney Studios Motion Pictures)

Manga Dimensions: Kabushiki Kaisha Banpresto

Neil George: Neil George Hair Products Inc

Perrier: Nestlé Waters

Maryland Cookies: Burton's Foods

Alice in Wonderland: Disney Enterprises Inc (from the novel by Lewis Carroll)

Mrs Overall: A character from 'Acorn Antiques' written by Victoria Wood

Miss Marple: A character from the 'Miss Marple Series' written by Agatha Christie

Hetty Wainthrop: A character from 'Missing Persons' written by David Cook

Stella Gibson: A character from 'The Fall' written by Allan Cubitt

Harry Potter: JK Rowling and Warner Bros Entertainment Inc

Starbucks: Starbucks Corporation

As a courtesy, the author would like to acknowledge the following celebrities mentioned in Best Foot Forward:

Jamie Dornan

Chris Hemsworth

Julia Roberts

Gino D'Acampo

Take That

Ed Sheeran

Cameron Diaz

Queen

Dolly Parton

Meatloaf

Phillip Schofield
George Clooney
Barbara Cartland

Also
Battersea Dogs and Cats Home -
https://www.battersea.org.uk/

DISCLAIMER: SETTING THE RECORD STRAIGHT ONE STEP AT A TIME...

The author would like to make a few issues perfectly clear in the interests of fairness (and not getting sued).

Best Foot Forward is purely a <u>work of fiction</u> and should be treated as such. To this end, there are some trademarked items mentioned which *could* be interpreted as not having been shown in their best light – this is just part of the storyline and should <u>not</u> be taken as an insult by readers or – heaven forbid – manufacturers.

Please note that:

<u>Step 1</u>

Christian Louboutins <u>do not</u> leave red paint on the floor. The author went to great lengths to emphasize that it was the <u>fake ones</u> in the story that shed the paint, <u>not</u>

the real ones. As a company, **Christian Louboutin Ltd** dedicates a lot of effort to identifying and eliminating imitations of their work in order to preserve their reputation and registered trademark, as well as helping their customers. They even have a 'STOPFAKE' page on their website to emphasize ways of spotting a counterfeit. One of the main tell-tale signs of a replica pair is the poor quality of the red sole. This story serves to highlight this fact, <u>not</u> to condone it. **Christian Louboutins** are fabulous shoes and the author (as well as Libby Lawrence) hopes to have conveyed this .

Step 2

Not all **Ford Focus cars** are old, as is James Harper's. There are many newer models out there, and older ones that don't look quite as decrepit as his. **Ford Focuses** are wonderful cars, and no insinuation is made to the contrary. Apart from James's one. Which is fictional.

Step 3

Toyotas aren't all in need of repair. Although the one being fixed at B M-W Car Repairs and Valeting definitely is. The fictional one is described as 'battered' and 'old', which may be the case in <u>some</u> real ones, but is definitely <u>not</u> an accurate portrayal of <u>all</u> **Toyota** cars, nor is it intended to be. **Toyota** makes lovely cars and no implication to the contrary should be interpreted.

Step 4

The author in no way implies that **Nutella** is a poisonous substance – just that it contains nuts and if one is allergic to them it might be best to choose jam.

(Unless, as in this case, it's smeared over the bonnet of a car, in which case one might not get the option). However we would like to point out that **Nutella** is delicious – especially on crumpets – and so offers a perfect choice to those who <u>don't</u> suffer a nut-allergy.

ABOUT THE AUTHOR

BEA STEVENS

Bea lives in the beautiful countryside of Shropshire, England, but is never averse to taking a trip to the local (and not-so-local) towns to check out the big stores for new shoes and bags (all in the name of research, of course).

She has worked mainly in catering and admin, but had to give up her job when her fight against breast cancer took another downward turn. An eternal optimist, she took the opportunity to write – something she has always loved. Every cloud... and all that!

She hopes very much that you share her sense of humour and that you enjoy her first Chick Lit novel, Best Foot Forward.

Feel free to follow her at:
https://www.facebook.com/AuthorBeaStevens

ALSO BY BEA STEVENS

Link to book 2: mybook.to/SteppingItUp

Book 2 of The Liberty Lawrence Series is entitled **Stepping It Up** and will be available in May 2018 – here's a peek:

STEPPING IT UP

CHAPTER ONE

I'm beginning to wonder if it might have been more useful to get my 'A'level in Running instead of English. I've worked for the *Chronicle* for two weeks now and I really enjoy it. I'd like to say my feet haven't touched the ground, but that, unfortunately, would be totally inaccurate. My feet haven't *stopped* touching the ground —at a rapid pace!

I was expecting to spend my time interviewing celebrities—or at least *interesting* people. I hoped to be trying out all the latest fashions and learning new make-up tricks. It would've been nice to work with Siobhan, the beautiful fashion editor, or Tammy, one of the junior editors who has her own quirky sense of style, to put it mildly. Ha! No such luck.

They put me with Dave, who is almost seven foot tall, three or four years older than me and a hundred per cent fitter. His skin is naturally tanned, he's bald—which he insists is by choice, but the jury's out on that one—and he's got a smile that shines in the dark, he must have Simon Cowell's dentist. I just wish he'd point that delightful beam in my direction a bit more often, instead of always rolling his eyes and frowning at me.

Dave could give Mo Farah a run for his money, he's so fast. I once spied Mo running around the track at St. Mary's University when I was on a course over in Twickenham. He winked at me, although my friend Trinny reckoned he just had something in his eye. She's not my friend anymore.

'I hope you're not planning to eat that.' Dave's just watched me place a ham and cheese sandwich on our desk.

I stare at him in dismay. 'What did you think I was going to do with it?' I hardly dare ask.

'We need to get across town.' He's already pulling on his hoodie. 'Something's going down.'

I take a quick bite of my sandwich before sealing it back in its plastic box. I suppose one advantage of bringing your own lunch is that you can eat it anytime. And I guess it will save money, as James insists. It's just such a chore.

My feet are already aching as we exit the *Daily Chronicle* reporters' office and head for the lift.

'I thought you'd take the stairs,' I grumble as he stoops to get in beside me.

'This'll be quicker as everyone's going for lunch around about now,' he says, pressing the button for the ground floor. 'Besides, I'll need my energy to get there. We're better off on foot than taking the Tube at this time of day.'

My heart sinks and I look down at my Kurt Geigers. The first day I worked here I wore my Karen Millens, which have always been ideal for work. Ruined! Not only did I almost break my neck running to an impromptu press conference in Westminster—when Dave said we were in the area I didn't realise he meant it was a flipping mile and half away—but he insists on taking back alleys and muddy paths to save time. They don't save shoe leather, though.

I actually had to go out and buy some flat shoes after that. They're really nice, I have to admit, plain little pumps. I got them in nude so they'd go with anything. They would have cost sixty quid but they were half-price in the sale. I don't think I'd have got them otherwise. James is a bit strict about money —even mine.

They don't look like two-week-old shoes, though. And they certainly don't look nude. I sigh as we get out of the lift and exit the huge office building. I tried my best to hide the scuff-marks, but all the dirt has stained the leather.

'Is it another drugs bust?' I'm hoping all this effort will be worth it. And I could do with impressing my new boss with a great story.

'Yep. But we have to be quick.'

I roll my eyes. *Since when has Dave ever not been quick?*

'This way,' he says, dashing through a crowd of Japanese tourists. I follow, glad I'm wearing comfy trousers and a chic light jacket, even though it is October.

'Gomen'nasai,' I say with an apologetic smile, as the tourists abruptly stop taking photos of a passing red bus and stand back to let us though. It's amazing how many languages I've learned to say 'sorry' in since I've been working with Dave. He's so tall no-one's going to argue with him so he just pushes his way through, leaving me straggling in his wake.

I wear a black Radley cross-body bag (one that Cassie, my bestie, doesn't need any more) which houses my phone, cash, chocolate bar and a small tablet, along with a notebook and pen—just in case. This is much more practical than the Marc Jacobs tote I used on my first day. It's a gorgeous bag, in tan leather, and held everything— make-up, lunch, Lindsey Kelk's latest novel, the usual pack of tissues, manicure set, decent-sized mirror— as well as all the stuff I've got with me now. Only trouble was when I had to make a mad dash across town it was too heavy and cumbersome to run with. I'm still using it—after all, a girl needs all this stuff—but it stays in the office now while I'm chasing stories.

Talking of chasing, I appear to have lost Dave. We were heading towards Earl's Court along the main road, but I can't see him anywhere. There are plenty of side streets he could've taken. Crikey, you'd think being so tall it would be hard to miss him, but he's got a nasty habit of just diving down any old alley and vanishing.

It gives me a chance to stop and catch my breath for a minute, as I escape the lunch-time crowd and move over to lean on the wall of an office-block. I'm sure I must have lost at least four stone in the last fortnight with all this exercise. Oddly enough my clothes don't seem to have had the memo, though. I'm even working really hard to keep my carbs up, like Dave does. Actually it's probably time I had more sugar to keep my energy up—after all, I missed lunch, didn't I?—so I delve into my bag for a Mars bar.

'You haven't got time for that!' Dave suddenly appears through the crowd, glaring at me. 'Come on, we'll miss it. Tom's already there.'

I didn't even get chance to unwrap it, before I have to stuff my little bar of heaven back into my bag and take off after him.

We enter a maze of side-streets and back-alleys, and I'm sure at one point we cut through someone's garden, before reaching a really nice cul de sac where some not-so-nice men are being led into the back of a police van.

'Over here.' Dave pulls me through a throng of on-lookers to where a police spokesman in a Chief Inspector's uniform is making a speech. Or, at least, he *was* making a speech—it looks like he's just finished.

My heart sinks. This was my fault for being so slow. Dave's going to be mad with me. I watch as a young guy with greasy, sandy-coloured hair tries to pull away from the officer who's leading him to the van. I push through the crowd to get closer.

'I didn't do anything,' he's insisting, 'I wasn't involved.' He sounds really desperate, and almost in tears.

I frown, marching over to the officer who was making the speech. 'Excuse me, why is he being arrested?'

The guy's eyebrows knit together so tightly they could make a jumper. He's clearly never heard of waxing, or even tweezers. 'He's a suspect.'

'But he's not with the rest. At least, he doesn't appear to be. Did you see their designer shoes? And the gold chains? This guy's got none of that.'

'Did you see his Rolex?' The Chief Inspector rolls his eyes at me. 'Of course he's one of them.'

'I saw a pitiful *fake* Rolex. And none of his clothes are designer, like theirs were. Are you sure he's involved with them?'

Something about the guy didn't seem right. He might have been a criminal of some kind, but he seemed terrified at being lumped together with those men in the van. And I was sure he wasn't one of their gang. He just seemed so different.

'Just let us do our job, will you?' The officer says, wearily.

I catch the young guy's eye as he's about to climb into the van. He looks like he's pleading with me to do something. But what *can* I do?

* * * *

I thought Dave would be furious with me, but when I catch up with him he's chatting quite happily with Tom, the photographer.

'I'm really sorry,' I tell him. 'Did we miss everything?'

'*I* didn't,' Tom pipes up with a grin. 'I got some great shots. In fact, I was surprised how early I was. I thought all the action would be in full swing by the time I arrived, but I got here just at the same time as the cops came rolling up. I saw them knocking down the door and everything.'

Tom's about twenty-five and quite good-looking, with black hair and a neat moustache. He's over six feet tall, and far too skinny for my taste, but he seems like a nice enough guy. He clearly loves his job and takes pictures even when there's nothing to see.

'Yeah, and I managed to find out most of the facts from one of the other reporters,' Dave tells me. 'It's a good job I've got friends, isn't it?'

'Who was that, then? I didn't see you with anyone.' Tom frowns.

Dave gives him a blank look at first and then shakes his head. 'You were taking more snaps at the time, I think.'

'*Photographs*,' Tom corrects him. 'Snaps are what

amateurs take, professional photographers take photographs. The clue's in the name.'

Dave rolls his eyes. They often have this conversation. I'm sure Dave just says it to wind Tom up—and it works every time.

'It's a good job your contact at the police station's on the ball,' I remark, smiling at Dave.

'Yeah, he told me all this was going down before they'd even finished their briefing. The man's a diamond.'

'I'll say.' I can't help being impressed. Dave's got some great mates all over the place, and the guy at the station gives him some brilliant tips. It's probably how Dave's become an award-winning journalist. He's climbed the editorial ladder quite quickly, and is very well thought of in the office. 'What's his name?' It suddenly occurs to me that this guy might be a friend of James.

'I can't divulge my sources,' Dave says, shaking his head. 'It's unethical.'

'Just like a cop informing a newspaper reporter that something's about to happen and where to go to get the scoop,' Tom points out, his eyebrows raised.

'Sometimes the cops actually *need* stuff to go into the papers. It can help flush out criminals and all sorts of stuff.'

'So why don't they tell *all* the reporters then, get it in all the papers?' I ask. 'I mean, if they need word to get around that's got to be the best way; get it into as many papers as possible. And the radio and TV, of course. They should tell everyone.'

'They *do* get it out on all the media. That's what *we're* here for. To report on it to the masses.' Dave almost snaps at me.

'But they should tell everyone when they tell you, so all the different reporters can get here from the start.' I'm frowning at him now. Can't he see that I'm making perfect sense?

He shakes his head. 'You don't get it. If everyone knew then they'd all get the scoop. This way, I – I mean *we*—get the best coverage and boost the Chronicle's readership. And talking of which, it's time we were heading back to get all this down on paper. We've missed the early edition but we can get it in tonight's if we hurry.'

He turns and breaks into a sprint in the direction we came. I can just see his head bobbing above the crowd who have clearly realised there's nothing more to see and have made their way to the mouth of the cul de sac where several people are huddled together chatting.

I get a sinking feeling, knowing how far it is to get back to the office. And if I don't keep up with Dave I'll get lost. Glancing back at Tom, I'm surprised he doesn't seem to be in such a rush to leave, as he slips his mobile back into his pocket.

'Aren't you coming?' I ask, hoping he knows the way. I look back up the road and notice that Dave's already disappeared.

'Do I look stupid?' Tom asks incredulously. 'The

taxi'll be here in three minutes. We'll probably get back about the same time as Usain Bolt over there'—he gestures towards the last place we saw Dave,—'but without the sweat.'

My heart lightens. 'I love the way you think, Tom.'

I spend the afternoon writing up the story from my notes and looking over Tom's shoulder at the photos he took. Dave also writes up the story. I don't know how he does it but his has much more detail in it than my version—I suppose he must've got the information from his journalist-friends. I wish I had contacts like that. I also wish I had a row of trophies lined across the front of my desk, like Dave. He's obviously worked hard to get so much recognition.

I can't help thinking how lovely it would be to attend an award ceremony. The men all wear black tie and the women have gorgeous designer dresses. The thought suddenly loses its appeal as I remember something.

'I just need to make a call,' I tell Dave, pressing the 'send' button on my computer. I'm secretly hoping that if the editor reads mine first he might be so impressed with it that he won't even bother to look at Dave's. I'd love to have my name in the paper as the writer. Heck, I'd like to have my name in the paper for anything.

He grunts in response and I dive out of the door and head for the staff room. It's late so there shouldn't be many people around. I'm right, the room's empty. Good. I quickly call Cassie, my best friend and flatmate.

'Shouldn't you be working?' She sounds cheerful.

'I meant to tell you something. I've seen the perfect dress for the policeman's ball next week,' I tell her, then bite my lip.

'It's not a bloody policeman's ball, you idiot. I keep telling you it's a charity gala night. It said so on the ticket.'

'Well, it's the same thing, isn't it?' I frown.

'No. Policemen don't have balls anymore,' she says with a giggle. 'Remember the joke? Woman pulled over for speeding offers to buy a ticket to the ball as a bribe but the copper tells her policemen don't have balls?' She's gone off in hysterics again. She does this every time anyone mentions that joke. She thinks it's funny because James is a policeman and we haven't 'done anything' yet. She reckons... well, you can guess.

'About the dress.' I need to keep this conversation on track; I haven't got long.

'How much?' I can tell she's rolling her eyes without even seeing her.

'Just under £700.'

Silence.

'I know,' I say, 'but I need to make a really good impression. James is a sergeant, after all. As his partner I need to look the part, don't I? I can't let him down.'

'You can't let him know how much you're planning to spend on the dress, either,' she says.

'I have to. It would seem like going behind his back

otherwise—and besides, he's bound to ask. You know how he is with money.' I feel a lurch in my stomach. James is a lovely guy but he has a real thing about not spending too much. It's not as if he's poor or anything —he's got a good job and a nice little flat in Fulham. He's just waiting for the sale of his other house to go through and he'll be rich. In the meantime he seems to think he has to hang on to every penny.

'You know what he'll say.' Cassie's right. He won't be happy.

'But wait til you see it,' I whine. 'It's gorgeous.'

'Tell *him* that.'

'I will. Tonight. I thought I'd go 'round and surprise him after work. I'll make sure he's in a good mood and then I'll just casually drop it into the conversation. Maybe after a couple of drinks.'

'It'll take more than a couple.' Cassie doesn't sound convinced.

'I've got to try. I need to wear *something*.'

'Well, good luck. Rob and I are going to the pub tonight anyway, but I shouldn't be too late.'

'Okay, babe. Have fun.'

I quickly hang up as I see Dave loitering in the doorway.

'We should just make it in time for tonight's issue,' he says.

'Great.' I sigh with relief. I really thought I might have blown it for both of us. I walk towards him.

'I'm heading out,' he announces. 'Just a bit of networking.'

'Can I come? I'd love to meet some of your contacts.' I can feel my heart pumping a little quicker at the thought. This could be my big chance. Well—it could have been if Dave wasn't shaking his head and looking at me as if I'd gone mad or something.

'No, it's just a social thing really. I like to keep in touch with them—you know, oil the cogs and all that.' He's already walking towards the lift.

'Okay. I'll just hang around here then.'

I can tell he's not even listening; he's already on his way. I wander back into the newsroom.

'What's up?' Tom looks surprised to see me.

'Dave's just gone to meet up with some more of his contacts,' I tell him, glumly. 'I wanted to tag along— you know, see how he recruits them and what makes him choose them.'

Tom chuckles. 'He's never going to reveal his sources to you or anyone else,' he says. 'Why would he? He's got friends in high places who give him the nod whenever something interesting is about to happen. That's how he gets the best stories and earns the big money. He's not about to share that with anyone, don't take it personally, love.'

I huff. Tom sounds so patronizing. What makes things even worse though, is that it all makes sense. Why would Dave introduce me to the people who have helped him make such a big name for himself? It's clearly every man for himself in this business.

'What're you doing?' I ask, watching him scroll

through his screen. If I can't pick up anything from Dave, maybe I could learn a thing or two from Tom.

'Just having another look through these photos from today,' he says, idly.

'Can I look?'

'Of course.'

I'm glad to notice that he's not as secretive about everything as Dave. I grab my lunch from my bag and go and sit next to Tom at his little desk by the window.

I recognize the house in the cul de sac, tucked away in a lovely little area. I wonder whose ill-gotten gains paid for it. Any of the four guys being marched out the front door and over to the police van could be the owner. They all look really smar— not at all how I expected drug-dealers to appear.

'Who's this bloke?' I ask, pointing to the sandy-haired guy who was the last one to be taken in.

'One of those scum, I suppose.' Tom shrugs.

'But he doesn't look like them, does he? I mean, look at his clothes. And his hair's greasy and that watch is obviously fake. He doesn't look like he belongs with them at all.' I frown. The more I think about it, the less it seems like he's one of their gang at all.

'Perhaps he's a user. Probably buying off them at the time they got stung.' Tom looks disinterested.

'But why would the cops take him in as well? They'd have to actually have evidence of him buying the stuff off them to arrest him for that. They must know he's not one of the gang they've come to pick up.'

'I suppose so.' Tom purses his lips. 'I'd be surprised

if they saw anything like that, though. I was there just as they arrived and they were straight in and out. Picked up the scumbags and hauled them out to the van. I didn't see anyone hanging about in there to verify what they were actually doing.'

'The copper who gave the statement told me he was one of the gang, but I don't think that's right.' I remember the way that inspector spoke to me and shudder. He obviously didn't like me asking questions, but I think I had a valid point.

'Doesn't look that way to me.' Tom took a closer look, scrolling through a few pictures. 'The young lad was brought out a few seconds after the rest of the gang. I don't know what the hell he was doing inside that house, but he certainly doesn't appear to be one of that lot.' He points to the men in suits in the previous picture, as they were being marched to the van. 'I think you're right, Libby. Something's not right there.'

Lightning Source UK Ltd.
Milton Keynes UK
UKHW020611170419
341166UK00005B/107/P

9 781912 913053